# DEADLY PROOF

ATLANTA JUSTICE

BOOK ONE

# DEADLY PROOF

## RACHEL DYLAN

BETHANYHOUSE

a division of Baker Publishing Group
Minneapolis, Minnesota

© 2017 by Rachel Dylan

Published by Bethany House Publishers
11400 Hampshire Avenue South
Bloomington, Minnesota 55438
www.bethanyhouse.com

Bethany House Publishers is a division of
Baker Publishing Group, Grand Rapids, Michigan

Printed in the United States of America

Library of Congress Cataloging-in-Publication Data
Names: Dylan, Rachel, author.
Title: Deadly proof / Rachel Dylan.
Description: Minneapolis, Minnesota : Bethany House, a division of Baker
    Publishing Group, [2017]
Identifiers: LCCN 2017012338| ISBN 9780764231100 (hardcover) | ISBN
    9780764219801 (softcover)
Subjects: LCSH: Women lawyers—Fiction. | Private investigators—Fiction. |
    GSAFD: Romantic suspense fiction. | Christian fiction. | Legal stories.
Classification: LCC PS3604.Y53 D43 2017 | DDC 813/.6—dc23
LC record available at https://lccn.loc.gov/2017012338

This is a work of fiction. Names, characters, incidents, and dialogues are products of the author's imagination and are not to be construed as real. Any resemblance to actual events or persons, living or dead, is entirely coincidental.

Cover design by LOOK Design Studio

Author is represented by the Nancy Yost Literary Agency

17  18  19  20  21  22  23      7  6  5  4  3  2  1

# CHAPTER
# ONE

You can't call that a settlement offer." Kate Sullivan looked directly into the dark eyes of her opposing counsel, who represented a medical device company. Jerry had just made partner and thought he could play hardball, but she wasn't going to let him get the upper hand. "You and I both know that amount will never cut it. Come back to me when you have a number I can work with." She closed her laptop and shoved it in her bag.

"C'mon, Kate. Fifty grand is a good starting point," Jerry said.

"We're done here. Call me when you're actually ready to negotiate." She stood up and walked out of the conference room before Jerry could say anything else. He wasn't taking her client's claims seriously, so she wasn't going to waste any more time playing games. He'd come to his senses soon enough. This case shouldn't go to trial, and he knew it.

Making the quick drive from downtown to Midtown Atlanta, weaving through the usual traffic, she parked in her reserved spot in the garage under a tall office building. The large office tower was home of the world-class plaintiff's firm Warren McGee.

She spent more time at her office than she did at her own home, but that was by choice. Representing innocent victims was her calling.

When she walked out of the elevator and onto the twenty-third floor, her assistant, Beth Russo, greeted her warmly.

"How did it go?" Beth asked. Her fifty-five-year-old assistant had been working at the law firm for decades and knew the ins and outs of each case and every schedule. Kate would be lost without her.

"Still no settlement, but they'll cave eventually. They don't actually want to try this case."

"I hope so, because you need to get it off your docket and give your full attention to the Mason Pharmaceutical litigation. You deserve to be running that case."

Kate laughed. "Let me get on the steering committee first, Beth. Then I'll apply for lead counsel."

"Exactly. You're due in court in three hours for the hearing on the steering committee, and you've got calls piled up."

She smiled. "Thanks, Beth. I'll work through them." Calls meant business, and business was what kept her in good standing as a partner at the firm.

In the privacy of her own office, Kate stared out the large window that gave her a fantastic view of Stone Mountain in the distance. She'd earned this corner office by working hard, but she wanted more. Her goal was to be managing partner one day, and this litigation was huge.

Thousands of cases had been filed across the country against Mason Pharmaceutical Corporation, known as MPC. She was responsible for a large chunk of them, representing victims who had taken MPC's migraine drug and had died or been injured. She needed a spot on the exclusive committee of plaintiffs' lawyers that would dictate the entire direction of the case.

Her phone rang, but she let it go, knowing Beth would answer it. She had started flipping through her emails when Beth hurried into her office with a frown pulling at her lips.

"Kate, sorry to bother you, but there's a call I think you have to take."

"Who is it?"

Beth's brown eyes narrowed. "She won't give me her name, but she said she has information regarding the MPC case."

Once the litigation hit the news and the firms started advertising to find clients who had taken the dangerous drug, there was a constant stream of inquiries to be fielded. The firm couldn't turn them down without hearing the person out first.

"Why don't you have one of the associates take it?"

Beth shook her head. "She says she'll only talk to you."

Kate was listed as lead counsel on hundreds of the complaints, so it made sense that this person would want to talk to her. "Okay, put her through." She waited for her line to light up red, then picked up the phone. "This is Kate Sullivan."

"I have some critical information for you, but I can't speak over the phone," a woman said, her words rushed and breathless. "Is there a place we can meet?"

Kate needed more before she dropped everything to go on what might be a wild goose chase. "And you are?"

"I don't want to say right now." Her voice was hushed.

"You can come down to my office, and we can talk here."

"No, no. That won't work," the woman said. "It's too risky. Your office is the last place I can be seen."

"Ma'am, as you can imagine, I have a lot on my plate right now. So it would be helpful if I had some idea of what this is all about."

"I have information you're going to need," the caller whispered. "Things related to your case. Things I know because of my job."

That got Kate's attention. "Are you an employee of Mason Pharmaceutical Corporation?"

"I told you, I can't have this conversation over the phone."

Kate's heartbeat sped up at the strain in the woman's voice. "All right. There's a coffee shop in Colony Square on Peachtree and Fourteenth. Can you meet me there?"

"Yes. See you in ten minutes."

Kate hung up, and her mind went into overdrive. If this woman was truly an employee of MPC, then this meeting could be huge. MPC had corporate offices in multiple states, but the company headquarters and largest office was in Atlanta.

It was likely this woman was a disgruntled employee or that she was unstable. But something about her voice tugged at Kate. Her curiosity and desire to be thorough led her to take the meeting.

She made the short walk from her office across the street and down a block to Colony Square, which housed restaurants and shops catering to the Midtown Atlanta community. It was lunchtime, and there were plenty of people out taking breaks in the warm Georgia sunshine. Since it was June, the humidity made the air thick and sticky, but it was better than being locked inside a stuffy office all day.

As Kate stepped into the coffee shop, she looked for someone who could potentially be her tipster. Not seeing anyone promising, she took a seat at the table in the back corner and waited.

After a few minutes, a woman who was probably in her mid-forties took the seat across from her. She had brown hair cut in a no-nonsense bob and wore simple wire-frame glasses that only partially obscured her bloodshot eyes.

"You're Kate Sullivan?" the woman asked in a low voice. Then she turned and looked over her shoulder. Nervous—and paranoid.

"Yes. And you are?"

"Ellie Proctor."

"Nice to meet you, Ellie. Why don't you explain to me what this is all about."

"I'm scared," Ellie said as she clenched her pale hands together in front of her.

"There's nothing to be afraid of. You're safe with me."

"No, you don't understand."

Was this lady a conspiracy theorist? Kate had no idea what she was dealing with. "Just take it one step at a time. Do you work for MPC?"

"Yes."

"And what is your job there?" Kate felt like she was conducting a deposition, trying to get information out of a witness.

"I'm one of the senior R&D scientists." Ellie shivered, but the coffee shop's air conditioning was barely functioning.

Kate pressed on. "What do you work on?"

"A variety of testing and product development for different drugs."

"And you think you know something about Celix? The drug involved in my cases."

Ellie nodded. "Yeah. I did my research. I went onto the law firm websites and read all the information about the litigation."

"And what do you think?"

"It's so much bigger than what you and the other lawyers around the country are saying about Celix."

Now Ellie had Kate's undivided attention. "How so?" Celix caused brain tumors, so she wasn't sure how much bigger this could get.

Ellie looked down. Her brown eyes not making contact.

"Listen, Ellie, I can't help you if I don't know what the facts are." She needed to be patient. This woman seemed like she might go off the ledge at any minute.

"You need to dig deeper." Ellie wrapped her arms tightly

around herself as she shook. "A lot deeper, but you have to be careful."

"The case is just starting, but I'm always very thorough."

As Ellie's eyes darted back and forth, Kate began to wonder if Ellie was strung out on something. The red eyes, the shivering, the paranoia. Did this woman even work for MPC?

"The lawsuits say that MPC should have known through its testing that brain tumors were a potential side effect, but . . ."

"What?"

"I've already said too much out in the open like this, but you need to go beyond Celix. This is bigger than Celix. You have to look at other MPC drugs. Get your hands on all of the testing records for Celix and the emails about the test results. I can't provide them to you. My computer has highly restrictive security protocols. I'm hoping you'll be able to get them through your case, but I know some of the documents have already been shredded or deleted. I don't even know what's left on our servers. I think this goes up to the highest levels of the company." Ellie glanced furtively around, then leaned over the table and whispered, "I know it sounds crazy, but I'm taking a risk even coming here to meet you."

Kate looked around, and no one in the coffee shop seemed even remotely interested in what they were talking about. But even given how weird this all seemed, she couldn't just push it under the rug and walk away. "How about we set up a time and place to meet? Your choice. Somewhere you're comfortable talking openly with me, so I can gather more facts."

Ellie let out a long sigh. "Thank you. I think that's for the best. I thought I might be able to talk here, but it just doesn't feel right. Can we meet the day after tomorrow at 7:00 p.m. at the entrance of Piedmont Park?"

"Sure. I'll be there."

Ellie reached across the table and gripped Kate's hand.

"Whatever you do, you can't bring my name into this. I'm coming to you because it's the right thing to do. I can't sleep at night with all of this on my conscience." She took a deep breath.

"I'll be discreet." Kate didn't want to jeopardize Ellie's livelihood, but she definitely had to get to the bottom of this.

"I have to get back to work before my lunch break ends."

"Can I get your contact information?"

"Yes. This is my business card. I'll put my personal cell on the back." Ellie took a pen out of her small navy purse and, with a wobbly hand, wrote down her number. Then she scratched through her work contact information. "Please don't ever contact me at work."

"You did the right thing by coming to me, Ellie. I'm going to figure out what's going on here."

A few hours later, Kate returned to the office after the steering committee application hearing in front of the magistrate judge. The cases against MPC had been consolidated into a multidistrict litigation called an MDL. And that meant the judge was going to pick the plaintiffs' steering committee—known as the PSC in the legal world.

There wasn't room on the committee for all fifty attorneys who'd applied, and most of her competition was male. But she didn't want to be put on the PSC because of her gender. She wanted to get a spot because she was highly qualified and would be an asset. All she could do now was wait to hear the judge's choices for the committee.

Her phone rang, and she looked down. She instantly recognized the number as Ethan Black, her longtime friend who also happened to be opposing counsel in the MPC case.

"Hey, Ethan," she said.

"I hear you did well in your application hearing today."

"Word travels fast, doesn't it? I just got back to my office. Did you guys have spies planted in the courtroom or something?"

"I'd much rather it be you on the steering committee than someone else."

"Just because we've been friends since law school doesn't mean I'm going to go easy on you." They'd met during their first year at the University of Georgia and quickly become close.

"Yeah, but in contrast to most of the crazy plaintiffs' lawyers I have to put up with on a daily basis, you have the ability to act rationally. It's probably because you started on the right side of things before you switched over to the dark side."

She laughed. "You're the one on the dark side, Ethan. Don't forget, I lived in your world for three years. You're defending a pharmaceutical company directly responsible for thousands of deaths."

"That's a baseless allegation," he shot back.

"No, it's a fact." Why was she fighting this now? It wouldn't matter.

"The fact is that MPC's drugs are lifesaving. You're forgetting how much good their drugs do. The innovation MPC has attained is unmatched."

"One good drug or a hundred good drugs doesn't outweigh all the bad they've done by putting Celix on the market if they knew it had life-threatening side effects." She tapped her pen on her legal pad, starting to lose patience. "But I know we aren't going to agree on any of this. It's just like the old days on the mock trial team. Do I have to remind you who was on the winning side then?"

He laughed loudly. "You always find a way to fit that into conversation. Want to grab dinner and catch up? I promise we won't talk about this case."

"I'm sorry, but I'm slammed right now. Can I get a rain check?"

"Of course. And we'll be seeing a lot of each other very soon."

After she hung up, she closed her eyes for a moment and asked God to give her the strength to get through this litigation. It was going to be her toughest yet.

# CHAPTER
# TWO

The next morning, Kate knew she needed a plan. That was why she was sitting at her desk, anxious for her meeting with a new private investigator. She didn't use PIs often, and her normal guy was out of the country, but he'd given her a recommendation. She needed someone who could determine what was happening at MPC, and fast.

Beth knocked and opened her office door. A tall dark-haired man stood next to her, wearing jeans and a leather jacket. "I have Mr. James here to see you."

"Thanks, Beth." Kate stood to greet Landon James.

He took her hand in a firm handshake. "Nice to meet you, ma'am."

"Thanks for coming on such short notice. I've got a situation on my hands I need your help with. You come highly recommended by Peter Myers."

She watched as Landon took a seat across from her. His dark brown eyes locked onto hers. He was younger than Peter—probably in his late thirties, just like her.

"Tell me how I can help," Landon said.

She gave him their standard confidentiality agreement, and he looked it over quickly and signed. "Let me give you some case background. I'm working on a large consolidated litigation against Mason Pharmaceutical Corporation, or MPC for short. Their drug called Celix is used to treat migraines, but MPC should have known through its testing that the drug actually leads to brain tumors. MPC failed to warn the public and medical professionals about this danger. We represent the individuals who took Celix and formed tumors, or the estates of victims in cases where the tumors led to death."

Landon nodded. "Sounds like a typical case against Big Pharma."

"You're right. But I had a brief meeting with an MPC employee named Ellie Proctor yesterday. She was very secretive when it came to setting up the meeting. She didn't want to talk on the phone or come to my office."

He raised an eyebrow. "What did she tell you?"

"That's the thing. She didn't divulge much specific information at all. She claims she's a senior R&D scientist at MPC, but she seemed paranoid and shifty. Maybe even strung out on something."

"You're questioning her reliability?"

"Of course, but I also wonder if there's anything to what she said. It was clear to me that she believed something was going on. She said the case was much bigger than any of the lawyers realized, and that I needed to look beyond Celix to examine other drugs."

"You think that means that other MPC drugs also have dangerous side effects?"

"That was my thought. I'm obviously not sure, but it's enough to make me curious."

He scribbled down some notes. "Where did the two of you leave the discussion?"

"I'm going to meet her tomorrow after work at Piedmont Park."

"You want me to start doing the deep dive on her?"

"Absolutely. Here's a copy of the business card she gave me." She slid the copy over to him. "I need you to figure out if she is who she says she is and gather any information you can about her. I haven't scared you off yet, have I?"

A slight grin crept over his lips. "No, ma'am. I don't scare easily."

"You can call me Kate."

"Sorry. It's a habit."

"Were you in the military?" That wasn't in the brief bio that was sent over, but from the way he carried himself, he had a strong military vibe. And he was built more like a soldier than an investigator.

"Yes."

Before she could say anything else, he shifted the conversation back to business.

"With people like Ellie, credibility is everything. Whistle-blowers can either be completely legitimate or just disgruntled employees."

She ran a hand through her hair. "She said I needed to get my hands on the testing documents. I'll have to rely on the document discovery process to get access to those."

He continued to take notes. "And can you explain what you mean by that?"

"In litigation, we have a phase called discovery. Each side has to turn over documents to the other side, respond to written requests, and we also have depositions of witnesses. All of that takes place under certain rules of discovery, and we're on a specific timetable for getting it done. The stakes are very high in this case, with huge implications."

"What kind of implications?"

"We're talking about thousands of people who died from brain tumors or are currently sick. I'm fighting for those people and their families. They deserve justice, and MPC shouldn't just get away with it."

He set down his pen. "I can get right on it."

"This has to be completely discreet. I don't want MPC to fire Ellie because she came to me."

Landon nodded. "This could all be a big mistake or misunderstanding on her part. Sometimes employees think they hear or see something, and then their imagination goes wild. Or she could have an ax to grind—being passed over for a promotion or a raise will do that to people."

"Yeah. I'm taking all that into consideration and trying to keep an open mind. I need to run down every lead to do the best I can for my clients. I hate to put added pressure on you, but I need you to find out the facts as quickly as possible."

"Understood. I'll call you as soon as I have something."

"Thanks for making this a top priority. I look forward to working with you."

"I can see myself out. I know you have other work to get to." Landon rose from his chair and left.

He seemed on top of things and ready to get started, which was exactly what she needed. While she would be anxious to hear the results of his investigation, she couldn't allow herself to become too preoccupied. She had her own work to get done to prepare for the discovery phase of the litigation. Because once that started, it would be nonstop.

Ethan splashed water on his face and looked in the mirror. He straightened the red-striped tie he had paired with one of his favorite black suits. But the bags under his green eyes gave him away. He'd barely slept last night, and now he had a full day ahead at work. Exiting the men's restroom, he walked back to his office and shut the door behind him.

He steadied his breathing as he read the emails from his client, CEO Royce Hamilton. Ethan had landed this case after pitching to Royce and the executive team at MPC. He knew this litigation would be taxing, but he needed to figure out a way to manage expectations. They were the defendants. Juries hated big drug companies. Their best option was likely settlement, and he had to find a way to convince Royce that settling actually meant victory for MPC. Royce was hardheaded and had made it perfectly clear that he wanted to win jury verdicts because he was adamant that MPC was in the right.

Since Ethan had only been an equity partner at his firm for two years, he was still under the microscope. He'd had a big defense victory in his first year as partner, but last year he'd had a critical loss. The victory had given him a little cushion, but the message that he couldn't lose another case anytime soon had been loud and clear. In Big Law, one day you were on the top of the world, and the next day you were kicked out of the partnership and stripped of your equity.

He pulled up the report of billable hours from last month. His numbers were solid, and he had enough work to keep a team of associates busy. But MPC was a mega company with more litigation coming down the pike, and he needed that work. So as much as he cared for Kate and their friendship, he was going to use it to his advantage. Kate was smart but too kindhearted for her own good, which was why she was now working for plaintiffs instead of defending big companies. There was no place for feeling or emotion in corporate defense.

As Ethan scanned his emails from Royce, he figured it would be easier to pick up the phone. He dialed Royce's number and waited to be put through by his assistant.

"This is Royce."

"Royce, it's Ethan. I'm reading your emails and questions and thought I'd just give you a call."

"What is all of this legal mumbo jumbo you sent over? I need you to give me the bottom line. When I ask for summaries, I don't want ten-page legal memos."

"I understand. I just wanted to provide you with the full picture in case you need all the details."

"What I need is a status report that I can read and comprehend quickly. I've still got a company to run."

Royce was clearly going to be a very high maintenance client. "The bottom line is that the judge heard from the applicants who want a spot on the plaintiffs' steering committee."

"Why do I need to care about this committee?"

"Because they call all the shots on the other side. We'll have to deal with the committee during the entire discovery process and for the bellwether trials."

"And the bellwether trials are basically the test cases, right?"

"Exactly. The judge will determine how many we have, but I'm guessing three to five. If we can win or at least split those, it will go a long way toward pressuring them to settle."

"Don't you dare say the *s*-word. Settlement isn't an option. We need to win. That's why we're paying you so much."

Ethan kept trying. "Remember what I said, though. This isn't a single case. This is thousands of cases around the country consolidated into one court. Settlement would actually be a good option if we got the number low enough."

"Let's win the bellwether trials first. Then we can talk about that. Anyone in the running for this committee that we need to be concerned about?"

"Concerned might be too strong a word, but there's one attorney I think will get on the committee. I've gone up against her before, and I've known her personally for years. We were in the same law school class. She's formidable, but I'm already working on her."

"At the end of the day, a victory is all I want. I don't care

22

how you get there. Do whatever it is you have to do. We can't get to where we need to be as a company as long as this case is dragging us down."

"We'll do our best."

"It better be enough." Royce hung up.

Ethan needed MPC as a client, but he was starting to question if the hassle would be worth it.

Landon didn't waste any time jumping into his new assignment. He'd run some basic computer searches and was ready to get out in the field. His meeting with Kate had been productive, but she hadn't been what he was expecting.

He generally didn't like lawyers. The attorneys he'd dealt with previously were slimy and untrustworthy. Always focused on how much money they were going to make from a case.

There was something different about Kate. The retainer agreement she'd emailed to him was entirely reasonable. And on top of that, she actually seemed to care about the people she was representing. It was a refreshing change of pace to work with someone like that. But the petite, auburn-haired attorney with the big hazel eyes might be stepping into trouble, and his protective instincts had kicked in. He had to figure out exactly what they were dealing with here.

Ellie's story sounded suspicious to him, but it was his job to question everything. There was often so much more to it than the facts as first presented to him. And his decade and a half in the military meant he was always looking over his shoulder.

Now that he'd done the requisite initial research, he wanted to get eyes on his subject of interest. He made his way down to MPC's headquarters, where Ellie currently worked. Her background check had raised a few red flags, and he'd emailed the info to Kate so she would have it ahead of their meeting. Ellie had been through some bad financial struggles over the years and she'd gotten a DUI a year ago. His research had confirmed that she was indeed a scientist at MPC and had been for years. She was forty-six, divorced with no children.

As he neared the parking garage next to the MPC office, he saw police lights and officers swarming the area. Something was always going on in downtown Atlanta. He would just park in a metered spot and try to get where he needed to go on foot.

For a brief moment he thought about saying a prayer but then reconsidered. God had abandoned him when he needed the Lord the most out in the Sandbox. Why would He listen to Landon now?

He parked his black Jeep Wrangler, fed the meter, and started toward the MPC building. More police cars arrived on the scene and parked in front of the garage next to MPC. Landon got about a block away from the building before an oncoming officer stopped him.

"I'm sorry, sir. I can't let you pass. We're working an active crime scene."

"I'm just trying to get into the MPC building."

The stocky bald officer shook his head. "There's been an incident in the garage, and we're locking down this block. No one can go in or out of these buildings right now until we've secured the area."

"What happened?"

"Can't say that either at this point. If you have business to take care of at the MPC building, I suggest you come back tomorrow. We're going to be here for a while."

Landon was frustrated, but he knew the officer was just doing his job. "Thank you, sir." He turned and walked away, but he wasn't going to give up that easily. He'd circle back around and come up the other side of the street.

Kate had made it clear that this was important, and he didn't have any time to get sidetracked.

He noticed a local news truck had also arrived, and that gave him an idea. He jogged toward the reporter and her cameraman. Best to go with the direct approach.

"Ma'am?" he said to her.

The young blonde looked at him and smiled. "Yes?"

"Can you tell me what's going on?"

"I'm going live in two minutes. You can listen in."

"Thank you." He stepped aside to make sure he wouldn't be in the camera shot and watched as the reporter fluffed her hair and reapplied bright pink lipstick before looking directly into the camera.

"We're live in thirty seconds," the cameraman said.

Landon waited patiently for her to start speaking.

"This is Analise Jenkins reporting live from downtown, where a lockdown is currently in progress after a shooting in the Wallace Street parking garage. Police are not giving many details, but we will provide updates as soon as we have them."

Unfortunately, this wasn't the first time someone had been shot in an Atlanta parking garage. But given the seriousness of the crime, it probably wasn't worth trying to get into the MPC building right now. He'd just have to come back in the morning like the officer had suggested.

Once the reporter was off the air, he approached her again. "Ma'am, do you have any other information?"

"Not yet. But I'm about to go talk to the police again. Why are you so interested?"

"I'm a PI working a case, and this has thrown a wrench into my investigation."

"Ooh, give me your card. Never know when I'll need a PI contact." She smiled at him again, and he got the sense she was really more interested in him than in his work. But he gave her his card, because he could always use a friend in the media. His business was all about connections.

An officer approached Analise, and Landon stayed close by to see if he could learn anything from their conversation.

"We've identified the victim and have completed the family notifications."

"Can you give me a name?" Analise asked the officer.

"Yes. An MPC employee by the name of Ellie Proctor."

Landon stared at the officer as Analise asked several more questions but was politely rebuffed. When the officer left and Analise went to talk to her cameraman, Landon jogged off toward his car, still in shock. Kate would want to know this right away. There was no way this could be a coincidence.

"Ellie's dead?" There had to be some sort of mistake. "We were supposed to meet tonight." A knot formed in Kate's stomach as she looked across her desk and into Landon's eyes, hoping there was a mix-up.

"I'm sorry," Landon said. "I came right over once I heard."

"And you're sure about this?"

He nodded. "There's no mistake. I heard the officer tell a reporter her name, but I don't have any details on the shooting yet."

"I know the crime rates in Atlanta are high, but this is just sickening." She was still reeling from the news. How could this have happened?

He looked down at his notepad. "Kate, I need you to hear me out on something."

"What?"

He leaned forward in his chair. "I think there's a possibility this wasn't just a random act of violence."

"I don't follow."

"You said yourself that Ellie seemed scared and highly paranoid about talking to you. MPC could've discovered that she was about to blow the whistle and decided to take her out."

She gasped. "No. That's too much, Landon. MPC wouldn't kill one of its own employees. That's crazy, like something you'd see in a movie. This is real life. Stuff like that doesn't happen."

"I think you're being a bit naïve about a company like MPC."

She thought he was overreaching. "But killing one of their own in cold blood? That's on a totally different level."

"I know it's a lot to take in, but we need to consider that this is much bigger than you initially thought, more than Ellie even uncovered." He paused. "I don't mean to scare you, but if I'm right and MPC is involved in this, then there's a likelihood that you could be in danger too."

Her heartbeat began to race. "Why me?"

"If they're willing to take her out, then you're also a target, since you're the opposing lawyer."

A chill shot down her arms at the word *target*. She practiced corporate law, not criminal. Suddenly she felt very out of her element. "You said yourself that Ellie had reliability issues."

"You're right, but now she's dead. I think that says something. We at least have to consider the possibility that she was onto something, even if she wasn't one hundred percent reliable."

Her phone rang and she ignored it, but a few seconds later, Beth was on the intercom. "Sorry to interrupt, Kate, but it's a call from Judge Freeman's clerk."

"Give me a second, Landon. I need to take this call."

"No problem."

She picked up the phone and heard the voice of the judge's clerk. "Ms. Sullivan, I have news for you. You have been selected to be a member of the plaintiffs' steering committee."

"Thank you." She enjoyed a little jolt of happiness that was immediately dampened by what she'd just learned about Ellie.

"Judge Freeman also wanted you to know that he will make his decision about who on the PSC will serve as lead counsel within the next couple days. If you have any supplemental information you think would inform his decision, please email it to me by close of business tomorrow."

Kate listened to the clerk give some further details, but her mind was already a few steps ahead. This was what she wanted. She ended the call and looked up at Landon.

"Good news?" he asked.

"Yes. I got a spot on the plaintiffs' steering committee."

He smiled at her. "Congratulations."

"Thanks. But now really isn't the time to celebrate." As much as she wanted to enjoy the moment, she couldn't.

"Which brings us back to your situation."

"Find out what you can, but be careful, okay? I'm still not willing to jump to the conclusion that MPC was involved in Ellie's death, but I don't want to take any unnecessary risks."

He closed his notepad. "I'll develop a plan and be in touch."

"Let me know as soon as you find out anything. No matter how small the development."

"You got it."

Once she was alone in her office, she put her head in her hands and let the tears flow freely. She'd only met Ellie once, but that didn't change her emotional reaction. Drug companies were known for putting profit above all else, but murder was hard for her to believe. Ellie Proctor had been following her conscience—and now she was dead.

*Lord, what have I stumbled upon?*

# THREE

Nicole Sosa blinked a few times as she tried to read her emails. She looked at the time and saw it was 10:00 p.m. But as a midlevel associate at Peters & Gomez, she wanted to stay a step ahead of the competition.

Miles Patterson sat two offices down, and she could hear his grating voice. She hated leaving the office before him. They were the same year and both gunning for the partner track. The sacrifices she'd made were enormous, but in the end, wouldn't it all be worth it? She hoped so.

No matter how hard she worked, Miles always seemed to be half a step ahead of her. His father, a retired federal judge, was buddies with several of the senior partners, so Miles got his pick of the best assignments while she had to fight and claw for each small thing. Her reviews had been stellar, but she couldn't help but feel that when the time came, Miles would make partner first even if she deserved it more.

As a fifth-year associate, she had at least three more years before she would be considered for partner, and she needed to shine on the MPC case. A case to which both she and Miles had been assigned. Of course, she would be managing the document review team, while he had somehow scored the more prestigious deposition preparation team.

But tonight she was preoccupied with the latest decision of the court. She reviewed the court order that appointed the twelve members of the PSC. Ethan had tasked her with diving into their backgrounds. It always helped to know the opposing counsel and identify any potential weaknesses. And it was never a good idea to underestimate a plaintiff's lawyer. Especially ones like these, who were the top attorneys from the most renowned firms in the country.

She enjoyed the challenge of being on the defense side, but she also hadn't had any choice in the matter. She had over two hundred grand in student loans from Emory she had to pay off. Getting a job in Big Law, as it was known, had been a necessity.

"What're you up to, Sosa?" Miles stood in her doorway with his arms crossed. He always called her by her last name.

"Researching the PSC members."

"Anything exciting?"

"Not yet." She studied him carefully. His movie-star boy-next-door looks had gotten him far in life. He wore his blond hair short, his eyes were as blue as the ocean, and he always wore tailored suits. Unlike hers, which she bought off the clearance rack at Macy's. She was on a tight budget because of her loans.

"Did you draft the document review protocol?"

She was immediately suspicious of his question. Why did he care about the protocol? He wasn't going to be the one managing the review team. "Yes. I sent it to Ethan for his review. Do you want to join my team?" she asked, knowing that document review was beneath him.

He let out his typical boyish laugh. "You know me, Sosa. I'm the best at getting out of document review assignments. Remember when we were second years and that huge doc review came in late on a Friday for the Martinez case?"

Did she ever. Miles had suddenly developed an acute case of food poisoning. "I do. I also remember seeing pictures of you partying on Facebook later that weekend when you were supposedly deathly ill."

He grinned, showing the dimple in his right cheek. "That's the difference between you and me. You're the rule follower, but you don't play as smart as you could. It's not too late to learn how to game the system here."

But he didn't understand. Gaming the system only worked for those who had connections and could make power plays because they had family to fall back on. Unlike her. "I'll just keep being myself, Miles. I work as hard as I can, and that's all I can do."

"The word among the associates is that the MPC case is going to be our biggest of the year. All the associates are posturing to get on the team—even if it's just to do the grunt work."

"It's high profile and big exposure. I got the sense that Ethan is going to be very hands-on." He'd called her into his office earlier and reiterated what the stakes were. She wouldn't forget his words. *I know you'll put in the time and effort, Nicole, to get this right. We cannot drop the ball.*

"I'm just glad that you and I already have our spots on the team locked down. Working for Ethan has been one of the best moves I've made."

Miles liked to take credit for helping her get her first assignment from Ethan. Maybe he had opened the door, but Nicole believed her work ethic was what kept her in Ethan's good graces. "We'll have to wait and see how much infighting there is, but I'd prefer to keep my head down and stay out of it."

"Of course you would, Sosa. Drama is not your style." He looked at his fancy watch. "It's late. Why don't we get out of here? Want to go grab some food?"

Miles always had an angle, but what had become clearer to

Nicole over the years was that Miles was also lonely. "No, I'm beat. I think I'm just going to call it a night."

"At least let me walk out with you. Since that woman got shot downtown, they're asking us to walk out in pairs. Especially at this time of night."

She could say a lot of things about Miles being pompous, but at the end of the day, he had been raised right as a southern gentleman, and she was grateful for his offer. "Thank you, that'd be great. I still can't believe one of MPC's employees was shot. Their office is just down the street." Just the thought of it was enough to make her check her locks twice tonight.

"I know. Last I heard, they're calling it a robbery gone wrong."

"I can't imagine she would've had that much of value on her. People don't carry much cash anymore."

"It's awful. But it's downtown Atlanta. You always have to be careful around here."

Nicole nodded, but she couldn't help thinking that she had much more to fear from the man standing before her than any random criminal lurking in the night.

Kate was accustomed to working long hours—coming in early and leaving late. Today was no exception. She rubbed her eyes and saw that it was past ten o'clock, but even though she was tired, her anxiety level was making her uneasy and restless. She didn't want to go home. As long as she was at work, she felt like she maintained some control over her life, the case, everything.

After she'd made the transition to plaintiff's work, she definitely enjoyed her job much more. No one in her life had any clue that she still dealt with bouts of loneliness and depression—not even her closest friends. She put on a brave face and got the job done and had never told anyone about her struggles with depression.

When she took on huge cases like this, it tended to amplify her emotions. The highs were very high, but the lows were incredibly low. Another reason she didn't want to leave. The office was more of a sanctuary for her than her home.

"Kate."

She looked up to see William Kirk—her mentor and one of the senior partners—standing in her doorway.

"William, you're working late." He didn't look tired, though. His dark brown eyes were still filled with energy. He was known as a health nut and took incredible care of himself.

"We had a big brief in response to a motion to dismiss to file. I wanted to stay here until I made absolutely sure that we made the deadline."

"I'm glad you made it."

He walked in and took a seat. "That brief has been taking all my time and attention today, but I did see the court's order hit my email. I wanted to congratulate you on getting a spot on the steering committee. I think you're ready for the lead counsel role. I hope you're going to throw your hat into the ring."

"Absolutely."

"Anything I can do to help?"

William had thirty years of experience under his belt, and he'd taken her under his wing from day one when she lateraled over from her old firm. "The clerk says we can submit supplemental information, although it's not required. Any advice on what I should include?"

"Honestly, you can submit an additional statement, but I think Judge Freeman already has a good idea who he's picking. And from what I'm hearing through the grapevine, you hit it out of the park at the application hearing."

She felt her cheeks redden, as she wasn't used to such praise. "Thanks for that, but I just did the best I could."

"Regardless of whether you're lead counsel, though, we need

to start putting together our internal team. Since you're on the committee, we'll have control over a large chunk of work. Even more so, if you make lead. You can have your pick of associates for your team, but we should talk about additional partner staffing."

She knew that on a case like this, at least one other partner would be included. They always had to have coverage, and one person wouldn't cut it. But there were some people she'd much rather work with, and one person she really didn't want to deal with at all. "I think you know my feelings on that subject."

"I hear you, and I know what you're thinking, but Bonnie has extensive experience in this type of litigation. You don't have to be best friends with her. It's all about winning the case."

She and Bonnie had butted heads since Kate arrived at the firm. Bonnie was a few years older, and Kate had hoped that Bonnie would be her mentor. But she couldn't have been more wrong. "Anyone else you'd like to recommend?"

"Adam. He'll be a good counterbalance to Bonnie. I think the three of you would represent the right mix of skills and experience. Of course, they're your cases, so it's your show."

"But you know I value your opinion."

He smiled. "And I know you'll pick the right team. I trust your judgment, and I want you to take control and lead this thing from start to finish. You don't need me looking over your shoulder. We want everyone to see that you did this on your own." With a final nod of encouragement, he stood and walked out, leaving her alone.

William was right. It was time for her to step out of her mentor's shadow. She wondered if she should have told him about Ellie, but it was too soon. First Landon had to find the answers she so desperately needed.

⊰◇⊱

The next morning, Landon sat in a Midtown coffee shop bustling with action and waited for Kate to arrive so he could update her on where his investigation stood. He watched as person after person dressed in a suit rushed in and ordered their fancy coffee drinks. It seemed, by the puzzled look on the barista's face when he'd ordered, that Landon was the only one in the joint who liked regular coffee.

No way could he imagine having an office job. He thrived on being out in the world, doing things, and would go stir-crazy otherwise.

He'd been talking to a bunch of his sources and doing good old-fashioned investigatory work. It was one of the many things he liked about his job. The pace was slower than being in the military, but he enjoyed being able to solve difficult problems.

When Kate walked in, she brought a huge ball of energy with her. He knew the long hours she worked, but she didn't appear tired—just the opposite. Wearing a black no-nonsense skirt suit and white blouse, she looked ready for the courtroom.

"Good morning." She smiled. "I've got to grab a latte first. Are you good?"

"Yeah. I got here early and have already had two cups of coffee." He looked down at the file in front of him, which he'd been reviewing in anticipation of the meeting.

After a minute, she joined him at his table by the window with a large cup in hand.

"How're you doing?" he asked.

"A lot of that will depend on what you're going to tell me."

"I've got a source inside the police department. Unfortunately, though, they don't have any new leads on the shooter. The garage surveillance tape shows a man dressed all in black leaving the garage shortly after what is believed to be the time of the shooting. No indication of a tie to gang violence, and definitely not a crime of passion."

"What does all of that tell you?"

She wasn't going to like where he was going with this. "It screams professional. The guy knew where the cameras were. He was careful to avoid them. He shot Ellie out of range of the video camera, so the actual shooting isn't on tape. This type of guy is a paid pro."

Her eyes widened as he spoke. "So you still think MPC is involved in some way."

"Well, I know the shooter wasn't a random criminal or a street thug."

Kate paled, and he had to remind himself that she was a lawyer. This world was totally foreign to her, but he felt right at home. As a former Ranger, he'd seen his share of violence. Enough to last him a lifetime.

"I'm not sure what to do with this information," she said quietly. "I still have such a hard time believing that someone at MPC would put a hit out on Ellie Proctor. I mean, isn't that what we're talking about here?"

He nodded. "That's exactly what I'm talking about, but there are a lot of missing pieces I'm still working through."

She picked up her cup but didn't take a sip. "I've been thinking about this a lot. Ellie said I needed to look at the testing documents. I'm going to have my team really focus on those as we start the document review."

He wasn't so sure about that. "Do you really think MPC would willingly turn over incriminating documents?"

She drummed her fingers on the table. "As attorneys, we're ethically bound to turn over relevant documents."

"You need to consider that this might not be like your normal cases. If I'm right about Ellie, then MPC won't have any qualms about hiding evidence."

"Hopefully, with enough documents, we can put the real picture together. Sometimes with huge corporations, there's so much data that even if they wanted to hide something, it could still come out, given the nature of how lawyers have to collect and electronically review the documents."

"You get the lead counsel role so you can shape the case, and I'll keep working this investigation." He didn't want her directly involved in his work at this point. Not while he was still unsure about the level of danger.

"About that. There are ethical rules involved in attorneys using private investigators. I want us to stay aboveboard on all of this."

He was seeing her feisty side now. "You realize the whole point of using a PI is to work in the shadows?"

"I don't have any problem with that, but I need to make sure we're not skirting the law. I want to figure out the truth and win these cases, but I still have to play by the rules. That's important to me."

"Roger that."

She cocked her head to the side. "There's that military thing again. How long were you in?"

"Fifteen years."

"What branch?"

"Army, with about nine years as a Ranger."

Her eyebrows rose. "That's impressive. I guess being a PI is pretty boring in comparison."

"Sometimes boring is better than the alternative of Iraq and Afghanistan." He wasn't about to get into a conversation about the wars he fought in and how it had impacted him. But Kate's straightforward and honest approach made her easy to talk to. Eager to turn the topic away from himself, he shifted direction. "And what about you? How long have you been doing the lawyer gig?"

Her eyes immediately lit up. It was evident how much she loved her work. "I've been a lawyer for thirteen years. I did three years on the defense side before making the switch. I made partner five years ago."

"Any thoughts on whether MPC's lawyers could be dirty?"

"No. I went to law school with their lead attorney. He just landed MPC as a client for this case. I know he isn't dirty. There's no way."

He feared Kate was too trusting for her own good and chose to see the best in people. Not a useful quality for a PI. "What's his name?"

"Ethan Black, from the firm Peters & Gomez."

He jotted that info down on his notepad. He'd take a closer look at Ethan to see if Kate's confidence in her friend was justified.

She looked down at her watch. "Anything else? I've got a conference call at nine."

"No. But I'll let you know as I find out more."

She reached across the table and touched his forearm. "Thank you, Landon. I appreciate all your hard work on this."

"You're welcome."

Kate stood up and walked out of the coffee shop. He had a lot of work to do to figure out just how corrupt MPC was and how far their deception went, but one thing was clear to him.

Kate Sullivan was one of the good guys.

# CHAPTER
# FOUR

That afternoon, Kate got the news from Judge Freeman's clerk that she had been waiting for. The judge had chosen her as lead counsel! It was a tremendous accomplishment, but with it came an enormous responsibility. She wanted to prove herself to the rest of the PSC members and other lawyers who may have doubted her.

Her struggles with confidence had gotten better over the years as she became more seasoned, but the little voice in her head still made her wonder if she was good enough to take on this big of a challenge.

The first thing she had to do was to get her house in order. The next morning, she sat with her fellow partners Bonnie Olson and Adam Fox in one of the firm's many conference rooms and prepared to bring them up to speed on the case.

Bonnie had a strong sense of style and today wore a heather gray fitted crossover suit jacket and pants. Her sparkling diamond stud earrings probably cost more than Kate's entire jewelry collection.

Adam was much more understated. The tall and lanky fifty-year-old attorney with thinning dark hair and glasses was often a bit disheveled. He focused much more on his work than his wardrobe, and it showed.

Bonnie and Kate had a lot in common, or so Kate had initially thought. They were both self-starters who had risen up through the ranks of a highly competitive plaintiff's firm. But their personalities and approaches were polar opposites. Kate had found that out the hard way.

Right after she arrived at the firm, she'd been a late addition to Bonnie's trial team and had suggested a strategy that Bonnie didn't agree with. Bonnie ignored Kate and lost the case. Some partners at the firm believed that if Bonnie had taken Kate's advice, it would've been a different story. Bonnie still held a grudge.

Kate smiled at her to try to break the ice, but Bonnie didn't reciprocate, her eyes showing no hint of warmth.

"Should we get started?" Kate asked.

"Sure." Adam's bright blue eyes confirmed that he was ready.

Unlike Bonnie, Adam was easygoing and a consummate team player. He had always helped Kate out in a pinch, and she had done the same for him. They were true partners. She couldn't say the same for Bonnie.

"We should get going, because I have other meetings I need to prepare for," Bonnie said.

Of course, it would always be about Bonnie's other work. Since Bonnie wasn't lead on this case, she wouldn't make it a top priority. Whether she wanted to deal with it or not, though, Bonnie was a highly skilled attorney, and Kate would utilize her if she could.

Kate recited the facts of the case as she knew them, leaving out the parts about Ellie. She didn't want to bring that up until she had a better grasp of the situation. It would just send the entire discussion into a tailspin that she couldn't afford.

"How can I help?" Adam asked.

40

"Would you take the lead on our expert witnesses?" One of Adam's strengths was his work with experts. He knew the medical field very well because he'd gone to a couple years of med school before he switched over to the law.

"Sure thing."

"And what about me?" Bonnie asked. "My time will be limited."

She decided to put the ball back in Bonnie's court. "What aspect of the case would you like to work on?"

Bonnie tucked her blond hair behind her ear, flustered by the question. "You're running the case, not me. I shouldn't be making those types of decisions."

Kate swallowed a sigh. "For now, please help Adam on the experts. I may pull you in on some of the discovery motions and document issues. There are going to be hundreds of thousands of pages produced by MPC."

"How many associates are you going to have working on this?" Bonnie asked.

"Well, from our firm, I plan on having ten, but we also have the resources of the entire PSC. I'd like to keep a tight grip on as much of the case as I can, though, and everything starts with the documents. I'm not willing to outsource that to another firm. A few of my PSC members have already offered their firms' services, but for the first bellwether trial, I want this to be a Warren McGee operation. That way we take full responsibility—big risk, big reward. And if anything goes awry, I'll get blamed anyway, since I'm lead counsel." She had another motivation too. She had to make sure she was on top of any connections to Ellie's warnings they found in the documents.

"That's smart, actually. Don't give away any of the work. Try to keep as much here as possible," Bonnie said. "We have the bandwidth to handle it, especially with our new crop of first-year associates. They're eager and ready to work."

Kate couldn't believe Bonnie had agreed with her on something. "From what I've told you, any potential pitfalls you'd be on the lookout for?" She looked at Bonnie and then Adam.

"Don't trust your friend," Bonnie said. "I don't care if he was in your section in law school. He's going to be out for blood. Drug companies don't play around, and if he doesn't deliver, MPC will drop Peters & Gomez without a second thought and move on to the next firm."

If only Bonnie knew exactly how cutthroat MPC might really be.

"I'll get right on the experts," Adam said.

"Thank you both. I'll email you the names of the associates I have lined up to work on this, and if you have anyone else you'd like to recommend, send them my way."

Adam gathered up his laptop and left the conference room, but interestingly enough, Bonnie didn't move.

Kate had to say something to break the awkward silence. "Is there something else you want to talk about?"

Bonnie flipped her laptop closed and made direct eye contact. "This is a big step for you, getting lead counsel on a case of this magnitude."

"Thank you. That means a lot coming from you."

"I'm not finished," Bonnie said. "If you truly want to succeed at this firm, or any firm like it, you've got to open your eyes."

"What do you mean?"

"Not everyone is like you, Kate. In fact, most people aren't like you. Let's get real for a moment. We're not here because of the victims, but because of our own overly inflated egos. And the money."

Kate fought to control her expression and let Bonnie keep talking.

"If you want to make it to the top, you need to start thinking about yourself more and less about others."

Kate shook her head. "The entire reason I became a plaintiff's lawyer was to help people and to advocate for those who don't have a voice. I could have stayed on the defense side if all I cared about was money and an ego boost."

Bonnie laughed. "That's the thing, Kate. Don't be fooled by our catchy slogans about victims' rights. It's all about money here too. We're a law firm—a business. And the sooner you figure that out, the better." She grabbed her designer laptop bag and left the room.

What had just happened? Was Bonnie trying to give her advice? Warped as the advice seemed to Kate, maybe that was Bonnie's way.

Kate didn't believe it was all about the money at Warren McGee. She personally knew lawyers like William who were passionate about their work, but she wasn't blind to the fact that it was still a business like Bonnie said.

As far as the MPC litigation went, Kate planned to push as hard as she could and do everything within her power to gain justice for the innocent.

She looked down at her watch and saw that it was almost time for her client meeting. Beth would be bringing Mrs. Wyman into the conference room for their discussion.

She represented many plaintiffs who were part of the consolidated litigation, but as lead counsel, it was her job to pick the candidates for the bellwether trials—and even more important to her, which plaintiff should be represented in the very first bellwether case. It was one of the most important strategic choices placed on her shoulders as lead counsel. She'd done the research in advance of getting the position because she wanted to be prepared for this very task. She'd made her decision. Now she just had to make sure that the family was on board. Nancy Wyman's sixteen-year-old daughter, Melinda, had taken Celix for migraines and developed an aggressive brain tumor that led to her death.

The tragedy of the situation made Kate physically ill, because for her, unlike what Bonnie had said, it really was all about the victim and the family. Not about the bottom line. Kate knew that to run a successful firm, you had to be concerned about money, but she believed it was possible to do both. And if people called her idealistic for that, then so be it.

*Lord, guide me. Give me the wisdom to know how to present this case to show the jury what MPC did.*

When Beth escorted Mrs. Wyman into the conference room, Kate's heart broke all over again. It never got any easier to see the grieving mother, and now with the possibility of something more nefarious going on at MPC, it made her even sicker.

She rose from her chair to greet Mrs. Wyman. "Thanks for coming down."

"Of course," Mrs. Wyman said. In her fifties, she was now not only a widow, but she'd lost her only child thanks to MPC.

"Please have a seat. Can I get you anything to drink?"

Mrs. Wyman shook her head. "No, I'm fine, thank you. Do you have updates on Melinda's case?"

"That's exactly what I wanted to discuss with you. I need to get your approval on Melinda's case being the very first one we take to trial."

Mrs. Wyman's eyes widened. "That's great, right?"

"I've selected your case because it's a very strong one both on the facts and the law, but also, your story is heartbreaking. I think a jury will identify with you and what you've been through. But that will mean you have to take the stand, and you'll have to relive this entire horrendous ordeal from start to finish. I need to make sure that you're okay with that before I push this case as the first one out of the gate."

Mrs. Wyman reached out and grabbed Kate's right hand.

"There's nothing MPC can do to me that hasn't already been done. They've already taken away the most precious person in my life, and I will do everything I can to make sure that they pay for their actions. No amount of money can ever bring Melinda back, but a company like that shouldn't be able to do what they did and get away with it."

"I also have to caution you that since this would be the first case, we might learn things as we go along. If we wait, the trial would probably go more smoothly." She wanted to make sure that Mrs. Wyman understood there were pros and cons involved in this decision.

"But you think Melinda's is the best one to go first?" she asked expectantly.

"I absolutely do."

Mrs. Wyman nodded. "Then I will be praying for you and your team. I've had to ask God many times to take away the hatred I feel for the people at that company who stole my baby from me."

Kate knew from previous discussions that Mrs. Wyman's faith was the only thing that sustained her through all of the tragedies she'd faced in life. "It's natural to be angry and hurt, but let me fight this battle for you in the courtroom."

"I trust you, Kate. From the day we first met, I knew that you'd do right by me."

"I don't want to take any more of your time today. I'll be in contact as the case progresses, though, especially when I need your direct involvement."

"Whatever you need, I'm available. I guess I don't have to tell you that this is on my mind every single day."

Kate felt her throat tighten at the raw hurt emanating from Mrs. Wyman. "I know, and I appreciate your dedication amidst all the pain. I'll have Beth walk you out."

Beth came back into the room, and Kate told Mrs. Wyman good-bye.

As she sat alone in the large conference room, fear started to creep in. Was she really up for this? What if she made the wrong decisions? What if she couldn't provide justice for Mrs. Wyman? She could only pray that she wasn't in over her head this time.

Landon decided it was time to call in some help. He needed to get an outside, objective perspective from someone he trusted. His college buddy Cooper Knight was just that man. Cooper had left the police force about a year ago to start his own private security firm.

Landon picked a table in the back corner of the restaurant that would give them the privacy they needed to talk. Taking a deep breath, he took a moment to embrace the aromas coming out of the kitchen. His stomach rumbled in anticipation of lunch.

Cooper joined him a couple minutes later, greeting him with a hearty handshake. "Good to see you, man. It's been a while."

And it had been. Landon had purposely avoided any of his friends when he returned from his final tour. It was just too hard. Cooper only knew that something bad had happened while Landon was deployed. He didn't know the details.

"I know. Too long, and for that I'm sorry."

Cooper nodded. "So what's up?"

"I'm working a case, and I'd like to bounce some ideas off you."

"I'm game," Cooper said.

The server came over, and they both ordered burgers with fried green tomatoes on top. Just one of the many things he loved about Atlanta—the southern food. Everything could be fried, and that was a huge plus in his book.

He turned his attention back to Cooper. "Hypothetically

speaking, how difficult would it be to get into the electronic systems of a large pharmaceutical corporation?"

Cooper's blue eyes narrowed. "Very difficult. And most likely illegal."

"I figured you'd say that."

"What's going on?"

"I've been retained by a law firm in a case against a pharmaceutical company. The main allegations surround one drug and its harmful side effects. I believe this company could have evidence on its servers that would be helpful."

"Wouldn't that come out during the litigation, when each side has to turn over documents?"

"Not if the company is dirty and refuses to turn them over."

Cooper let out a low whistle. "I get that you need the info, but hacking into the computer system is highly inadvisable. Even if you could get in, you'd be on the hook if you got caught. Don't you have a human source you could work?"

"We did, but she's dead."

"Dead? How?"

"Murdered, and I believe the company is responsible."

Cooper raised an eyebrow. "That might be a stretch, don't you think?"

"Normally, I'd tend to agree with you, but in this situation, I can't find any other rational explanation."

"You need to find a *legal* way to get at the information you need."

Landon already knew what Cooper was going to say, but he still needed to hear it. It didn't help resolve his problems, though.

"Maybe there's someone else on the inside who can help you," Cooper said. "It's worth digging around to find out. In my experience, if one person is willing to blow the whistle, there's likely another person as well."

"Let me talk to the attorney who hired me and is running the case. We might want to bring you on for some specific tasks."

Cooper smiled widely. "I'm always open for business."

Their burgers arrived, and Landon wasted no time taking a huge bite. When they were about halfway done with their food, Cooper set down his burger and looked at him.

"How're you doing?" Cooper asked.

Landon wanted to be honest with his friend, but it was hard to talk about his feelings because he tried not to feel at all. "The PI business is good. Staying busy on this type of work keeps me focused on moving forward and not dwelling on the past."

"A past that you can't change."

"I try to keep my mind on the present."

Cooper took a swig of his sweet tea. "I understand why you kept to yourself when you got back as you worked through stuff, but some time has gone by now. Over a year. I'd like to think that we could hang out again."

Landon felt like a jerk. "I know, Coop. I've been an awful friend."

"I get that it's pointless telling you that I'm around if you want to talk about it, but I'm going to offer anyway. I realize you went through some awful things in Iraq. I also know that you aren't one to talk about your personal stuff."

"Yeah, I'm not so good at that."

Cooper chuckled. "You're not the only one."

"So you're still working with Noah?"

"Yeah, and business is really taking off. When we started out, we focused on the tech side, but now that we've got that part of the business thriving, we're moving into personal security services too. But we're still trying to make sure we don't overstretch, building at a sustainable pace." Cooper paused. "And since we're here talking, I should let you know that we're considering opening up an investigation wing of the business, if you have any interest."

"Really? How do you think Noah would take that?"

"I'd like to think that the issues between the two of you could be put to rest. So that door is open. I'd much rather have us all working on the same team as opposed to being competitors."

Working with his old buddies could be great, but Landon wasn't in a position to commit to anything right now. And he'd have to deal with Noah. "Thanks for saying that. Let me think on it a bit."

"Of course. And if you need us for this case you're working, you know where to find me."

Landon hoped he wouldn't have to make that call, but he also felt that danger lurked around the corner.

CHAPTER
# FIVE

Nicole mentally readied herself for the team meeting. Things were heating up on the MPC litigation, and she planned to be ready to jump on any opportunity that presented itself. Since she knew battling Miles on his turf wouldn't work, she had to have something solid to show for herself on the substantive work. She'd never be able to play the political game like him.

She buttoned her black-and-white print suit jacket and walked into the large conference room, which was bustling with action. Of course Miles had already secured the seat next to the head of the long rectangular table. One of his typical power plays. She chose an open chair closer to the middle.

Ethan had called an all-hands-on-deck meeting. She wasn't sure what he wanted to discuss, but whatever it was, she was ready for the challenge.

Ethan walked into the room looking perfectly put together as usual. His short dark hair was neatly styled, and he wore a navy tailored suit and checkered tie. But she immediately noticed the dark circles under his eyes. She knew that being a relatively new partner at an elite law firm like Peters & Gomez was highly stressful. There was little room for error in this business when millions of dollars were on the line. She wondered if she was really cut out for that type of stress.

Ethan took a seat. "Thanks, everyone, for joining on such short notice. We need to start ramping up for the MPC case, and I want to make sure we're fully staffed and up to the task."

She looked around the room and saw a mix of associates at her level and those who were more junior. Ethan didn't have any senior associates on the case at this point. She liked to think that was because she and Miles already operated on the senior level even though they were technically still midlevels.

"The first case we're going to be trying is the Wyman case," Ethan said.

That statement set off chatter within the room. They'd developed a short list of the cases to propose for the bellwether trials. Each side got their first pick, and then the others would be negotiated. The Wyman case was one Nicole knew might be chosen by the plaintiffs, and she dreaded it.

"I can tell by your reaction that everyone has already read up on the facts of the Wyman case," Ethan said. "Yes, this is a big challenge, but if we can perform well on this case, it will shape how the entire MDL goes. There's no getting out of these bellwether trials, so buckle down and get ready for some of the most intense months of your life. For many of you, this will be your first experience with being on a trial team of this magnitude. These days, we don't see trials like we used to because most large corporations settle. But product liability is a different beast, and sometimes we have to go to court. So if anyone wants out, now is the time, because I can't have any excuses. This case will be your life for the next few months."

There was no way anyone was going to bail. That would be the easiest way to ensure a bad review and a closed-door meeting that resulted in being let go. Nicole had seen it happen one too many times.

Big Law had changed over the past few years. Gone were the days when you could slack off and still pick up the big paycheck as long as you did the bare minimum to get by. Now, with more lawyers than positions, they knew they were all replaceable and had to earn their keep. One misstep and they'd be shown the door.

Ethan crossed his hands together on the table. "Well, I see that you all want to be on this case, or you're just too scared to get up and walk away. Either way, you're stuck on this case until I tell you otherwise. Here's how we're going to divide things. Our outside vendor has done all the data collection from the systems at MPC—that includes hard drives, shared drives, the whole nine yards. We'll have to negotiate search terms with opposing counsel, but in the meantime, we're going to start our own internal searches. We need to identify any hot documents now so we can figure out how to work them into the storyline of our case."

Nicole had learned her second week as a first-year associate that a hot document was basically one you didn't want to exist. But there were ethical rules about what lawyers had to produce in litigation, and she believed Peters & Gomez would follow them. At least, she had on every other case she'd worked on for the past five years.

"The document review team is going to be led by Nicole Sosa. She'll manage the team and handle all of your day-to-day questions. We're looking for a minimum of ten hours of review a day. And before anyone starts moaning and groaning behind my back, yeah, I know it sucks. But if you want to work at a firm like this, it goes with the territory. I sat in your exact seat once."

That was true, but not everyone would end up in Ethan's partner seat. The competition was fierce—and that was for those who made it through the grueling years of being an associate. At Peters & Gomez, there was only one type of partner, and that was equity. Which meant that once you were in, you were a full partner and entitled to your piece of the pie. And at a firm like this, it was a substantial piece of pie.

"Each day you'll report your progress to Nicole, and she will keep me briefed on how things are going. If you find any hot docs, tag them in the electronic review database and let Nicole know immediately. Nicole, anything else to add?"

She wanted to set expectations up front so there would be no surprises. "Our vendor is conducting mandatory training on the database tomorrow morning at eight. Everyone must attend that meeting. I'll distribute the document review protocol after this meeting is done. We have a ton of docs to get through, so like Ethan said, we need everyone to be a team player." She looked over at Miles. He wouldn't be in the trenches, but she had to get over that. They were never going to be on a level playing field.

Ethan gave her a warm smile. "Thanks, Nicole. Our other team is the deposition and witness preparation team, and that's going to be led by Miles Patterson. The doc review team will feed the dep team the key documents so we can start preparing for deps and trial testimony. I'll send out specific team assignments when this meeting is over. Each team is vital, and neither is more important than the other. So regardless of which team you're assigned to, I want everyone on top of it. Any questions?"

The room was so quiet, it almost made her uncomfortable.

"All right, then," Ethan said. "I'll stick around for a few minutes in case anyone has questions they'd rather ask one-on-one."

Ethan was a nice guy, but he was still intimidating, especially to the younger associates. Not surprisingly, everyone filed out of the room except her, Miles, and Ethan.

"Did I scare them too much?" Ethan asked.

"Nah," Miles said. "They need to know how much work this is going to be."

She held back a laugh, given the comment was coming from Miles.

Ethan turned his attention to her. "Nicole, you need to rule your team with an iron fist. We can't afford to miss any key documents."

He'd reiterated this multiple times, which made her think he was worried about what they were going to find when they dug into MPC's computers. "Don't worry. You sent a strong message today, and I will reinforce that at our training tomorrow. And if there are any problems with their work ethic or competency, I'll let you know."

"We have two other huge cases happening right now, so I had to do some negotiating with other partners to make sure we had enough solid junior and midlevels to get this done. We could've contracted out the document review, but the client was insistent that everything was reviewed in-house, given the sensitive nature of the data."

"That's great for billable hours," Miles said.

"Yeah, but it means we'll be under even more scrutiny if something goes wrong. We won't be able to blame it on the outside vendor," Nicole said. "I had a document review that went sideways two years ago, but it was all the vendor's fault. We inadvertently produced privileged material to the other side because of the vendor's incompetence."

Ethan's face noticeably reddened. "I don't even want to know how that one ended, Nicole."

"Sorry," she said. She didn't need to add to his stress. Sometimes she needed to think more before she spoke.

Ethan ended the conversation by standing up and walking toward the door. "Keep me posted."

"Will do." She stood and walked out with Miles.

"How do you feel about the first case being Wyman?" he asked her.

"It's not good for us at all, but maybe having the hardest one first will end up working out. If we can mitigate the damages on this one, then maybe we have a fighting chance for a low settlement deal."

He nodded. "The jury is going to eat this one up. The woman's husband died of cancer ten years ago, and then she loses her only child to a brain tumor. They're going to make us out to be the big, bad drug company."

"Isn't that what we are?" she asked.

"Look, I'm under no delusion that MPC's hands are clean here, but we have to do our job as attorneys and defend them. That's part of what we do, working in a firm like this. We don't have time to get emotionally attached. Leave that to the plaintiffs' lawyers." He gave her a little punch in the arm. "Don't go soft on me, Sosa."

She looked up at him. "You don't have to worry about that."

"Good. Then let's get to work taking down these plaintiffs."

Kate ushered Landon into her office and eagerly awaited his update. Today he wore a gray button-down shirt and dark jeans. She looked up at him, expecting him to smile, but he did just the opposite. Something was wrong.

"What do you have for me?" she asked as he took a seat.

"You're not going to like it."

"What?"

"My police contact said the trail has run cold on Ellie's case and that while there is obviously a desire to pursue, he isn't optimistic on coming to a resolution any time soon—if ever."

She groaned. "They're not just going to give up, are they?"

He shook his head. "No, nothing like that, but when there are absolutely no leads, it puts law enforcement at a disadvantage. It's like they're chasing shadows. That's why professional hits are so hard to track down, and it means we don't have any ability to tie MPC to what happened to Ellie. We need to start thinking about other ways to get to the truth. I've got a few ideas I'm working on."

"Thanks for keeping me updated." She took a few deep breaths, but her heart still ached for Ellie. "Given that you and the police think it was a professional hit, is there any doubt in your mind that this is all connected to what Ellie knew about Celix?"

"I've thought about it long and hard and examined every angle, and I do believe it's all connected. The big problem is that we have no proof. There's nothing beyond our suspicions that I could take to law enforcement—and that's even if you wanted to go that route. I'm not knowledgeable enough on all the legal issues to understand how any criminal actions would impact your civil case."

She'd had those same thoughts. "At the end of the day, my ethical obligation is first and foremost to my clients. I need to see this through and put on the strongest case I can to advance their rights, because that's what I was hired to do, and it's the right thing. But what happened to Ellie has hit me hard. I feel like if we can gain justice for these victims, though, it would be the best way I could honor Ellie's memory. I have to leave the law enforcement efforts up to the experts. And like you said, what would we tell the police? They'd want to know what evidence we have, and all we could point to is my conversation, but that doesn't rise to the level of actionable evidence they'd need to open an investigation into MPC."

"You're right. Just because we strongly believe MPC is involved doesn't mean that law enforcement would see it that way. We're talking about a huge and highly respected company. None of the executives have any criminal records. I did that research as part of my investigation—the CEO, COO, CFO, all the members of the leadership team are squeaky clean and extremely wealthy. Men like that know exactly how not to get their hands dirty, but the end result is still the same."

"So what would you suggest we do?"

"Let me work some other avenues and see if we can go about getting more information. Hopefully, between the two of us, we'll be able to come up with something."

"I have a meeting with Ethan tomorrow to go over the discovery items. Things are about to jump into high gear on the litigation side."

"How are you holding up?"

"Why, do I seem like I'm frazzled?" She wondered if her stress was beginning to show.

He smiled. "Not at all. Just the opposite. You don't seem fazed by anything."

"Then I guess I'm a good actress, because this entire thing has shaken me quite a bit. I'm trying to remain focused on each task and take one step at a time because I care so much about getting this right."

He studied her for a moment. "You're really different than most lawyers."

"You think so?"

"Yeah. Most attorneys I've known are obsessed with lining their pockets, but you don't seem to be that interested in money."

"I'm interested in justice." She looked at him and realized she had put a lot of trust in him. That was something she didn't do easily, but he had a way of making her feel safe and comfortable. It wasn't just the fact that he was a former Army Ranger, though. It was something else she couldn't put her finger on.

"Your clients are fortunate to have you, Kate."

"I hope they feel that way after the first of the bellwether trials."

"I don't have any doubts about your skills. From everything

I've witnessed, you've got all the regular legal stuff completely under control."

"Thanks for the vote of confidence. Let me know when you come up with other strategies to vet the information that Ellie gave me."

"Will do."

The next day, Ethan sat in his law firm's conference room, waiting for Kate's arrival. He wanted their first discovery meeting to be on his turf, and she hadn't complained about his request to meet at his office. The conference room he'd chosen was one of the smaller ones, since it was just going to be him and Kate.

He'd become spoiled by all the law firm's amenities. Nice conference rooms were just the beginning of what he had tied up in his life at the firm. He stared out the window into the Midtown skyline and the other large office buildings filled with lawyers, accountants, businesspeople, and consultants.

Atlanta might not be New York City, but it was like the NYC of the South. Major corporations from various industries had made their home in Atlanta, including MPC. Ethan's goal was to become one of the biggest movers and shakers in the Atlanta legal community. One of the first steps was to achieve a huge defense victory in this litigation. Winning jury trials was the name of the game.

He'd come up with a game plan. It included being as aggressive as the law would allow. His career and lifestyle depended on the success of this case. When he'd made partner, he had bought a very large home in the suburbs and treated himself to an apple-red Maserati. They were big splurges, but he was also pulling in close to a million dollars a year now. That could all change in the blink of an eye if he messed things up. He couldn't allow that to happen.

When Kate walked into the room, he rose to greet her. She looked great as always, wearing a black-and-white polka dot jacket. "They just let you wander around this place unaccompanied now?" he joked.

"Yeah, you know how tight I am with Karen. I've been here enough to know my way around."

"Except, unfortunately, this time it isn't a social visit. Please sit and let's talk."

He looked at his longtime friend. Kate was one of those women who had no idea how pretty she really was. Her big hazel eyes always held so much kindness. He'd never had any romantic feelings toward her, but she was a close friend who had always been there for him. That was going to make this all the more difficult.

Sometimes life wasn't fair, and that was especially true in cutthroat, high-stakes litigation. Litigation that your career and paycheck depended on. He had accumulated a large amount of debt, thanks to his extravagant purchases, and he had no intention of turning back to his old life. If that meant he had to compromise his friendship a little, then that was what he was going to do, because this case meant everything to him.

So now he had to start putting on the hard sell and see if Kate would buy it.

"First, I should congratulate you on being tapped as lead counsel in this case. As a friend, I couldn't be happier for you. I know how hard you've worked to get to this point in your career, and this is a big payoff."

"But as opposing counsel, you're ready to rip my eyes out."

He laughed. "You know how it is." He opened his laptop. "But I could never rip your eyes out. You're the last person in the world who deserves that type of treatment. I think we can keep things friendly, even if we're on opposite sides."

"I'll definitely give it my best shot. We respect each other and understand the situation. And we've got a lot to discuss. Do you want to get started?"

"Yeah, I'm ready when you are."

"Where is your army of associates that I know you have working on this case?"

"I thought this first meeting would be more productive if it was just you and me. We can cut through the silly issues and get right down to it."

"You know I'm not going to cut you any slack, right?"

"Right back atcha."

She pulled a stack of papers and her laptop out of her bag. "Are we going to go through the document requests one by one?"

"Yeah. But I have to start out by saying that this is a crazy fishing expedition, Kate."

"Instead of making broad statements, let's stick to the specifics. I'm here, and we can walk through each item. I'm confident about all the requests I've made."

"Fine, then. Let's talk about search terms first and then go through the requests from the top."

After two hours, they'd butted heads on each and every document request Kate had submitted. Some more than others. They had come to somewhat of a resolution, though, on the first round of keyword search terms that his document collection vendor would use to identify the documents his team of associates would review. Given how much data was collected in these types of cases, it was standard procedure for each side to agree on what keywords would be searched. But they still had major disagreements over the scope of the doc requests.

It was time to play hardball. Especially after Kate threatened to file a motion to compel.

"Kate, if you do that, you'll lose and make yourself look bad in front of the judge, and you don't want that. I don't even want that."

"So you're giving this advice out of the goodness of your heart?"

"Your requests are way too broad and cover multiple other MPC drugs. This case is about Celix, not about any other MPC product. That's a line we need to abide by to keep this thing manageable for both sides. This is just your attempt to explode the case, put extra pressure on us, and hike up the legal fees by forcing us to look at thousands and thousands of pages of additional documents. Judge Freeman is going to be sympathetic to our position on this." There was no way he was going to expand this case to other MPC drugs. There were already enough obstacles in his way with Celix.

"That's your opinion, Ethan, but we don't know what we don't know. As plaintiffs, we reserve the right to examine all the relevant facts—including looking at other drugs."

"The key word being relevant. And other drugs are not relevant to this litigation, Kate, period. Unless you know something that I don't?"

She opened her mouth but then shut it. He didn't know what she was going to say or why she stopped.

"Go ahead. It's not like you've ever held back on me before."

"What have you got to hide?" she asked.

He held back a laugh. "Nothing, but it's ridiculous to expect a huge pharmaceutical company like MPC to freely give out information on drugs that aren't even remotely connected to this lawsuit. Putting aside the cost and resource issue, it just doesn't make good business sense."

She frowned but didn't say anything as she typed away on her laptop.

He watched her as she gave him the cold shoulder. But they weren't done talking.

"So the Wyman case as number one, huh?" he asked.

"You'll get your pick for number two."

"Yes, we will. But I don't think the Wyman case is as strong as you do."

"You have to say that, Ethan. You're the defendant."

He shook his head. Now was the time to play games to try to shake her. "My team is finding interesting things in the documents, and our experts are going to have a field day with the decedent's prior medical conditions."

Blotches of red started to spread up her fair neck. He'd gotten the reaction he wanted.

"The decedent has a name. Melinda. A sixteen-year-old girl. An innocent and vibrant girl whose life was taken from her by MPC. A girl who leaves behind a mother who had already lost her husband. Melinda was an only child."

He lifted his right hand. "Hey, I'm not heartless. I'm not saying her death isn't tragic, but I am saying that you're going to have a very tough time proving that Celix was the cause of that tumor. You don't have the science and law behind this to back up your story."

"That's not true," she shot back.

"You've examined her medical history, right? Her father did die of cancer." In truth, there was nothing that linked the father's cancer to the girl's tumor, but he wanted to send Kate on a wild goose chase and plant seeds of doubt in her mind.

"Of course I have."

"Good. Then let's turn to any other topics you'd like to discuss."

"I think we're at an impasse here." She paused. "When do you plan to have your first set of documents produced?"

"Very soon. But they'll come in waves."

"And all the first ones will be totally useless."

"Your words, not mine."

"Remember, I was on your side of the fence for a few years. I know the drill, but I think you also know me well enough to

63

realize that I won't relent in getting what I need to try this case. If I have to file every discovery motion that I can think of, I will."

"And if you do that, the judge will hate you."

"Not if I can show that my arguments have merit. If you hold out on me, I'll do it. Don't force my hand, Ethan, and make this uglier than it needs to be."

"Litigation is always ugly." That was just the truth of the matter.

"I'd like to think we'll be able to remain friends once this is over, but so far, I'm not feeling too good about that."

He'd pushed too much, too quickly. He still needed her to trust him if he was going to use their friendship to his advantage. He walked over to her side of the table and sat down beside her. "Kate, our friendship is stronger than any of the cases we work on. Yes, we're going to fight tooth and nail, but at the end of the day, I'm never going to give up on you or our friendship. We've been through too much over the years."

And just like that, he saw her eyes soften and knew he had her. It was almost too easy.

## SIX

Landon stood outside the deli, waiting for his target to arrive. His investigation had led him to a man named Pierce Worthington. He worked in the same department as Ellie at MPC.

His approach had to be cautious, and he might get shut down, but he had to try. Based on his recon, Pierce came to this deli every day for lunch and sat at the counter.

It was risky to go after a current MPC employee directly, but like Cooper had said, there was always a chance that someone else felt the same way Ellie had.

*Bingo*, he thought, as Pierce approached the deli at 11:45. Just like clockwork. Landon hung back for a minute and then walked in to ensure he'd be able to get a seat beside Pierce.

There were a couple of ways he could play it, and it would depend on how Pierce responded to the initial contact. He listened as Pierce talked to the waitress for a few minutes.

After the waitress left, Landon decided it was time. "Seems like you're a regular here. Any recommendations?"

Pierce looked over at him. The almost sixty-year-old scientist adjusted his glasses. "Eggs are the best thing on the menu, especially with the homemade biscuits and gravy. You won't be disappointed."

"Thanks." He figured he didn't have much in common with Pierce—a highly educated scientist with a PhD—but he had to try to form a connection. "I'm sure anything here is better than an MRE."

"You're military?" Pierce asked.

"Yes, sir. No longer in service, but I was army."

"My son's in the Marines."

"Deployed?"

"Yes, he's in Afghanistan right now. Been on a couple of tours."

"And what about you? Did you serve?"

Pierce shook his head. "No. I'm not built like you or my son. I'm a scientist."

"Really? Where do you work?"

"MPC, the drug company."

"Oh," Landon said.

"You know them?"

"I've heard of them, yeah. Drug companies aren't exactly popular in this country. With all the skyrocketing prices and everything."

"Yeah, but we do a lot of good too."

*Uh-oh.* Pierce was drinking the Kool-Aid. "I just heard on the news about that poor woman who got killed in the parking garage. Did you know her?"

Pierce looked down. "I did. It's a shame. Ellie was a sweet lady and a brilliant scientist. Such a senseless murder. I hear the police are no closer to finding who did it."

"Did you work on projects together?"

"Oh yeah. She was top-notch."

"Do you think she was happy with her job?"

"Ellie was very serious about her work. It consumed her life. But scientists tend to be that way."

This was quickly leading to a dead end. This guy didn't seem like he would be willing to blow the whistle—assuming he even knew what Ellie had known. "Do you like working there?"

"Yeah." Pierce tilted his head to the side. "Why're you so interested?"

It was time to take a different road. This could change everything, but he didn't have much of a choice. "I should be honest with you. I'm actually doing some digging around about Ellie's murder."

"You a cop?"

"No, sir. Private investigator."

"Then I'll give you a piece of advice. Leave the investigation up to the police."

"And why do you say that?"

Pierce looked around the diner before leaning toward him. "Because you don't want to get on the wrong side of MPC."

Ah, how quickly Pierce had changed his tune. Maybe Landon could get somewhere with him after all. "If you know something, anything, no matter how small, about what happened to Ellie, it could be helpful to me."

"I don't know anything, you hear me? Nothing."

Those words told Landon that this man definitely knew something but was afraid to talk.

*Jackpot.*

When Ethan had received an invitation to Royce's home for dinner, he hadn't known what to expect. As he drove through the Buckhead neighborhood and located Royce's address, he knew he was going to be in for an interesting evening.

The house wasn't a house—it was a mansion. Even bigger than those of the senior partners at Peters & Gomez.

He'd tried to talk himself down about this case, to convince himself it was just like the others he'd worked on that were high profile, but he knew otherwise. He was the originating partner for this work for MPC. That meant that if MPC hired the firm on other matters, even if they were totally unrelated, he would get credit for bringing the client in to the firm. And at the end of the day in his world, that meant more money, which led to more power.

On the other hand, if MPC never used them again, he'd get nothing further from this case than the disdain and mockery of the other partners, who would question how he'd messed it up. And the worst-case scenario was if he lost a jury verdict for MPC. The managing partner at the firm had given him a stern warning, since he was still one of the newer members of the partnership. A big loss would put him on probation, and he couldn't afford that, so he was willing to push things as far as necessary.

Royce was a fickle man. He'd fired his former law firm, which had worked for him for years, without a second thought. That made Ethan nervous, because it suggested Royce had zero loyalty, but he would just have to roll with it. Opportunities like this didn't come around very often. Most large corporations were set with their regular lawyers and didn't deviate.

He rang the doorbell and waited for a brief moment. A gray-haired man dressed in a dark suit opened the door and greeted him with a warm smile. It didn't surprise Ethan that Royce had a staff. In a house this big, he probably had quite a large one.

"Mr. Black, please come in. Mr. Hamilton is waiting for you in the formal den."

He was led through a large living room with ornate crystal chandeliers and then down a long hallway.

The butler opened another door, and Royce rose from his plush maroon chair to greet Ethan. With him was Matt Canton, MPC's Chief Operating Officer and Royce's right-hand man.

The den was the largest one Ethan had ever seen. It was bigger than his one-bedroom apartment during law school.

Royce gave him a warm handshake. "Ethan, so glad you could come to dinner. I thought we'd chat a bit about business beforehand."

"Of course."

"And I'm sure you remember our COO, Matt Canton."

Ethan reached out and shook Matt's hand. "Very nice to see you again."

"Likewise," Matt said. The lean, dark-haired man was probably a decade younger than Royce but very knowledgeable about the business from the discussions Ethan had had with him. Matt had been the executive lead for several drugs, including Celix, so he knew the facts of the case very well.

"Do you need anything, Mr. Hamilton?" the butler asked.

"No. We'll be in for dinner in just a bit," Royce responded.

The butler left the three of them alone, and Ethan turned back to Royce. "What a magnificent place you have."

"I'll give you a full tour after dinner."

"How long have you lived here?"

"For about ten years, but I did major renovations five years ago." Royce paused. "I know you probably think it's a bit much for a single man, but I do so much hosting and entertaining."

"You work hard. There's nothing wrong with having nice things as a result of that."

"I did this all on my own. I didn't come from a wealthy family."

"That makes it all the more impressive." Ethan was laying it on a bit thick, but that was par for the course. Royce was the client, and that was how the dance worked.

"Enough about me. We're going to bore Matt to death. Let's talk about where we are on the case."

"I have a few developments to update you both on. First, the judge appointed lead counsel for the plaintiffs."

"Who is it?" Matt asked.

"My former classmate, Kate Sullivan from the firm Warren McGee."

Royce leaned back in his chair. "Interesting they didn't choose a senior partner, isn't it?"

"This judge is all about picking who he believes is the right fit and giving people chances to succeed. She's female, from a top firm, and known as a rising star in the legal community. It was her time."

"I sense you have a real soft spot for this woman," Matt said. "Is that going to be a problem? If it is, we want to know right now before we move any further."

Ethan couldn't give them any reason to doubt him. "I plan on leveraging my friendship with her to our advantage. Kate is an excellent attorney, but she doesn't have an edge. She's as straitlaced as they come."

Royce scoffed. "That doesn't sound like someone who's cut out for this type of work."

If only they knew the real Kate Sullivan. "That's why she's on the plaintiff's side. She believes she's fighting for those who can't fight for themselves. That she's making a big difference in the world."

Matt laughed. "She's in for a rude awakening when she finds out that's not how to get things done."

"One other thing. She's chosen the first plaintiff for our bellwether trial."

Royce leaned forward. "Which one?"

"It was on the short list we went over last week. The Wyman case."

"I knew it," Royce said. "They're going to make the jury feel sorry for the poor little sixteen-year-old and her widowed mother. I assume you have a strategy to neutralize those facts?"

"We're going to do a mock trial to get a feel for how the jury will react to different strategies."

"How do you find jurors for the mock trial?" Matt asked.

"A company we hire runs and organizes the whole thing. I've used them before, and it's definitely worth the money. It gives you a real-time sense of what average people think about the case. We'll have a good idea before we go into the Wyman trial as to where our weak spots are. And remember, Royce, this is just the first bellwether trial. We'll have more, but this one sets the stage for everything else to come."

"Don't even start talking settlement again," Royce said. "We should win this thing straight up."

At some point, he hoped to wrap Royce's head around at least the idea of talking settlement numbers. "I'm not bringing it up, at least not now. But the results of the Wyman case will have to inform our decision and strategy going forward."

Matt fiddled with his cufflinks. "We have to show that girl's death had nothing to do with Celix."

"And that's my job. We're closely examining medical records, and our experts are already on the case. But from everything I've seen and heard so far, we don't have another explanation. She was a healthy sixteen-year-old before she started taking the meds."

"Obviously not that healthy, or she wouldn't have had the migraines to begin with," Royce shot back.

"Valid point. Don't worry. I'm going to find an expert who will argue that the tumor was hereditary, given her father's cancer, but that's going to be a stretch. We're going to run down every theory possible. The plaintiff still has the burden of proof. I

71

just have to poke holes in their case to make the jury question everything."

Royce looked at him. "I'll be honest, when I hired you and your firm for this case, I went out on a limb. I wasn't happy with our past representation and wanted a fresh, new approach. You and your firm came highly recommended to me."

"That's good to hear. We want to do everything possible to ensure a robust defense."

"I'm glad you said that, because robust is exactly what Matt and I are looking for. We need to know that you're going to be out there on the front lines, fighting the plaintiffs each and every step of the way."

Ethan nodded, wanting to make sure they understood his enthusiasm. "Of course. That's my job, and I take my obligations to you very seriously."

"Your firm has a reputation for being cutthroat, but can I speak frankly?" Royce asked.

"Absolutely. If you can't speak frankly with your attorney, then who can you speak frankly with?"

"We need you to be willing to push the boundaries beyond what you'd normally do. Do you understand?" Royce gave him a pointed look.

Ethan's pulse kicked up as he processed what Royce had just said. "Yes, but is there something specific you had in mind?"

Matt exchanged a glance with Royce then said, "I think we need to be a bit more aggressive in screening documents before turning them over to the other side than you're probably used to in your other cases."

That put Ethan on alert. "You're worried the document discovery is going to uncover something you would prefer wasn't produced to the plaintiffs."

Royce crossed his arms. "You catch on quickly."

Ethan took a deep breath. "I think I see the direction this is going. For this relationship to work between all of us, I need you to be completely honest with me."

"We get that," Royce responded.

"What is it that you don't want to see the light of day? For me to be able to protect you and MPC, I need to know the facts. If I'm in the dark, it will make it harder on all of us."

"I'll let Matt answer, since he's a bit closer to the details on this than I am," Royce said.

Matt's dark eyes fixed on Ethan's. "As initially developed, Celix did have some questionable side effects—not brain tumors, of course, but still dangerous side effects nonetheless. As we went through the testing and development process, though, we resolved those issues. There could be, however, older documents out there that could be misconstrued if you don't have the full context. That type of information would be harmful to the case and the company if it got out."

He wished they had told him this sooner, but he couldn't really say he was surprised. This was pretty standard stuff in this kind of business. If there wasn't any evidence at all, there probably wouldn't be a lawsuit to begin with. "I know you're both concerned about this, but what you're telling me right now is typical of every single big case I work on. There are always going to be what we call hot documents. That's why we get paid the big bucks to handle them. I'll argue motions and make objections to fight these things."

"But that's what we need to discuss." Royce cleared his throat. "I don't want you to treat this like all your other cases. I hired you because I thought you'd be willing to take a different approach. A more aggressive tack, doing whatever it takes to win this thing. I don't want you to handle these 'hot documents' by arguing motions and making objections. I don't want the documents to ever see the light of day. They don't even matter, because we fixed the problems anyway."

Ethan raised an eyebrow but then immediately regained his composure. He couldn't let them think he was weak. "I understand your concern, and we'll conduct any document reviews with a careful eye to sensitive issues and react accordingly."

"I don't need to tell you how damaged MPC would be if those documents got out," Matt said. "All the good that MPC does, all the drugs we've developed that have saved thousands of lives, would be put in jeopardy. And we have more cutting-edge drugs set to hit the market soon that can't be impacted by this litigation. We need to have a clear path forward."

"I hear you loud and clear. Drug companies like yours are put in very difficult situations. To make the next cure-all drug, there will always be some type of collateral damage."

"I think we're on the same page, then," Royce said. "Let's stop talking shop and go have some dinner."

"That sounds good to me." Though Ethan couldn't help but feel like he may have really crossed over to the dark side.

After a long day at work, Kate pulled into a parking lot in downtown Atlanta. She had an evening board meeting for the Atlanta Women Attorneys group. She'd considered not re-upping her board position with AWA because of time constraints, but she enjoyed the work, and it allowed her to spend time with other women in the profession.

Outside activities were a struggle for her, though. Sometimes finding the energy and motivation to get out and do something that wasn't part of her work at the firm was tough. It helped that her two best friends also served on the AWA board, but even they didn't realize the battles she had faced with depression over the years. They were both so upbeat and vibrant. She didn't think they'd get it, even if they had the best of intentions.

It was easier to keep her issues between herself and God. Her faith was the only thing that kept her from falling into a deep bout of darkness, curling into a ball, and never leaving her house. She was much stronger now. She tried to take it one day at a time.

AWA brought together women lawyers in Atlanta from all practice areas, including the private sector and government. Not all female attorneys had the same experiences, but it was unquestionable that Kate had a special bond with many of the women who were striving for the same goals.

She walked into the conference room of the law firm that was hosting tonight's meeting. The board members who were at law firms rotated hosting the monthly meetings.

She set down her bag and turned to see Sophie Dawson, who grabbed her in a big hug.

"I feel like I haven't seen you in forever, Kate," Sophie said.

"I only missed one meeting." She'd had a trial in Savannah in the Southern District of Georgia last month.

Sophie frowned. "I know, but it's impossible to see you unless it's at our meetings. You work way too much these days."

Kate did work all the time, but she didn't know how to operate any other way. "You understand how much I love what I do."

"I do too, but all work and no play will make you go crazy. There is such a thing as burnout."

To deflect attention from her crazy work schedule, Kate took a step back and made a show of looking Sophie up and down. "Look at you, rocking that white pantsuit! It's perfect for this time of year and looks amazing on you." She'd look like a fluffy marshmallow in it, but not Sophie. "And you chopped your hair off. What, maybe five inches?"

"Yes, isn't it crazy?" Sophie flipped her blond hair, which now barely hit her shoulders. "I thought summer was the perfect time to do it."

Mia Shaw walked up to them and smiled widely. "If it isn't my two favorite attorneys stirring up trouble."

"Mia, so great to see you." Kate gave Mia a hug. She stood between her two friends and was reminded again that she was always the shortest in the group. Mia was only a couple inches taller, and then there was Sophie.

"Big congrats on being named lead counsel on the MPC case." Mia's dark eyes beamed with excitement. "We're both so proud of you. Your hard work is paying off."

Kate's cheeks flushed. "Thanks. I just hope I can do right by these families."

"You've got this," Mia said. "I have no doubts about it. Are you about to dive into the discovery phase?"

Mia worked at a large firm too, so she was very familiar with the challenges Kate was about to face. "Yeah. I've already started negotiating with Ethan. It's strange to have to face off against a friend."

Mia twisted her long dark hair into a bun. "It would almost be like you and me on opposite sides of the table."

"I hope that never happens." It was one thing dealing with Ethan, but being adverse to Mia might be too much. "I'd probably ask someone else at the firm to handle it. I wouldn't want to risk our friendship. It's too important to me."

"I feel the same way. You've helped me so much along the way."

She was a few years ahead of Mia and had offered her help and advice as much as she could. Thriving in a big law firm was a difficult task.

"All right, ladies." The chair of the board was ready to get the meeting started. "If everyone could grab your food and take your seats, we'll begin."

Kate listened attentively as they went through the agenda. But almost two hours later, when the meeting adjourned, she was exhausted and ready to head home.

"Kate, I know you're going to be busy on the MPC case, but do you think the three of us can grab dinner this weekend to celebrate you making lead counsel?" Sophie asked.

"Yeah, that would be nice. You guys need to drag me out of the office more often, because I always come up with some excuse."

"We can handle that," Mia said.

"It's been a long day for me. I'm going to call it a night and head home," Kate said.

Sophie grabbed her laptop. "All right. Mia and I are going to work on the scholarship program."

"See you ladies this weekend. Text me details on where we're going. I'll let you decide."

Mia and Sophie laughed. Kate was famously indecisive about picking restaurants. She gave them each another hug before walking out of the room.

She exited the building and briskly walked toward the parking lot. It was almost ten, and dark. She hated walking to her car alone in downtown at this hour, but she didn't have much of a choice. She moved quickly across the parking lot, grateful it was a well-lit area, but she couldn't shake the feeling that someone was watching her.

She looked over her shoulder and saw several other people walking down the street, but none of them had any interest in her. They were going about their own business. Why was she so jumpy?

When she made it to her Grand Cherokee, a knot formed in the pit of her stomach as she looked at her Jeep. Was this really happening to her? She'd parked in this lot multiple times before and never had any problems.

She had an internal debate for a minute before pulling out her phone and calling Landon. He needed to know.

He answered on the second ring. "Kate, what's going on?"

"I'm at the Peachtree flat lot downtown at the corner of Ivan Allen."

"Are you okay?"

"Yes, I'm fine, but my tires are slashed." She took a deep breath. "All four of them."

"I'll be right there. Get in your car and lock your doors. Don't wait out in the open. We can't assume that this is random. You may have been targeted by MPC."

# CHAPTER
## SEVEN

Landon arrived at the parking lot to find Kate sitting inside her Jeep just as he had instructed. He pulled up beside her and jumped out of his car. The humid night air filled his lungs.

Her eyes locked onto his, and he saw a familiar expression—fear. His muscles tensed. Seeing her that way made his blood boil.

She opened the car door and stepped out.

"Are you okay?" he asked.

"Yeah. Just a little freaked out."

"That's understandable." He put his hand on her shoulder and gave it a comforting squeeze.

"Could this be random?"

"It's possible, but you've been named lead counsel against MPC. Given what we believe about what they're willing to do, you need to be more alert. I don't think it's wise to be out alone at night like this while you're in litigation with them. We should call the police." He looked at her tires. "There's no hope for the tires. You'll need a tow."

She looked up at him in defiance. "This only makes me want to work harder."

# DEADLY PROOF

"I guarantee they're smart enough not to have this tied back to them in any way."

About an hour later, the police had come and gone, and Kate's Jeep was towed away.

"I'll give you a lift home," he said.

"Thanks."

"Also, you should let me check out the security situation at your house."

Her eyes widened. "You don't think they'd come to my home, do you?"

He didn't want to scare her, but he needed to be honest. "If MPC sent a hit man to kill Ellie Proctor, then there's really no limit to what they would do."

She gave a quick nod but didn't say anything.

They drove mostly in silence to her house. It only took about fifteen minutes from downtown, since there was no traffic at that time of night. She lived in a nice neighborhood near Emory University.

He pulled into her driveway and eyed her ranch-style home. He'd expected a law firm partner to have a bigger house, but he was learning that nothing about Kate was stereotypical. She broke a lot of his preconceived notions.

"Do you have a security system?" he asked.

"Yes. It's a good neighborhood, but we still have crime. Since I live alone, I feel like it's for the best."

"It's just you, then?" He didn't want to be too presumptuous.

"Me and my cat, Jax."

"Ah, a cat person?"

"I like dogs too, but having a dog isn't practical with my job. Jax is very loving and understanding of my schedule, so we have a great relationship." She laughed.

He could see that she welcomed the moment of levity after the night she'd had. "Can you show me around? I'll sleep bet-

80

ter tonight knowing that I made sure your home was secure."
He might be overly cautious, but he didn't want to take any
chances. It wasn't worth it. He'd learned the hard way that
taking chances could get people killed.

"Sure," she said.

"Too bad there's no garage." He would have preferred one,
but it wasn't the end of the world. At least she had a security
system.

"No. A lot of the houses in this neighborhood don't have
garages."

She unlocked her front door and started to step into the
house, but he grabbed her by the arm to stop her. "Please let
me go in first. Just in case."

"You're beginning to worry me," she said softly. But she let
him walk in front of her.

She flipped on the lights, and he saw Jax dart out. The black
long-haired cat walked toward Kate, but he seemed to be limp-
ing.

"Is he okay?"

"Yeah." She leaned down and picked him up. "Jax is a tripod."

"A tripod?"

"Yes. He was a stray, and I started feeding him one day when
he showed up under my carport. He never let me get close to
him, but he always came back for food. Then one day I saw
him, and he was barely able to walk." She rubbed Jax's head
and the cat started purring.

"I bought a trap at the hardware store, took him to the vet,
and found out that the poor baby's leg was shattered. They
had to amputate, and I brought him inside. Now he runs the
house. Only having one back leg doesn't slow him down a bit."

Just when Landon thought he couldn't be any more surprised by Kate, she'd taken in a three-legged cat. Talk about

having a big heart. He wasn't used to dealing with people like her. After all the heinous things he'd seen, she was a breath of fresh air.

He took a step toward her. "Please stay here and let me check everything out."

"Sorry that it's not cleaner."

He looked around, didn't see a speck of dirt, and had to laugh. "You should see my place if you have worries about your house."

He went room by room through the split-level ranch home. He didn't like that there was easy window entry on the first floor in a couple of rooms, but he felt confident that no one was in the house.

He joined her in the living room once he had completed his inspection. "Are your windows wired to your alarm?"

"Yes. When I got the system, they recommended that, given where the windows were located."

"Great." That, at least, made him feel a little better.

"I'm sure I'll be fine," she said.

He couldn't help but notice that she didn't say the words with her normal level of confidence.

"Promise you'll call me if anything at all happens. No matter how small."

"Of course."

Kate had gotten new tires and her car back, but there was no resolution on the matter. She doubted the police would ever find the culprit, and it wasn't exactly a top priority, which she fully understood.

When Landon had invited her to dinner, she'd initially turned him down. She knew he wanted to check up on her, but her MO was to either be at work or at home. She'd prefer not to go out at all, but after some prodding, she had relented because he said he wanted to talk about the case.

She arrived at a Midtown Atlanta restaurant known for its chic southern food with flair. She could already feel her thick hair starting to frizz as she made the short walk over from her office. She loved living in Atlanta, even though the summers were super hot and humid. It didn't matter that it was seven o'clock. There was no break from the sweltering heat.

Landon stood in front of the restaurant, waiting for her. Tonight he wore khakis and a light blue polo shirt. His face looked freshly shaved, and there was no hint of the stubble she'd seen before. Although she had to admit that the stubble look also suited him very well.

He smiled, and butterflies swirled in her stomach.

She felt her step hitch in surprise. Since when did she have this type of reaction to him? Normally a guy wouldn't get a second look from her because she was so focused on her career. A fact her friends reminded her of often, but she had other priorities.

Yes, Landon was incredibly handsome and smart, but there was so much riding on this case. Why did she have to start crushing on this guy now?

This wasn't like the other litigation she'd worked on. Someone was dead—a person who had trusted her and come to her for help. And now it appeared that she might be a target as well. It needed her full attention. She couldn't afford to be distracted.

Pushing down those thoughts, she walked up to Landon. "Hey there," she said.

"You actually made it out of the office." He laughed and then grinned at her.

"I do leave the office, you know."

"I was beginning to wonder."

"You told me it was safer there," she said in a lower voice.

83

"That's true, but I wasn't expecting you to go on lockdown."

The hostess interrupted their discussion. "Mr. James, your table is ready."

As Landon placed his hand on her lower back to guide her toward the table, she fought another rush of butterflies and tried to relax. She wondered what he needed to talk about.

They were seated upstairs at a secluded corner table with a nice view of the summer evening in Atlanta. "Have you been here before?" she asked.

"Yes. I love the bacon mac and cheese and the cheddar biscuits. I'm not exactly known for having a balanced diet."

He didn't look like he ate many biscuits. Oh, to have a man's metabolism.

"I also love the shrimp and grits with corn bread," he added. "I'm assuming you've been here too?"

"Yeah, we come here on a lot of business lunches because it's so close to the office." Although at lunch she usually opted for the boring and healthy kale salad with salmon.

The server arrived, and Kate ordered southern-style trout, which she figured was only a half step healthier than the shrimp and grits with extra corn bread that Landon ordered.

"What's going on?" she asked once the server left.

"I want to talk to you about something I'd like to do, but first, how are you doing? Any further issues?"

"Nothing. But the more I think about it, I believe MPC is engaging in scare tactics as we kick off the discovery phase of the litigation. If they can rattle me, it's to their advantage. I've also decided which case is going to go first in the bellwether trials. But what is it you want to talk about?"

"I'd like to hire a security consultant to work with me on an as-needed basis."

"Why would we need that? You're a PI with a strong military background. I think you probably have the security situation covered. You've dealt with much more dangerous situations than this."

"This is a bit different. I can't be at all places at all times, and I'd like to bring in some experts, especially on the technical and computer side. You said yourself that you think what you find in the documents is going to be important. We may need someone on our side to help us determine if there's been any wrongful destruction of documents."

"You're right, but we're not at that phase yet. To even get that far, we'd have to get through some of the document production and then file a specific motion to compel or a spoliation motion."

"Spoliation?" he asked with a furrowed brow.

"It's a fancy way of saying that the documents were somehow compromised." She thought for a minute. "Is there something else you'd like them to do in the meantime?"

"Nothing that's legal," he said flatly.

"Landon, we've already discussed this." She leaned forward in her chair. "Absolutely no going outside of the law here. That's not how I'm going to run this case. We will not stoop to MPC's level under any circumstances. Are we clear?"

He smiled again, and it knocked her off her game.

"This isn't funny, Landon."

"It's fun to get you riled up, Counselor. Don't worry. I talked to my guy, and he isn't down for breaking into their systems anyway."

"Well, that's good, I guess. And who is this guy? How much did you tell him?" Immediately, concerns of client confidentially worried her.

He put his hand on her arm. "You have nothing to worry about. I was completely discreet and didn't reveal specifics to him. I know he'd have to sign a retainer and confidentiality agreement if you wanted to use him, just like I did. I was just bouncing ideas off someone I trusted to see what they could offer."

He sat back in his chair, and she wished he hadn't moved his hand away from her arm. His touch had actually been nice. "How do you know this guy?"

"We were college roommates. He and his business partner, actually. His partner has mad technical skills."

"Ah." Well, that changed things a bit, but she still wasn't convinced.

"Their firm specializes in security issues for the corporate world and then also in personal security services. I'm perfectly capable of keeping you safe, but I don't want to take unnecessary risks."

The hairs stood up on her arms. "Do you think I'm in real danger?"

"I don't know, but I like sticking close just in case. The tire slashing might just have been a warning shot and nothing more. But you're the enemy because you're the opposing lawyer. These guys seem intent on doing whatever it takes to prevail and keep their dirty secrets out of the public eye."

"That's assuming Ellie was telling us the truth. You're still working on getting to the bottom of what she was so concerned about."

"That's the other thing my friend's company could help with. He suggested I look into other MPC employees who may flip. I met with a scientist who worked with Ellie. He tried to warn me off, but I'm not going to give up trying to get him to blow the whistle."

"Wouldn't that put him in danger?"

"I'll be on top of that."

"Do these guys at the security firm have names?"

The corners of his mouth turned up. "Yes, Cooper Knight and Noah Ramirez. Cooper is a former Atlanta police officer, and Noah worked at ATF. They have stellar credentials. Their company is called K&R Security. I'd be happy to set up a meeting so you can talk to them about the case."

"I'm still not convinced you need them. If you can present me a specific issue to bring them into, then I'd be happy to consider it. Remember, as a plaintiff's firm, we pay for everything upfront, and we only get paid back if we win. I have to take a cautious approach to expenditures."

"You hired me."

"Yes, because I felt like it was a necessity."

"I'll come through. I just need a little time to work on this Ellie angle."

"I'm not questioning your timing. I knew we wouldn't crack the case overnight."

"Thanks. So what's your update?"

She filled him in on the facts of the Wyman case and the reasons she'd chosen it.

"What happens now?"

"We jump into discovery. I had my first discovery meeting with Ethan. After a few hours locked in a conference room, we came to some areas of agreement, but there are plenty of areas where we don't see eye to eye. He doesn't want other drugs included in the document requests, but I need to run down every possible scenario, especially after what Ellie said."

"If MPC is up to no good, what's the likelihood they would have filled Ethan in on all of their plans?"

"I actually think it's low. They haven't worked together that long, and it would be a big risk, opening up to Ethan so soon."

"And what if in response to all of your document requests, they don't turn over any questionable documents?"

"That's when we start filing motions and arguing about computer forensics. Also, if there is something bigger like Ellie alluded to, we need to determine if it goes all the way up to the CEO, Royce Hamilton. Ellie said it went to the top levels of the company, so if Royce has knowledge about all of this, it will come out in his deposition."

Landon shook his head. "If the CEO is up to his neck in this, he'll probably lie in the deposition. Think about it, Kate."

She frowned. "I guess you're right, but I want to put him on record. That way he'll be stuck."

When they'd finished dinner, she decided to go back to the topic of the security firm. "Have you used this security firm before?"

"Actually, I haven't. In general I prefer to work alone. It's easier that way."

She sensed there was something deeper going on, but she didn't want to push. "I also like working alone, but cases like this require teamwork. There are far too many moving parts to be a lone ranger. No pun intended."

He laughed. "You know, Sullivan, you have a wry sense of humor."

"Sullivan?" She raised an eyebrow.

"It's a military thing, but I think Kate suits you much better."

"Do you miss it?"

"I miss some parts of it for sure, but it was time for me to leave when I did. Things got difficult at the end."

His dark eyes told a story that his words couldn't. This man had put his life on the line to protect the freedoms that she enjoyed every day. She wished she could help him get through whatever was responsible for those dark shadows. She went down the only path that she knew. "My faith is what has gotten me through difficult times in my own life."

"Faith can only get you so far. It can get pretty dark when God turns His back on you."

Her heart broke. "You don't really believe that God abandoned you, do you?"

88

"I don't have any other explanation for it, but I don't want to cause a rift between us. There's too much on the line here."

She didn't want to back down. This topic was also important. "There's not going to be a rift. I'm an attorney—believe me, I can handle a debate."

He crossed his arms and leaned back in his chair. "All right. If you want to go there."

"Yeah, I do."

"It's easy to sit here in this nice restaurant and say you have faith and that you believe God is good. It's much harder to be out in the middle of the Iraqi desert, witnessing unspeakable atrocities, not being able to help—or even making things worse—and knowing that God isn't there." His deep voice cracked. "He's not answering you. He's not helping you. You're completely on your own."

The pain in his eyes stole her breath. And who was she to tell him how to feel? But at the same time, she had to speak up, because she'd experienced a lot of pain in her life too. "This world is an evil place, Landon. To those of us who believe, we're not promised an easy road—just the opposite."

"I can't unsee what I saw. I can't undo what I did. All I can tell you is that God wasn't there when I needed Him the most."

"And all I can tell you is that even in the darkest times, He is there. Even when we may not feel His presence or hear His voice."

He leaned forward. "Have you ever had any hardships in your life? You work in a fancy law firm, drive a nice car, and have a great house."

If only he knew her real struggles. The darkness she faced. The depths of despair that she'd lived through. The days when she didn't even know why she was still on this earth. But she couldn't explain all of that to him. "Just because I seem to have it all together now at thirty-eight years old doesn't mean that I've always had it easy."

His shoulders slumped. "I'm sorry. I shouldn't have made assumptions about your life."

"It's okay. We all do it." She took a deep breath and wondered if she could open up about a part of her past that had impacted her entire life. "My childhood was great. I had two loving parents and was oblivious to most of the world's problems. Then one night when I was sixteen, it all changed. My parents were out at dinner, and on their way home, a semitruck crossed into their lane and struck them head on. My mom and dad were killed instantly."

"Kate, I'm so sorry." He reached out and took her hands in his.

"My uncle took me in, but he didn't have his act together. And he definitely didn't know how to handle a sixteen-year-old girl. I went off the rails for a while. When I went to college, I stepped into an even more rebellious phase. I still did my schoolwork, because I wanted to get into law school. It had always been a dream of mine since I was little. I had actually talked to my dad about it a lot, and I felt like I had to become a lawyer or else I would be letting him down. But I wasn't living a life I was proud of. It wasn't until my third year of law school that I found faith. I'd gone to church on and off growing up, but I didn't have a real relationship with God. And then after the death of my parents, I was angry. Really angry and confused. I kept asking, why me?"

"I know a thing or two about being angry, but the last thing I wanted to do was dredge up painful memories for you."

"It's all part of me, and those experiences shaped who I am today."

"So then you got your law degree and threw yourself completely into your career?"

"I make no excuse about the fact that I'm all-in where my work is concerned. When I made the switch to plaintiff's work,

it was like I finally found out what I was supposed to do with
my life. Helping those who can't help themselves. Fighting for
those who have been wronged. That's why this case is more to
me than just racking up large verdicts and getting a piece of
the pie. It's people's lives and justice for those who have been
hurt or worse." She looked down at her watch. They'd been
at the restaurant for over two hours. "Wow. I didn't realize it
was this late."

"I'm sorry. We started talking, and I lost track of the time.
We need to get out of here so you can get some rest."

"Thanks for the dinner invitation. It was nice to get out."

"And sorry things took a turn to the serious."

"Don't be."

As they said their good-byes at the restaurant door, she looked
at this man she was learning more about and felt a bit sad that
the night was ending. Was it possible he was in her life for a
reason?

# CHAPTER
# EIGHT

Landon hadn't given up on Pierce, so he showed up at the deli the next day and waited for him to come in and have lunch.

When Pierce entered and made eye contact, he immediately frowned, but he still walked over and took a seat beside Landon.

"You shouldn't be here, soldier."

"I can't just walk away. You should understand that."

"What do you want from me?"

Before Landon could answer, the waitress came over and took their orders. Once she brought back their drinks and walked away, Landon answered Pierce's question.

"You could help in several ways."

"Like what?"

"Do you really think Ellie was randomly murdered in that parking garage?"

Pierce took a sip of his sweet tea before he answered. "No reason to think otherwise."

"You're saying that, but I don't think you believe it."

"You're not suggesting I had anything to do with it?" His voice cracked.

"No, not at all, but I think you may know something to help

me figure out who is behind it. What do you know about the other drugs Ellie was working on?"

"Well." Pierce rubbed his chin. "She worked on a variety of drugs. That's the way it works."

"All right." Landon felt certain that Pierce knew more, but now wasn't the time to turn the screws. He needed to build up a level of trust first. "Can I ask you something on a completely different topic?"

"Yeah," Pierce said softly.

"Is your CEO hands-on?"

"Oh, definitely. He's involved in every aspect of the company."

"You tried to warn me off before, but I need to understand how far you believe the company would actually go. Do you think anyone at MPC would be capable of ordering a hit on Ellie?"

Pierce's eyebrows shot up. "Are you being serious?"

"I know this might be difficult to talk about, but I need your feedback."

Pierce crossed his arms and avoided eye contact. "MPC is really locked down on the legal stuff—keeping their scientists on a short leash, making us sign very aggressive noncompete agreements and confidentiality provisions. But what you're insinuating is pretty drastic. I'm not saying that the company executives don't bend the rules—that's just the nature of corporate America and Big Pharma. They might even go outside the law, but I don't think they'd go that far. It's just too much."

"You clearly don't want to get sideways with them, though."

"I need my job, and the last thing I want to do is call attention to myself or create any unnecessary drama. What happened to Ellie is tragic, and if there is an ounce of truth to your allegations, then that's even more reason for me to keep my head down and stay out of it."

Their food arrived, and Landon decided to shift the conversation to small talk. If he could keep getting information from Pierce piece by piece without scaring him off, it would be worth it.

Kate had stayed true to her word to go out with her friends Saturday night. Both Sophie and Mia were more sociable than her. Once she'd turned her life around at the end of law school, she'd actually made a concerted effort to not go out as much. It was easier that way to make a clean break from some of the bad habits she'd formed in college. Partying had only made her depression worse. At least now she was able to face it straight on with a clear head and with a faith that grew stronger with each passing year.

Given the fact that she didn't have any family—her uncle having passed away a few years ago—it was nice to have girl-friends to lean on and celebrate the victories with, like making lead counsel for the first time. It bothered her that she couldn't fully open up to them about what was going on in the case.

As usual, Kate was early and the first to arrive. Her friends had chosen a nice seafood restaurant in Buckhead. She was seated and started perusing the menu while she waited.

After a few minutes, Sophie and Mia joined her at the table. They lived close to each other, so it wasn't surprising that they had ridden together. She stood and gave them each a quick hug.

"We would've been here sooner," Sophie said, "but Mia couldn't get her act together."

"Don't listen to her, Kate. I was ready in plenty of time." Mia gave her an I'm-your-best-friend type of smile.

Kate enjoyed their friendly banter. She knew that between the three of them, Mia and Sophie were closer than she was to either of them, but she was okay with that, since she knew it was her own doing.

"I can't believe you actually showed up," Sophie said. "Mia and I were putting it at about seventy-thirty odds that you'd cancel at the last minute."

"Am I really that bad?"

Her friends exchanged a glance and then laughed loudly at their inside joke.

"I'll take that as a yes."

"But we didn't come here tonight to harass you. This is your night to celebrate! It's not every day that you get tapped as lead counsel on a case this large, and it's your first one," Mia said. "It's a big deal, and we want to celebrate this milestone with you. You work harder than any other person I know."

Sophie raised her glass of sparkling water. "I'd like to make a toast to Kate, our friend and the fearless attorney who is going to take down MPC. Watch out Big Pharma, Kate Sullivan is coming for you."

Kate lifted her glass. "Thanks, ladies. You can both relate to how hard this job is. Now I just have to actually get it done."

"You're going to do great, Kate." Mia said. "Everyone in the Atlanta legal community knows you're the real deal."

At the end of the day, it mattered the most to her what a jury would think—not her peers. "Thanks, but I'm under no illusion that this is going to be an easy case. Just the opposite."

"I know you can't talk specifics, but anything interesting you can share?" Sophie asked.

Kate thought for a moment and then decided to tell them, since it wasn't confidential. "I hired a private investigator to run down some things for me."

Mia took a sip of her drink. "Someone you used before?"

"No, this is a new guy. He's actually a former Army Ranger."

"How old?" Sophie asked.

"Around my age."

"Oh, now this is starting to get interesting," Sophie said.

"Come on, Soph," Mia said. "There's no way Kate is interested in this guy. Remember, she doesn't have time for a love life."

Her friends were constantly giving her a hard time about not taking the time to date. Both of them did, but neither had found anyone they wanted to settle down with. They were a few years younger than her, though.

"I don't hear her denying it," Sophie said.

"Guys, I'm still sitting right here. And there's nothing going on between Landon and me. But he is a very interesting man."

"Does interesting include attractive?" Mia grinned widely.

Kate couldn't lie. "Yes, very. But that doesn't mean anything."

Sophie twirled her straw in her drink. "I don't know, Kate, that look in your eyes says otherwise. You know you can level with us."

She relented. "All right. I am attracted to him, but going down that road would be really messy."

"Life is messy," Sophie added. "You can't hide behind that excuse, or you'll just continue to be alone."

"I'm not hiding." Kate paused and wondered if she actually was hiding. "And anyway, even if I were interested, which I'm not saying I am, this is a two-way street, and he's done nothing to make me think the attraction is mutual."

"You shortchange yourself," Sophie said. "Any guy would be nuts not to want to date you."

Kate decided she'd had enough of the romance talk. "This case is hectic with all the discovery we're looking at. You two understand how that can be."

"All too well," Mia said. "I assume you've assembled a team to review all the documents that MPC is going to dump on you?"

"Yeah. That's a work in progress. We're waiting on the first big wave of production. But enough about me and my case. What's going on with the two of you?"

"Mia's pitching for a big case next week," Sophie said.

"I hope you land the client," Kate said. "I know how much pressure there is to bring in business. And it's even more pressure for you, since you mainly work on the defense side. Landing big corporations as clients is hard, and that's exactly what the firms expect."

"Especially when it's an old boys' club. Breaking into some of those places is nearly impossible," Mia added. "But that doesn't mean I'm going to stop trying."

"Another reason I'm glad I'm not in a law firm," Sophie said. "The two of you can have all of that."

Kate understood why Sophie would say that, but Sophie had her own challenges. "But you have to deal with a completely different set of problems as a prosecutor. I can't even imagine the types of pressures you face in the courtroom." Her friend had been a prosecutor since graduating law school. "I have a tremendous amount of respect for the work you do. You work just as hard as we do but for a fraction of the pay."

"True enough," Sophie said. "But I have a big safety net to fall back on."

Sophie's father was extremely wealthy. So much so that Sophie didn't even need to work, but she still did. That fact only made Kate respect her more.

Kate laughed more at dinner that night than she had in a long time, and being surrounded by friends made her realize that she needed to make more of an effort to spend time with them.

By the time the meal wound down, Kate was tired from all the talking but energized from the conversations.

As they were saying their good-byes, she looked over at Sophie. "See you in church tomorrow?"

"Yeah, I'll be at the early service as usual."

"Me too." Kate looked over at Mia. "The invite is still open, Mia."

"Thanks, ladies, but you know church isn't my thing."

Kate and Sophie had been unsuccessful at getting Mia to accept their invitation to attend a church service. But Kate never wanted to be pushy, so she said her final good-byes and headed home. She hoped to get a good night's rest and was glad she had opted for decaf after dinner.

She pulled up into her driveway and started planning out the rest of her weekend. Stepping out of her Jeep, she made a mental to-do list of everything she needed to accomplish, including making a run to the pet store to pick up more food for Jax.

Digging in her purse, she found her house key just as strong hands grabbed her from behind. She let out a shriek before the attacker put his right hand over her mouth, muffling her voice.

With his left arm, he pulled her dangerously close to him, pinning her arms to her sides. She struggled to turn and get a look at his face, but it was so dark she couldn't tell what he looked like. She continued to fight in vain against him.

Not willing to give up, she bit down hard on the fingers that covered her mouth. He responded with some foul language, but clamped his hand harder on her mouth so she couldn't bite him again. He squeezed until she writhed in pain.

"You have the power to influence how this case goes." He spoke directly into her ear, his voice deep and ragged. "Every decision you make has consequences. So think long and hard about how you handle things." He tightened his grip. "You don't want to meet me again."

Fear shot through her as she fought to get away from him, but he was easily a foot taller than her and much stronger.

"Now, if you don't want to get hurt, unlock your door, go inside, and think about what I've told you."

He loosened his grip. She couldn't move at first, her hand shaking as she tried to put the key into the keyhole. What if he came inside the house once she unlocked the door? Her heart pounded, but she didn't have much of a choice. She tried to steady her hand.

Before she could think through how she should handle him, he let go of her completely, leaving her free to move. Immediately she spun around, but he was already sprinting off into the night—approximately six three, over two hundred pounds, but that was all she could discern.

For a moment she considered running after him but then realized that was a completely stupid idea. She wasn't equipped to handle a man like that.

Quickly, she got inside and rearmed her alarm system. Her entire body continued to shake as she attempted to steady her jagged breathing. The attacker didn't mention MPC by name, but it was clear that was what he meant. They wanted her to slow walk this thing and go easy on them. They obviously weren't afraid to use violent tactics to get their way, but she couldn't even consider their suggestion. Besides being unethical, it was unthinkable for her.

She tasted blood in her mouth and realized she must have bit her cheek during the attack. *Lord, thank you that it wasn't worse.*

As she stood there, she could feel the man's breath on her neck, his tight grip around her waist, and she thought she might be sick.

She took a moment and continued to pray—not only for her safety, but also for guidance on how to handle this situation. She simply wouldn't abandon her clients because of some vague threat. They'd come after her directly, but would they take it even further, like they had with Ellie? She didn't want to find out the answer to that, but she had to move forward.

Pulling out her cell, she dialed Landon and waited for him to answer.

"Hey," he said. "What's wrong?"

He must have known it would be strange for her to call at almost ten o'clock on a Saturday night. "Can you please come over to my house?" She could hear her voice cracking, but she had to keep it together.

"Are you all right?"

"Yes. I'll explain everything when you get here."

Horrible thoughts raced through Landon's mind as he broke the speed limit in a desperate race to get to Kate's house. She said she was okay, but the shaky sound of her voice told him otherwise.

He considered trying to say a prayer. Not for himself, but for Kate. Ever since he'd met her, he found himself thinking about his faith—or lack thereof. He thought he'd never be open to believing that the Lord would be there for him again, but a strange tugging at his heart and mind continued to make him wonder. And even if God wasn't there for him, would He be there for Kate? Landon hoped so.

What could have happened to her? Whatever it was, he knew it was related to the case. Attorneys shouldn't have to worry about their safety, but after what he believed happened to Ellie, nothing was off the table.

When he arrived at Kate's, he jumped out of his car and ran toward the front door. He knocked loudly, and a moment later, the door opened and Kate let him in.

He followed her into the living room, but neither of them took a seat. Just seeing her standing there, alive, sent a flood of relief through him. But her red, puffy eyes told him she'd been crying. "Kate, what happened?"

"I was out to dinner with my friends, and when I got home, just as I was about to open my door, a man came up behind me." She paused, struggling with her emotions.

"It's all right, Kate. You're completely safe right now." He clenched his fists by his side even though he wanted to wrap his arms around her.

"He grabbed me. He basically told me to go easy on the case, and that all my decisions had consequences. He didn't mention MPC, but I'm certain that's the case he was talking about. Then he told me to unlock my door and go inside. I was worried he was going to follow me in, but he took off running."

The thought of a man putting his hands on Kate made him sick. He had to keep his temper in check, because going off the handle wouldn't help her. "Did you get a good look at him?"

She shook her head. "No, it was dark, and I couldn't see his face. He was a big man, though, at least your height and weight, if not bigger. And very strong. If he'd wanted to really hurt me, it wouldn't have been any issue for him."

"They're trying to spook you. First, your tires, now this. They want to send you a message. This is becoming way too dangerous. We need to come up with a plan for your personal security."

"I need to sit down." She walked farther into the living room and collapsed onto her large beige couch.

It hit him that he was being far too cold about the entire situation. He was already in the mission mindset, but what Kate needed most right now was a friend and a shoulder to lean on.

He sat down beside her and took her hand in his. "Kate, we're going to get you through this."

"What does that even look like, though? Getting me through? It's not like you can shadow me around the clock. They came to my home."

"We'll come up with a strategy that works for you. Given

this escalation, I'd really like to bring in my friend's security company. I'll do all I can individually, but having some backup would be a good idea, especially as this moves forward. If MPC is trying to scare you off now, at these early stages, it will only get worse as the process continues. Especially when they figure out that you're not the type to back down."

She looked up at him. "I'm not a weak person, Landon. I'm very independent and driven, but right now I don't feel like my normal self."

He felt her shiver, but he didn't think she was cold—she was afraid. He let go of her hand and instead wrapped his left arm around her shoulders, providing her some assurance that he was right there with her. "Kate, after a traumatic event like that, it's perfectly normal to be scared."

"He was so strong, and there was nothing I could do. I was completely helpless. I tried my best to fight him, and I even bit his hand, but that wasn't enough. I prayed that God would intervene."

Could that be the case? Was God protecting Kate? Now wasn't the time to think about these things. He needed to gather more facts. "You said you were out with friends, but you came home by yourself?"

"Yes. Two of my best friends took me to dinner in Buckhead to celebrate me getting the lead counsel position."

"Did you tell your friends about your tires?"

"No. I didn't think it wise to involve them in all of this. They'd just worry. And I can only speak to them about the case in general terms anyway, because of confidentiality issues."

He nodded. "That was probably for the best, although I know it's hard, because you want to talk about what you're going through. Just know that I'm here for you, Kate." A strong desire to protect her surged inside of him, and the responsibility of it weighed heavily on his shoulders.

"So you think we need to call in reinforcements?"

"Before this happened, I would've said that I could go it alone, but the circumstances have changed. We should also call the police so you can file a report about what happened."

"Do you think it's a good idea to bring in the police?" she asked. "I don't want to draw more attention to my situation than is needed."

He quickly ran through the pros and cons in his head. "Between your tires being slashed and this, I think it might lead them to open a more active investigation."

"But I don't want that. You know how word gets around. The last thing I want to do is to impact my case or have unnecessary attention drawn to me. I can just see the news headlines now. I think we realize who we're dealing with, and for now we just lay low and get our work done. No police. I would like to meet your friends, though."

"I'll stick by whatever decision you make, but you may want to sleep on it."

"That's fair. But I don't think I'll be getting much sleep tonight."

"You should try. I'm going to be right outside in my car keeping watch, so you won't have to worry about anything else happening here tonight."

She looked up into his eyes. "No, Landon, I can't possibly ask you to do that."

"You didn't ask. I offered. Believe me, I can handle pulling an all nighter."

"You're going way above and beyond what I hired you to do for this case."

"This isn't just about the case. It's about you and making sure you're safe."

She stood, and he joined her. "I'll personally pay you for this additional work."

"No way. Kate, I don't want your money. I'm offering my help as a friend. Let me give that to you."

She smiled at him. "As you can probably tell, I'm not that great at accepting help from others."

"I can relate. You and I are a lot alike."

"That isn't such a bad thing, is it?"

As he looked down at her, he realized that he needed to keep himself in check. He wanted to keep this woman safe, but could he actually be developing feelings for her?

That seemed like an even more dangerous proposition than anything else that had happened so far.

CHAPTER
# NINE

The next morning, Kate took a quick shower, made herself presentable, and set out to find Landon. She couldn't believe he had insisted on staying there all night to protect her, but she would be forever grateful. She had thought she wouldn't be able to sleep at all, but knowing that Landon was there watching over her lightened her burden, and she had actually slept through the night.

When she peeked out her front window, she didn't see Landon, but another man leaned up against a large black SUV parked in front of her house.

She took a quick step back from the window and tried to steady her ragged breathing. Her pulse began to pound, and her hands shook. Where was Landon? Why was this strange man outside her house? Had he been sent by MPC? But then again, if he were there to hurt her, would he be waiting around in broad daylight?

She pulled back the curtain to look again. He was probably in his mid- to late thirties, tall, with short blond hair and a muscular build.

He made eye contact with her and smiled. There was no

sinister intent in his bright blue eyes—just the opposite. He started walking toward her front door.

"Ma'am," he said, from the other side of the door. "I'm Cooper Knight, a friend of Landon's."

Relief flooded through her. So this was one of Landon's college buddies who owned the security business. She disarmed her alarm system and unlocked the door to let him inside.

He walked in and offered his hand. "Nice to meet you," he said. "Landon contacted me last night and updated me on your situation."

"Where is he?"

"He'll be back soon, ma'am. I insisted that I take the second shift so he could get some rest."

"You can call me Kate, and thank you for your help. I didn't even want him to stay all night, and now I have both of you to thank."

"Your safety is top priority."

As she processed his words, a chill shot through her. "Would you like some coffee?"

"That would be great, ma'am—I mean, Kate." He smiled.

"Come on in the kitchen." As she prepared the coffee, she looked over her shoulder. "I understand that you and Landon were college roommates?"

"That's right, along with my business partner, Noah Ramirez."

"Since you're here, I'd love to hear more about your company. Landon has been pretty insistent that we retain you for the MPC case."

He nodded. "I'm happy to tell you more about what K&R does, but first you should know that I think Landon's right. I'm not saying this because I'm trying to get business. Even if you don't choose our security firm, I seriously suggest you hire someone, given the threat assessment. Landon has only been able to tell me a limited amount, but I'd be happy to sign a nondisclosure agreement to get more of the download from you, with absolutely no obligation on your part to hire us."

"I already owe you for last night," she said.

"No, that was me doing a friend a favor. It had nothing to do with being on the clock."

"You two must be very close."

She saw him hesitate for a brief moment, but it was long enough to realize she'd hit a nerve.

"When you go through the college experience together, you build a bond. But since Landon left the military, he's been focused on his PI business, and I've been working with Noah on our company. We haven't had much interaction lately, but when he reached out to me about your situation, I was there in a heartbeat."

There was much more to this story than Cooper was saying, but it wasn't her right to pry—and definitely not with Cooper. If she wanted more answers, she should go to Landon directly. "Please tell me about your business. That will help me decide if we need to move forward and sign an NDA."

"We started primarily as a private security firm working in the tech space. If a company has security concerns with their systems, they call us. We can build from the ground up or work with whatever the company has in place and upgrade them to state of the art. Our clients range from small start-ups and family businesses to huge corporations. We also do computer forensics—the type of stuff you'd hire an expert for if you were trying to find or recover data from a system or trace what happened to certain data."

"That's very impressive."

"We've also branched out into personal security services. The type of work I did here last night. Mainly our clients are celebrities or other VIPs."

She laughed. "Well, that wouldn't be me."

"From where I sit, it seems you fit the VIP mold pretty well."

She shook her head. "No way. I'm just a lawyer trying to get justice for my clients."

"And you have no chance of succeeding if you aren't alive and well to do so."

Another chill shot down her back at his words. She'd never thought about it that way before. She ran her hand through her hair and let his words sink in. "I guess you're right."

She took two big mugs out of the cabinet and poured coffee for them both. "Need cream and sugar?"

"No, I take mine black."

She gave him a steaming mug of coffee before fixing her own. She dumped some sugar in her cup. "Sounds like I should get you that NDA to sign. I can print one off from my home office if you give me a second."

"Sure."

She took her coffee with her to the office down the hall. A knock on the door almost made her spill coffee on the hallway floor.

"Let me check that out," Cooper said. Immediately he was at her front door. He looked through the peephole, and his shoulders visibly relaxed. "It's Landon."

Cooper opened the door, and Landon entered, walking directly toward her. "How're you doing?"

"Pretty good, thanks to both of you. I was just about to print Cooper an NDA so I could get him up to speed on the case and the investigation you're running."

"Seems like perfect timing, then." Landon looked at Cooper. "Coop, can you give us a second?"

"Sure. I'll be in the kitchen, getting back to my coffee." Cooper walked down the hallway toward the kitchen.

She turned her attention to Landon. "Are you okay?"

"Yes, I wanted to explain why Cooper was here this morning. I figured you might not be too happy about that."

"Why? You guys are putting yourselves on the line to help me. I appreciate it, and I'm thankful for what you're doing. All of it."

He took a step closer to her. "I didn't want you to think I was abandoning you."

"I would never think that. You've been here each step of the way. Cooper told me that he offered to take over so you could get a few hours of sleep. I understand that. He seems completely capable, and you'd already told me about him and his background as a police officer."

He gently placed his hand on her shoulder. "Yes, that's what I wanted to make sure you understood. I would've never left you in just anyone's hands. I trust Cooper with my life."

She hesitated a moment, then said, "Cooper told me that since you left the military, he hasn't seen you very much."

"Did he say anything else?"

"No. I got the feeling he didn't want me to pry."

"I told you that I had a rough time during my last tour in Iraq. When I came back stateside, it was easier just to separate myself from everyone I cared about."

"I'm sorry to bring up such a painful topic." She regretted saying anything at all.

He squeezed her shoulder before dropping his hand. "It's fine. But for now, I'd like to focus on our current situation."

"Understood. Let me get that NDA, and then we can fully brief Cooper. Did you actually get any rest?"

"I did. Sleeping is a skill I developed as a Ranger. You might only have thirty minutes, and you have to be able to nap on command. I appreciate Cooper stepping in."

"If everything goes as I expect it will, it looks like I'll be retaining his company to help us out."

Nicole knew by the tone of the email she'd received from the first-year associate that the newbie thought she'd found some hot documents. Nicole had to take it all in stride, because this was about the fiftieth time she'd been alerted by a junior associate about supposedly hot documents—and not a single one of them rose to that level.

But she appreciated that these young lawyers were taking it so seriously. She'd much rather have a million false alarms than the alternative—missing key documents and then being blindsided in depositions. Heads would roll if that happened, and that would include her own.

She gathered up her patience and grabbed an espresso from the break room before heading back to her office to meet Julia. One of the perks of a large firm like Peters & Gomez was the amenities. They had a gourmet coffee bar and an endless supply of snacks to fuel lawyers who often worked around the clock.

When Nicole got back to her office, Julia stood eagerly waiting for her, notebook, laptop, and a stack of documents in hand.

"Come on in," she told the junior associate.

"I'm sorry to bother you, Nicole, but I really thought you needed to see these docs. I printed out copies for you."

"Thanks, Julia. Let me take a look." She took the pages from Julia and started to scan them. Initially nothing too troubling, but as she flipped to the next page, the email exchange became more interesting. "Did you bring the list of key players with you? Do you know who all of these people are?"

"Yes, and yes."

Julia provided the list, which was essentially a cast of characters of everyone in the litigation. It grew daily as the team learned more about the people involved and all the MPC personnel and their specific roles.

"Tell me what you know," Nicole said.

"This is an exchange between two senior research scientists—Pierce Worthington and Ellie Proctor. Ellie tells Pierce that she thinks the repeat tests for Celix will confirm that the drug has harmful side effects."

Ellie Proctor was the woman who had been killed in the parking garage. Nicole flipped from one document to the next and read them, first quickly skimming, and then rereading in a more careful way.

Finally, she looked up at Julia. "Good work, Julia. Thanks for bringing these to my attention. I'm assuming you flagged them in the system for my personal review too?"

"Yes, definitely."

"Keep an eye out for anything else like this."

"Will do." Julia got up and left her office.

Nicole needed a few moments to gather her thoughts. The email exchange between the two scientists was troublesome. She read the worst of the documents again. The other side would use this conversation to demonstrate that two top scientists at MPC at least had some concern about the possibility of dangerous side effects to using Celix.

She checked the date on the exchange and saw it was before the release of Celix. This document could be used to show prior knowledge, and that in turn would boost the plaintiffs' failure-to-warn claim.

She marked up the documents with highlights and notes. How they approached this issue ultimately wasn't her call. Those decisions were way above her pay grade. She picked up the phone and dialed Ethan's number.

Landon took Cooper along with him to scope out Ellie's apartment in the popular Virginia-Highland neighborhood.

113

He hadn't invited Kate because he thought she might not be comfortable with some of his plans. It was better to keep her out of the loop until he had something to tell her. Her firm was paying him to investigate, and that was exactly what he was doing.

"What's your angle here?" Cooper asked.

They stepped out of Landon's Wrangler and started walking toward the apartment complex office.

"I'm going to try to sweet-talk the apartment manager into letting us into Ellie's apartment."

"And you think that will work?"

"It depends on who the apartment manager is." A bead of sweat rolled down his back as he walked toward the office. He was eager to get inside to the air conditioning. "You might actually be the one to get us in there."

Cooper raised an eyebrow. "How do you figure that?"

"Because if it's a woman, you'll have a better chance than I will."

Cooper laughed loudly. "Whatever you say, bro."

It was fun giving his old college buddy a hard time. Landon realized he had missed hanging out with Cooper. It was sad that it had taken circumstances like these to bring them back together. "I was thinking we could say that either we're friends of Ellie's or friends of the family. Something like that?"

Cooper stopped walking and turned toward him. "What about the honest answer? That we're investigators and want to find out what happened to her?"

"That might spook them. They may call the cops." That was the last thing Landon needed to explain to Kate.

"I could bring up the fact that I'm a former cop," Cooper said.

"That actually might be the best strategy." Why hadn't he thought of that?

Twenty minutes later, Kim, the forty-something office manager, was opening Ellie's door for them. When Cooper had told her that he was former Atlanta PD, Kim was instantly put at ease.

"I hope you guys find something that will help. Ellie was a nice woman and a good tenant. Kept to herself and didn't cause me any problems. I'm having some trouble getting in touch with her family, though, and if I don't hear from anyone by the first of the month, I'm going to have to clear out the place myself so it can be relisted."

"Thank you, Kim," Cooper said with a wide smile. "We really appreciate it."

"Stop by on your way out so I can lock up again."

"No problem." This had worked out even better than Landon expected. Kim trusted them implicitly because of Cooper's law-enforcement credentials.

Kim shut the door on her way out, and Landon looked at Cooper. "Time to get to work."

Landon walked into the kitchen. "A pile of unpaid bills are stacked up here." He flipped through them. "She was having financial trouble. No doubt about that."

"A lot of people have financial trouble," Cooper said. "That doesn't mean she was lying."

They went through the one-bedroom apartment in a methodical manner, room by room, leaving no inch of the modest apartment untouched.

"No laptop that I can find," Cooper called out.

"Yeah, nothing for me either."

Landon started to examine Ellie's small bathroom. He opened her medicine cabinet. It looked like she was running a pharmacy. Bottle upon bottle of pills. The entire cabinet was completely full.

He pulled out his phone and took pictures of all the drug labels. Kate had said that Ellie seemed like she could have been on something when they met. Had the stress of the job done this to her, or was it totally unconnected?

Landon finished up in the bathroom and started on Ellie's bedroom. He opened her nightstand drawer and found a notebook. He flipped it open and started reading. The notes were scribbled in awful handwriting and used a lot of shorthand.

His eyes scanned each page, hoping he'd find something. There were a ton of notes and what looked like some chemical equations, which wasn't surprising for a scientist.

From what he could tell, the first part of the notebook was all about Celix. When he was about halfway through, as he flipped to the next page, he saw that one phrase was circled and starred on each side: *Look at Acreda.*

He kept reading, but the rest of the notebook appeared only to talk about Celix. No other mentions of Acreda.

"Hey, Cooper, come in here," he yelled.

A moment later, Cooper walked into the bedroom. "You find something?"

"Any idea what the word Acreda means? The spelling is A-C-R-E-D-A."

"No. Never heard of it." Cooper pulled out his phone and started typing. Then he let out a low whistle.

"What is it?"

Cooper looked up at him. "Acreda is a drug manufactured by none other than MPC."

# TEN

When Ethan got a concerned voice message from Nicole, immediately his stomach sank. Nicole wasn't the type to sound a false alarm. If she said they needed to talk ASAP, then she meant it. He cut his outing short after lunch and returned immediately to the office. He'd have to pick up his dry cleaning later.

When he walked into his office, he picked up the phone and called Nicole's cell. He told himself the good news was that whatever the reviewers had identified in the documents, at least they had found it, and he could develop a strategy to handle it.

Less than two minutes later, Nicole walked in, her face flushed.

"I hope it isn't so bad that you had to run up here?"

"I was downstairs in the cafeteria."

It wasn't a good sign that she'd dropped everything to come to his office. "Sorry, I didn't mean to interrupt your lunch."

"No, this is far more important. I ran by my office to pick up the documents. Take a look at these."

She placed a manila folder in front of him, and he opened it to examine the contents. He skimmed the email messages. With each additional word he read, he could feel his pulse thump more quickly.

"As you can see, these are bad for us," Nicole said. "They show knowledge of side effects. Check out the date. This is between two top scientists. And what's even worse, one of those scientists is Ellie Proctor, the woman who was murdered. She isn't around to testify and explain this email away or provide more context. We're toast." Her voice shook as she spoke.

He put the emails down and focused on his associate. He had to calm her down and get control of the situation. "Take a few deep breaths, Nicole."

She clutched her phone in her hand. "I'm trying, but I know how high the stakes are here. Please tell me how we're going to explain this one away."

"Let me be the one who loses sleep over this—not you. Once you make partner, things like this will become your problem, but for now I bear that burden."

Her big brown eyes didn't break contact with his. "But I can't forget I know about this."

"Let's take it one step at a time. First of all, we need to examine the context around this email. I need you to pull all the documents that fall anywhere around this one and develop a chronology. We can't look at this doc in a vacuum."

She lifted one of the documents in her hand. "I bet the plaintiffs will put this in their opening statement."

"Nicole, this is what we do. If it were an easy case, MPC wouldn't hire a firm like ours. They brought us on because it is difficult and there will be challenges, but that's why we have to be better and smarter than the other side. You understand?"

She nodded but didn't say anything. Her lack of response concerned him.

"And we clearly aren't handing this over in our early docu-

118

ment productions," he said. "We'll wait until we have a strategy developed."

Nicole bit her bottom lip. "That makes sense. There's no rule that says we have to produce in some sort of order."

He wondered if she was mentally and emotionally tough enough for this type of work. She needed to get her head in the game. "You can't let one bad document throw you off. There are hundreds of thousands of pages to review. This is only one tiny piece of the story. We'll have a hundred good documents to tell our version of events for every bad one. Don't ever forget that."

"You're right. I was much calmer before I came in here and had to explain this to you. I just got so worked up scenario-building."

Over the years he'd learned that there was never just one bad document. "You did the right thing by bringing this to me. Have you told anyone else about this document?"

"No. The only people who have seen it are me and the attorney who found it."

"Let's keep it that way for now. I don't want to send the team into a panic, but do tell everyone to redouble their efforts and make sure they stay focused and on the lookout for anything potentially damaging."

"I'm on it."

"Can you also start working on that chronology right away?"

"Of course."

"I'd like you to be personally responsible for constructing the chronology. I know you have tons on your plate, but I need to get the bigger picture here, and quickly." Channeling her nervous energy into a big project would be a good idea.

"That's no problem. I'll make it my top priority."

"Good work as always, Nicole. I'm fortunate to have you on my team."

She smiled. "And I'm glad to be on it."

"All right. Go grab your lunch now."

"Thanks." She walked out of his office, and he turned his attention back to the documents in front of him.

This was the exact type of thing Royce and Matt had warned him about. He hoped this was as bad as it got, but he figured he might be in for more surprises. The bigger question was how he was going to handle it in the trial.

Royce had made it perfectly clear that he was fine withholding documents, but Ethan wasn't at that point yet. It was his duty to zealously advocate for his client, but it was also his duty to follow the rules of ethical responsibility for lawyers. He couldn't just hide evidence, could he?

But realistically, if the jury saw docs like this, he could kiss a defense verdict good-bye. Then it would be more about how much the jury would hit them for. That would not only be a disaster for MPC, it would be an even bigger one for his career. There was no room for a loss right now, not on his current trajectory.

He took a deep breath and decided that he didn't have to come up with the exact strategy at that moment. He needed to wait and see what else the team found in the documents.

And there was no way he was turning over this document anytime soon.

Cooper had invited Kate and Landon to the K&R office to talk about the MPC case. She'd given Cooper the factual background on Sunday, but now they needed to develop a plan to move forward.

The K&R office was downtown and only a few minutes from her building. She'd insisted to Landon that she didn't need a 24-7 bodyguard right now. The man who attacked her on Saturday night could have easily killed her, but he didn't. They were trying to scare her, and she refused to change her entire life because of it.

That didn't mean she was going to be reckless, but she wanted to maintain some semblance of normalcy.

Once she arrived at the building that housed the K&R office suite, Landon was waiting for her when she got off the elevator on the twentieth floor.

"How're you doing?" he asked.

"Ready to get to work." She'd had some time to process the events of Saturday night and felt much stronger than she had after it happened.

"Good. Let's go in."

They entered the suite, which opened into a small reception area. Landon told the receptionist who they were, and Kate enjoyed the city view out the large window. The office wasn't fancy, but she didn't think it needed to be for this type of work. It was a big contrast to the law firm offices she was accustomed to, as there was no modern artwork hanging on the walls or high-end furniture—just the basics.

After a moment, Cooper walked out into the lobby, accompanied by a tall, dark-haired man. She assumed this was Cooper's business partner.

Cooper smiled at her. "Kate, great you could make it. I'd like to introduce you to the tech brains behind this operation, Noah Ramirez."

She stepped forward and offered her hand, which he took. The brown-eyed man didn't smile back at her but wore a serious expression with pursed lips. His handshake was firm but not overly so. "Nice to meet you. Although, not under these circumstances." His voice was deep, but he was soft-spoken. Cooper seemed to be the more outgoing of the two.

"Let's go back to the conference room and talk," Cooper said. She noticed that Noah and Landon didn't exchange any words. In fact, they hadn't even looked at each other. She didn't know what that was all about, but she couldn't worry about it right now.

She was ushered into a medium-sized conference room that held multiple computers. This room also had the no-nonsense styling of the lobby—just the bare minimum in terms of furniture and décor. The dark tones also gave it a masculine feel that matched the company's owners.

"I've gotten Noah up to speed on the facts," Cooper said. "What we need to do is get a full strategy together to make sure we're using all of our resources and knowledge the best way we can."

"Agreed," she said. "There are quite a few moving parts."

"First, let me update Kate on a big development in our investigation," Landon said.

"What?" She could tell by the look on Landon's face that this was important. He was in all-business mode.

"Cooper and I were able to take a look inside Ellie's apartment," he said flatly.

Her heart sank. "I hope you didn't break in."

Landon smiled. "Nope. Perfectly legal and on the up-and-up."

She relaxed a little. "What did you find?"

"A few things," he said. "A pile of unpaid bills and a huge stash of prescription drugs to start."

"You think Ellie had a problem with drugs?" That would explain her behavior when they'd met.

"It's a possibility. People don't normally have that many drugs in their house. She had a combination of uppers and downers. Not a good mix. And if she was taking them with alcohol, that's especially bad. We know she had a DUI."

This was a hit to Ellie's credibility, but it didn't change Kate's opinion. At least not yet. "Ellie might have struggled with addiction, but we can't ignore the fact that she made those allegations and turned up dead."

"You're absolutely right. Which brings me to the biggest find we made at her place. A notebook on Celix. But on one single page, there was a highlighted phrase that said, 'Look at Acreda.' After further research, we found out that Acreda is a drug set to go on the market within the next six to nine months. It's produced by MPC and primarily used to treat various types of tumors, although it has other possible uses."

Her mind began to race. "I've never heard of Acreda, and I've read a ton of research about Celix. More than you can even imagine."

"I don't know yet how Acreda fits into this puzzle," Landon said, "but it certainly seems like something we need to focus on as one of our top priorities."

"Let's think this through. Ellie specifically told me that I needed to look at other MPC drugs." Trying to connect the dots, she started spinning out theories. "Maybe Acreda also has dangerous side effects, and she was trying to let us know. She said it was bigger than Celix. Maybe Acreda is highly dangerous too, and she was trying to warn us to stop it from hitting the market before it could harm people."

"At least we have a direction to go in," Cooper said.

"I agree," she said. "And if Acreda is a dangerous drug, we need to figure that out before it's too late." There could be an entirely separate class of people who would be harmed if it went to market.

"One other thing," Landon said. "I've made contact with Pierce Worthington, a scientist who worked with Ellie at MPC. I'm trying to develop a relationship with him, but he's hesitant. I still think he wants to do the right thing, and if I keep up with it, I hope he'll provide us with useful information or a way to get at some documentation—assuming it still exists."

"What has he told you so far?" Cooper asked.

"He doesn't believe MPC is actually behind Ellie's death. He thinks the company is cutthroat, but not to that level. He said they have a tight legal grip on the scientists, just like Ellie told us. It's not like they can just up and get a new job because of all of the restrictions they agreed to when they went to work for a company like MPC. Also, he said the CEO, Royce Hamilton is very hands-on."

"We should do an even deeper look at Hamilton." Noah typed up notes on his laptop.

"We will," Cooper said. "Kate, where are you on your legal stuff?"

"I expect to receive the first wave of documents today from Ethan. A team of people at my firm will review them. The best way to construct a legal case that MPC knew about the side effects of Celix and failed to disclose them is to find documents that show MPC's knowledge about the harmful side effects. But beyond that, we'll also search for information on Acreda. Since all the documents they're producing are in electronic format, our database has search functionality to look for certain keywords."

"That's also where you guys might come into play," Landon said to Cooper and Noah. "We'll need to be ready on the computer forensics side."

She jumped in to make the situation clear. "But I have to warn you, getting access to MPC's systems is probably never going to happen."

"Really?" Landon asked. "Are you sure? That doesn't seem fair. If we can make a good enough argument that they're hiding evidence, why wouldn't the judge allow that?"

Trying to explain all of these intricacies to nonlawyers was always a challenge. "Judges don't just give access to a company's data or systems to the opposing side. That's not how it works. Even if I can show that they're withholding evidence, the more likely remedy would be sanctions and an adverse inference instruction."

"What does that mean?" Cooper was taking a lot of notes.

"The fact that evidence was destroyed or not produced would be fair game at trial, and the judge would tell the jury that they can take that lack of evidence and construe it negatively against MPC." She paused at the blank looks on their faces. "Or to say it another way, the jury will be able to presume that MPC had something bad to hide because they destroyed or didn't produce documents. It's a very extreme remedy that isn't often used because the impact can be big. It could also be an issue raised on appeal."

"That does seem like a big deal," Landon said.

"If we really need the docs that badly, we could also try to breach their system," Noah offered.

That wasn't going to happen. "No way. I've already told Landon that we have to stay on the right side of the law here. I refuse to stoop to their tactics. And from a practical standpoint, we wouldn't be able to introduce any evidence you found through hacking anyway. So that is completely off the table."

"Kate's right." Landon gave her a reassuring nod. "She's convinced me that's a bad idea. But we have other issues to deal with. Given the attack on Kate Saturday night, I think we should discuss Kate's security protocols."

"I didn't realize I had any security protocols," she said, feeling her eyebrows rise.

"That's the point. You need some," Cooper said. "And to that end, we've been discussing a proposal we'd like to present to you."

"All right." Something told her she wasn't going to be a big fan of their suggestion. All three men had focused their attention on her, which made her nerves feel a bit frazzled.

Landon reached over and touched her arm. "Hear us out before you shoot it down, Kate."

"We all agree that you don't need around-the-clock protection," Cooper said. "But we do think you should have a security escort to and from work and any other places you go to ensure that you get safely to work and back home at night."

"I'd primarily serve this role, relying on Coop for backup," Landon said.

"What about you?" she asked Noah.

"I'll work on updating your home security system and provide any backup as needed to your security detail."

By the looks of him, he seemed perfectly cut out for the job. All three men had either a law enforcement or military background. She was fortunate to have them in her corner. "Thank you. After what happened Saturday night, I don't want to be put in that position again. If that means having an escort to and from work and beefing up my home security system, then so be it."

"Great," Cooper said. "I'll work out a schedule with Landon, and Noah will work on your security system. Sounds like there's nothing for us to do at this point on the computer forensics front, so we'll just wait and see if there ends up being any way to help on that end. Landon will keep working his source at MPC to see what comes of that. And most important, we'll do research on our end on Acreda."

"And in the meantime, guys, I need to get back to work." Kate looked down at her phone. "Looks like Ethan actually met his deadline with the document production. The first CD was just delivered to our office, and our practice support is in the process of loading it up for our reviewers."

That meant she could have her team start looking at documents right away. She needed to find the smoking gun. And fast.

# CHAPTER
# ELEVEN

Kate assembled her team of junior and midlevel attorneys who would be reviewing the documents. Much to her surprise, the first batch that Ethan sent over had been about a hundred thousand pages.

Even though that was a lot of volume, she assumed it would be junk. They were the types of documents that needed to be produced but wouldn't hold any particular significance to her case. But despite what she thought, she couldn't afford to act on those assumptions. In a case like this, where there might be foul play and a cover-up, she needed to be extra careful about examining every single page that Ethan turned over on behalf of MPC. And that was a message she had to convey to the team without telling them everything she knew.

Years ago, attorneys would have been locked in a room with tons of boxes, going through paper documents, but now in the digital age, it was a completely different ball game. Everything was electronic—the documents and the method of reviewing them. Thankfully, she was comfortable with technology, but she wasn't nearly as good at it as the junior associates.

She'd reserved one of the firm's largest conference rooms as their war room. It was fully set up with everything her team would need to review all the documents and start preparing for the Wyman case.

As the associates filed into the room, she waited for them to get settled. She'd also asked Adam and Bonnie to attend this kickoff meeting. She could only hope that Bonnie would be well behaved.

"Thanks to everyone for gathering on short notice. As most of you know, I'm Kate Sullivan, and I'll be leading this litigation. MPC dropped the first document production on us today, and our staff has been hard at work loading the data into our review platform. I know that all of you have been trained in our database and the document review tool, so we won't cover that ground again. I would like to make sure that everyone on the team knows the other two partners working the case with me." She looked over at Bonnie and Adam. "This is Bonnie Olson and Adam Fox. Both highly experienced litigators who will be doing a lot of work with our experts, but they can also serve as a resource for other aspects as well. Bonnie, Adam, do you have anything to add?"

Bonnie shook her head, but Adam stepped forward. "I'm managing all our expert efforts, so if any of you have a specific interest in doing work on the expert reports, I'd love to work with you. And for everyone here, my door is always open, so feel free to reach out if you want to discuss anything about the case."

Tellingly, Bonnie didn't make the same offer, but that was fine. It was enough just to have her on board. Kate would need her help at some point. She was thankful Adam was such a positive force for the group. Hopefully between Adam and her, they could balance out Bonnie.

"Well, then, let's get down to business. I circulated the document review protocol to the group a while ago. Hopefully everyone has had a chance to read it. I won't bore you with those details again, as each of you has had the case briefing. But I do want to take a moment and bring your attention to one thing."

She paused a moment to think through her words. She wanted to make sure they were extremely thorough, but she couldn't explain all of the reasons there was so much on the line here. "All of you have been on review teams before, and I know you're always told that you have to be on top of it and pay a lot of attention to detail. But I can't stress enough how important that is in this case. I believe there will be documents showing that MPC knew of the connection between Celix and the brain tumors, but it might not be as simple as spelling it out. I'll need each of you to read these documents with a critical eye toward our case—the central contention we need to prove is that MPC knew or should have known about the tumors. We can't afford to miss anything. It could be the difference between winning and losing the case. Anyone have any questions?"

One of the associates raised her hand.

"Yes, go ahead."

"As far as workflow, is this case our top priority right now? What if we get pulled onto other matters?"

She'd already cleared all of their schedules with the partners they reported to. "You shouldn't get pulled onto anything else. If you're sitting in this room right now, it's because you've been approved to work full time on this. I can't afford to have people popping in and out of the review."

The associate nodded. "I assume we should come to you if someone tries to get us to work on something else?"

"Absolutely," she said.

Another hand went up. "Are you saying we can't do any substantive work like writing briefs or memos while we're on this case?"

By the sound of his voice, he wasn't happy about being put on document review.

Bonnie stepped forward. She was tall, and her commanding presence filled the conference room. "Let me answer that. I know document review is looked at by a lot of you as grunt work, but it's absolutely critical to understanding the case and developing the strategy. All of you were selected because your managing attorneys thought you would bring value to this team. So if you're not in it to be a team player, you should walk out of this room right now."

Kate hid a smirk. Bonnie clearly had no trouble playing bad cop.

"It's just that I would hate to lose out on other opportunities," the associate said.

"What's your name?" Bonnie asked.

"Phil Gentry," he answered with a shaky voice. His initial show of confidence had been sapped by Bonnie's response. Kate didn't think this was going to end well for Phil. He should have just let it go and not challenged Bonnie.

"Phil, you should leave," Bonnie said. "We won't need you on this team any longer, and I'll personally have a discussion with your managing attorney about why you've been taken off this case."

"Wait a minute. I didn't say I wanted to be removed from the case," Phil said.

"You don't want me to ask you to leave again." Bonnie took another step toward him. "This little stunt will not be forgotten, either, when it comes time for performance reviews."

Phil muttered under his breath, gathered up his things, and walked out of the conference room.

Kate needed to change the mood in the room. She didn't want to start on such a negative note. "I'm guessing everyone else would like to stay here. You should all have your first review sets ready to go in the database. You're all very valuable members of this team, and I appreciate your commitment. So let's get to work."

Bonnie pulled her aside for a hushed conference. "You have to be tough with these kids, or they'll just run all over you. Millennials think they can have it all—a six-figure salary, a cushy schedule, and choice assignments. You have to work that out of them, and quickly."

"You and I have different management styles."

Bonnie laughed. "You can say that again, but I did you a favor with Phil. You don't want someone like that on your case. He's bad news."

"I don't want anyone on the team if they aren't going to give it their all," she said.

"As women, we have to be stronger, Kate. The soft touch just won't get the job done. The last thing you want is to be seen as weak."

"I don't think anyone would call me weak," she protested, keeping her voice firm and steady. "I wouldn't have gotten lead counsel in this case if I was."

"That's the fire I like to see." Bonnie smiled. "I'm going to get back to my other cases. You know where to find me."

Had Bonnie just said something nice to her? Kate saw that Adam had left as well. Now that she was the only partner in the room, it was time to give the team a pep talk. Because unlike Bonnie, she felt that people did their best work when they were motivated and valued.

—◁◇▷—

Landon arrived at Kate's office that evening to escort her home. He'd worked out a schedule with Cooper. Kate had warned him that there would be some late nights, but tonight it wasn't so bad. She'd asked him to pick her up at seven thirty.

He waited in the lobby as she had instructed, and it wasn't long before she stepped off the elevator. Her long auburn hair was down today, and it flowed past her shoulders. When she saw him, she smiled, and that, in turn, made him smile.

What was it about this woman that made him a bit crazy? It wasn't like she was doing anything special to try to get his attention—if anything, just the opposite. She was focused on her job, but he couldn't help being focused on her. The danger that she found herself in only fueled his already strong protective instincts.

He walked over to her. "Thanks again for agreeing to this new system."

"I should be the one thanking you. This isn't the best gig in the world."

"Being around you isn't exactly tough, Kate."

She laughed. "We'll see if you're still saying that by the time the trial is over. I'm starving. Can we pick up some takeout on the way to my house?"

"Sure. Just let me know what you're in the mood for."

"Thai would be great."

"Sounds good to me." He realized, once they started talking about food, just how hungry he was. It had been a long day, and he had skipped lunch.

"I'll call it in right now. It'll be ready when we get there."

"Thai on speed dial?"

She shrugged. "I order out a lot."

He could relate. He ate a ton of takeout too.

About thirty minutes later, they arrived at her house with a huge bag of Thai food, but his voracious appetite would have to wait. First things first. He had to confirm that Kate's home was secure.

He turned to her before she could climb out of the Jeep. "Stay put for a minute, and lock the doors when I get out."

"Do you really think that's necessary?"

"Humor me."

She nodded, and he stepped out of his Wrangler. She'd given him a key so that he could make copies for the team. Noah would be working on her security system, but that wasn't an overnight fix.

He unlocked the door, disarmed the alarm, and cleared the house room by room. Jax darted out in front of him, but everything seemed normal and in place. No sign of any intruders. He hadn't expected there would be, but from here on out, they weren't going to take any chances. Satisfied that all was well, at least for now, he went back outside to get Kate.

A little while later, they sat at Kate's kitchen table with their plates full of Thai food, including his hefty portion of spicy noodles. He looked up and found Kate staring at him.

"Uh-oh, what did I do now?" he asked.

She smiled. "I'm just wondering how quickly you're going to get tired of this setup. Having to babysit me and make sure that I'm safe. I mean, this goes way beyond your initial job description."

He paused for a moment before he responded, trying to gather his thoughts. "Kate, even if this wasn't a paying gig, there is no way I'd leave you to deal with these threats alone."

"That's sweet of you, Landon, but the firm is definitely paying you for your time."

"But I'm not on the clock right now." He wanted her to understand that this wasn't about obligation. Far from it. "We're having dinner, and it was my choice to stay. I could've just secured the house, made sure you were fine, and left. But I wanted to have dinner with you."

She cocked her head to the side. "I appreciate the company. I'm not going to lie. This entire situation has taken me out of my comfort zone. I've never dealt with security threats before."

"Which is exactly why I'm here, and why we now have extra help with Cooper's team." He took a bite of noodles and then continued. "Also, Noah will be here tomorrow to work on the security system."

"That's great. Will you make sure to warn him about Jax? I don't want him getting out. Post-surgery, he's purely an indoor cat."

"Yes. I'll do that." He pulled out his phone and shot off a text so he wouldn't forget.

"Did I sense some sort of tension between the two of you?"

"Me and Noah?"

"Yeah."

He really didn't want to have this conversation, but maybe he'd feel better if he opened up just a bit. "It's a long story."

"I have nowhere to go and a plate of noodles to get through."

Instantly, without even trying, Kate had disarmed him once again. "I met Noah and Cooper in the freshman dorms. We got an apartment together sophomore year and were very tight throughout college and over the years since then. But I had a falling-out with Noah last year."

"About what?"

Once he told Kate this, it would probably lower her opinion of him, but he wasn't in the business of being dishonest. "A woman. And he totally had the right to be mad at me. He was seeing someone but said it wasn't serious. Little did I know that he had completely fallen for her. Well, let's just say I made some extremely bad choices where she was concerned when I got back from my final deployment. He still hasn't forgiven me, and I can't really blame him. I was in an awful place and acting out in every possible way that I could, including moving in on his girlfriend. My bad decisions were just that—bad decisions. And I own up to that."

She moved her chair around the table to sit directly beside him. "We're all imperfect, Landon. I can't begin to tell you some of the things I did that I regret. I engaged in so much self-destructive behavior that I often looked in the mirror and was disgusted by the person I'd become. But once the Lord came into my heart, I was able to approach things with a different perspective. It's all a process, though. I still face ups and downs."

"Your faith shines through, Kate, but I don't know how I'd ever get back to a relationship with God, especially after the things I've said and done. The pain I've lived through. We're not talking about small bumps in the road here. More like life-altering detours."

"It's not that you doubt God's existence, then?"

"No, but I doubt that He has any real interest in me."

Kate slipped her hand into his. Her soft touch impacted him more than it should have.

"That's not true, Landon. God loves you, and He's there for you even when you don't think He is. You've shut Him out, but it only takes small steps to change and open back up to Him."

Listening to the longing in her voice hurt him, but she didn't understand the full picture. The horrors he experienced in the Sandbox—the pain, death, and destruction. And he wasn't sure he could bear to try to make her understand. "It's so messed up. Where I've been, what I've been through, how I've reacted. It's all just too much."

She moved even closer to him and didn't break eye contact. "You don't have to tell me everything. But know this—I'm praying for you."

Her words, spoken with such conviction, were like a punch to the gut. If only she knew just how broken he was. "I can't stop you from praying for me, but I should probably tell you not to waste your time."

"It won't be a waste. That much I know with all of my heart," she said quietly. She was still holding his hand.

The room was completely silent as he looked into her eyes. So many different emotions raged within him. Including the urge to pull her into his arms and kiss her. But he had to check himself.

He pulled back. "It's getting late. I should get out of your hair." He stood and threw his plate in the kitchen trash can. "I'll double-check everything once more before I go."

He walked out of the kitchen, needing a moment to gather his thoughts. Kate had a lot more faith in God and His ability to be there for him than Landon ever had. While he wanted to believe her impassioned positions, his past experience made him wary. And even if he had experienced that reoccurring tugging at his heart, that small voice in his head, what was he supposed to do with it?

He didn't even know how to begin to approach God again. It was easier to just bracket off that part of his mind, but he also knew faith was central to Kate's life. If he wanted to know her better, he would have to understand her ability to connect with God in a way he hadn't been able to.

Kate affected him unlike any woman ever had, but his feelings worried him. He was scared he would let her down.

# CHAPTER
# TWELVE

Kate couldn't believe how fast the past month had flown by, and thankfully there hadn't been any additional threats against her. She'd fallen into a good schedule with Landon and Cooper. After her heavy conversation with Landon, she'd tried to keep things lighter and give him time to open up to her at his own speed.

True to her word, though, she'd been praying for him daily. Even in the midst of all the legal work, she felt that God had placed Landon in her life for a reason. Yes, she needed him for his skills and protection, but she wanted to be there for him as a friend too. It was clear he was still dealing with the deep wounds of war. But the fact that he hadn't given up completely on faith made her believe there was still hope. God could work His will—she was sure of that.

Her team had combed through tens of thousands of documents. Ethan had kept additional productions coming. He was trying to drown them with documents, but she knew he had to be hiding something.

Which was why she was ready to file a motion to compel. He hadn't produced any documents in response to several of her requests, including the one that would pull in other drugs.

And given the warning in Ellie's notebook about Acreda, she had to find a way to get those documents.

She'd suffered a setback on the timing of the motion because the draft of her brief had mysteriously been deleted from the shared drive of the firm's computer system a few days ago. She'd worked with the IT staff for hours, but they had been unable to retrieve it. Unfortunately, they couldn't tell her how it disappeared.

And that wasn't the only weird thing that had happened. Over the past few weeks, her review team had reported that someone had taken their highlighted printouts of key documents. On top of that, a box of witness outlines had also been misplaced, and no one could find them.

If it had just been one thing, Kate would have overlooked it, but the fact that multiple documents had gone missing made her look over her shoulder. She didn't think MPC had anything to do with it, because their security inside the office was very tight. You had to have an authorized badge to get onto the floors that housed the law firm. So that meant it was probably someone on the inside. She had even started to question her own team—especially Bonnie. She hated to think that Bonnie would try to sabotage her, but she couldn't rule it out, given their history. Bonnie still held Kate's actions against her from when they worked together upon Kate's arrival to the firm.

She planned to keep an eye on Bonnie, and if things kept happening, she would confront the issue head on. It was ridiculous to think that any lawyer would try to sabotage someone else in the same firm, but she'd learned a long time ago that the legal field was cutthroat and far too shady.

But for now, she had to put that aside. She'd finished a new draft motion, and was ready to go. Court rules dictated that she make a good-faith effort to confer with Ethan about the issue to see if there could be any resolution before she filed the motion.

When he showed up at her office a few minutes later, she was ready.

"Beth escorted me back," he said. "It feels weird to shake your hand, and a hug probably isn't appropriate either, so I'll just say hello." He smiled.

"Thanks for coming over."

"What do you want to talk about?"

She hoped they could resolve this without going to the judge. "Ethan, my team has been diligently reviewing all the productions you've sent over in the past month."

"I would expect nothing less."

"Here's the thing—you still haven't produced a single document responsive to multiple requests, and most of the stuff you have produced so far could fall into the junk category. You have a duty not to produce nonresponsive documents just to make our lives more difficult."

He shook his head. "MPC is not producing nonresponsive documents. My team, just like yours, has been working very hard to identify documents responsive to your requests and to get them to you as quickly as possible. I think we have been successful at both."

"Do you need me to point out some examples?"

"Sure, that would be helpful."

She pulled out a stack of documents and placed them in front of him. They were all basically junk emails—employees talking about lunch plans, vacation ideas, pictures of their kids and pets. She let Ethan take a few minutes to review the pages, wondering what kind of explanation he'd have for them.

He crossed his arms. "Kate, we have hundreds of thousands of pages of documents to get through. The fact that you've been able to pull a few pages of junk out of the thousands we've given you doesn't mean that we aren't doing our jobs. It

139

just means that you're trying to pick a fight. I know you. This is one of your strategic power plays."

She balled up her fists and felt her nails dig into her skin. "You know that's not true. It's just how you're trying to spin this. Even if you put aside the issue of all the nonresponsive documents you've made my team sift through, what about the fact that you've produced absolutely nothing in response to multiple requests?"

Ethan didn't seem fazed by her accusations. "I told you that we would push back on some of those, just like I said in our written responses to the requests."

"You made general objections that they were unduly broad and burdensome, but you didn't specifically say you wouldn't produce anything in response to them. Look at numbers ten, fourteen, thirty, and thirty-six." She placed the specific document requests in front of him.

"We still have a few more productions to make."

His evasiveness was beginning to test her patience. "I need to know whether you will produce items responsive to these requests."

"And if not?"

"I'm ready to file a motion to compel."

He laughed, catching her off guard.

"You think this is funny?"

"A judge will be laughing too. There's no basis for that type of motion at this juncture."

"And I completely disagree."

"Where's this hostility coming from? Do you not trust that I will abide by my professional duty?"

She didn't want to offend her longtime friend, but she was also wary of what he might be willing to do. "I know you're under a lot of pressure and that you might not make the best decision. Regardless, discovery battles are normal in these types of cases, so I'm geared up for one. I wanted us to have our meet and confer, but it appears we're at an impasse, with neither one of us willing to budge on our positions."

He threw up his hands. "All I can say, Kate, is bring it on. I'm in the right here and willing to fight to prove it."

She hadn't meant for this to escalate so quickly. "Ethan, it doesn't have to be like this. Just meet me halfway. Try to be reasonable so we don't have to take this to the judge."

Ethan sighed as he fidgeted with his tie. "I don't like arguing with you about this stuff, but we knew when we took on this case that it was going to put us directly at odds with each other. I don't want you to feel like you have to advocate for your client any differently because of me, and I hope you feel the same on my behalf. I think it might be best to just take a step back and think this through again, and if you still want to file your motion to compel, I won't take it personally. I promise."

She sat back in her chair and deflated a little. "This would be so much easier if we didn't know each other." And wasn't that the truth. She hated being so adversarial with a friend, but at the end of the day, she believed that her clients deserved her best efforts. Even if it made her uncomfortable.

"It would be easier on us if you hadn't switched sides years ago. Just imagine, we could be working together instead of against each other."

She couldn't hold her tongue. "You really enjoy defending companies like MPC, don't you?"

His genial expression disappeared. "Aren't you on your high horse today," he snapped. "I enjoy what I do because, as much as you may think otherwise, the law is not black-and-white. You look at everything in stark moral terms, and in this case, you see a big bad corporation out to hurt the little guy. But that's a simplistic way to view things. That's not real-world."

His words hit her hard. "Do you really think my worldview is that simple?"

"Kate, you want to prance in on your white horse and save everyone, and it's a lot more complicated than that."

"I didn't realize you had such a low opinion of me."

He leaned forward in his seat, his demeanor softening. "I didn't mean it like that at all. Just that you have a completely different way of looking at the world and how you see your role as a lawyer. I don't share your views, and that directly impacts how I defend my cases and how you prosecute yours."

She let out a breath. "Well, Ethan, this is truly eye-opening. I had no idea you thought we were that different in our approaches. But I guess now I understand how you feel. Which brings us back to our impasse. I don't think there's anything left for us to discuss."

"I never meant to upset you, Kate. Keep everything I said in perspective. You do you, and I'll be me. We'll get through this and probably laugh about it one day regardless of how it turns out." He offered her a smile, stood up, and walked out of her office.

She stared despondently after him. Ethan couldn't be more wrong. There was nothing about this situation that would ever make her look back and laugh. If Ethan only knew the dangers she was facing.

—◁◇▷—

Landon had tried the deli again for the fifth time in two weeks, and there was still no sign of Pierce. Had Pierce found a new lunch spot to avoid having to deal with him?

Now he and Cooper were trying a different strategy. They waited outside the MPC building at five o'clock as most of the employees started to filter out. The summer sun was beating down on them, and Landon wiped a bead of sweat off his brow.

142

"He's probably not going to be happy that we're ambushing him," Cooper said. "But I realize you don't have much of an alternative."

"Pierce is a good guy, but I think he'd rather just stay out of all of this. I can't really blame him for that."

After waiting about twenty minutes, Landon laid eyes on Pierce walking out of the building and toward the parking garage. The same garage where Ellie was murdered.

"There he is," Landon told Cooper.

"Let's make the approach."

They easily caught up to Pierce before he reached the garage. When Pierce saw Landon, his eyes widened. "What are you doing here?"

"I need to talk to you."

"I told you that you should leave me alone and back off this thing," Pierce said. "And who is he?" He looked at Cooper.

"A friend and colleague."

Pierce's lips thinned. "Walk with me."

They did as he instructed and walked a couple blocks before Pierce turned into a coffee shop.

"So what is it you want with me?" Pierce asked them.

"Why did you stop going to the deli?" Landon asked.

"Isn't that obvious? I think you're poking your nose into things at MPC, and I want no part of it. Nothing you can do will bring Ellie back, and I think you're cooking up conspiracy theories to help your cause—whatever that may be."

Landon stifled a sigh. Pierce had taken a decided turn against him. "Do you know anything about the drug Acreda?"

Pierce's face paled. "I'm not the lead on that project."

"Do you know anything about possible side effects from taking Acreda that the tests would have shown?"

Pierce shook his head. "No, I don't. I haven't heard anything about that."

"Okay. Did someone at MPC start asking you about this case?" Landon asked.

"No, but we did have a meeting."

Cooper took a step forward. "What kind of meeting?"

"I shouldn't even be talking to you two. I could get fired for this."

"No one has to know," Landon said. "Let's grab you a cup of coffee and a doughnut, and you can tell us what happened."

Pierce reluctantly accepted the offer and took a seat at one of the tables in the back while Landon grabbed the food and drink.

He wanted to play this carefully, because Pierce was in a very awkward position. But the fact that he hadn't told them to pound sand gave him a boost of confidence.

A couple minutes later, the three men were seated at the table, and Pierce had the floor.

"Once again, I shouldn't even be talking to you guys," Pierce said.

"But you are, and we greatly appreciate that," Landon said. "This is my colleague Cooper. Like I told you before, I'm investigating what happened to Ellie."

Pierce nodded. "And like I told you before, I don't know anything about what happened to that poor woman."

"But you do know something. What kind of meeting did you have?"

Pierce took a bite of his glazed doughnut before responding. "My group had a meeting with the head of corporate security—a guy named Bradley Cummings."

"What happened?"

"He wanted to make sure we were all aware of the Celix lawsuit, and he gave us specific instructions not to talk to anyone outside of MPC about the lawsuit—no matter who it is. And that if anyone contacts us about the suit, we're supposed to let Bradley and his team know immediately."

"Don't you find that a bit suspicious?" Cooper asked.

"We're always told that if the media contacts us, we have a strict no-comment policy, but this felt like something else. Which makes me even more hesitant to talk to you guys, because I can't help but feel like this is all intertwined, given that Ellie worked on Celix and you're supposedly investigating Ellie's death."

Landon exchanged a glance with Cooper. "Pierce, doesn't it strike you as odd that the head of security of the company would gather the scientists to have a meeting like that? Have you ever had a meeting with him before?"

Pierce looked away. "Nothing like that, no, but I still don't see what you guys want from me. I really don't know anything about Ellie's murder."

"But you might know something else that will help us," Cooper said.

"You're asking me to put a lot on the line. It was clear from that meeting that we could get fired for talking to people. Our employment contracts are so restrictive that it's possible it would hold up too. Then what would I do? I understand that you fellows have a job to do, but so do I." He stood up. "So I'm going to have to ask you to please leave me alone. Please leave me be."

Pierce grabbed his coffee and walked out, leaving Landon and Cooper sitting there.

Cooper rested his elbows on the table. "At least we got one major piece of intel from this meeting. The head of corporate security is worried about something."

"Which means that Pierce and the other scientists have information that could harm the case. The only issue is figuring out what that is and how to get to it."

"Couldn't Kate call Pierce as a witness?" Cooper asked.

"I'll ask her about that. I'm not sure what the protocol is."

"Speaking of Kate, everything has been super quiet with

her. Maybe MPC was just blowing smoke to test the waters," Cooper said.

"Maybe, but I'm not willing to take that chance. And the thing is that, according to Kate, the case is really about to heat up. We need to be even more on guard than normal, because she said feathers are about to get ruffled."

"Over what?"

"She believes Ethan isn't turning over all the relevant documents and that he's stonewalling her. I think she's going to file something with the judge to argue that the documents have to be turned over."

"We'll be ready no matter what happens."

"Do you think we let go of Pierce or keep pushing?" Landon asked.

"Push, of course. We push until we can't push anymore."

"Agreed." They weren't in a position to just let things go right now.

"I notice you still haven't said more than a single sentence to Noah."

Landon lifted his hands in a helpless gesture. "It's not me, Coop, it's him. Clearly, he still hates me, so I don't want to make the situation any more awkward than it needs to be."

"The two of you should talk. It's been long enough for tempers to have cooled."

Landon highly doubted that. "I don't think Noah is going to move past this one."

"That's where I think you're wrong. Noah believes in forgiveness, but you need to put yourself out there. It's not his responsibility to come to you—just the opposite."

"I hear you, buddy. But easier said than done."

"Just try. I promise he'll meet you halfway."

Landon wasn't so sure.

## THIRTEEN

W hat's this court hearing you're talking about?" Royce
asked loudly.

Ethan was glad this was a phone conference and he
wasn't face-to-face with Royce. He wasn't really in the mood
to coddle his client.

"The other side has filed a motion to compel. Kate's arguing that we're not producing all the documents responsive to
her requests."

"Of course we're not. Those requests were outrageous. You
said so yourself. Won't a judge just toss this out? But what if
he doesn't? What can the judge do to us?"

Ethan let Royce get the questions out of his system before
speaking. "There's absolutely no cause for alarm here. She'll
get her shot, and I'll get mine. I can't imagine a world in which
the judge would agree with her requests, and they have zero
evidence to demonstrate that we're withholding evidence."

"You and I have already had a discussion about this, so I
assume there's no need for us to rehash that same ground."

Yes, Ethan remembered it quite well. Royce had specifically
told him that he wanted Ethan to blur the lines. "We're on the
same page. There's no reason for you to be worried. I'll let

you know if there comes a point in time when we should be concerned—this is not that time."

"Okay. Also, just to keep you in the loop, I had my security chief brief some key employees about the case and remind them that they're not supposed to speak with anyone about what they do at MPC."

That got Ethan's attention. "Did you have cause for concern?"

"A man in my position is always concerned and a bit paranoid. This case is high profile and in the news. I just want to make sure all my employees are buttoned down. The last thing we need is someone out there blabbing because they want their five minutes of fame."

Was that really what Royce was worried about, or was there something more? Ethan wasn't stupid. He knew Royce had secrets and he was only getting a partial version of the truth. And while he was used to that with most of his clients, he still didn't have to like it. "Royce, remember too, that I'm the company's advocate. I'm also the first and biggest line of defense. So don't feel like you have to rely solely on MPC resources and staff. I can do a lot of things beyond just speaking in the courtroom."

"I know, and I appreciate that. It's just that this case has me more wound up than normal."

Ethan had no trouble believing that. "And remember, if you include me more on these things, we can argue that these activities are protected by attorney-client privilege. For instance, that meeting your security chief had won't be covered, but it could've been protected if I had been there."

"You have a good point, Ethan. I'll do a better job looping you in on the MPC side of things."

"Thanks. And I'll let you know the outcome of the hearing."

"Shouldn't I attend?"

"No way. This is not a CEO-level hearing. That would only give the other side's argument more credence if you show up. I can handle it."

"Call me right when it's over."

"Of course."

"And as always, don't screw this up."

The dial tone let him know how serious Royce was.

Kate walked into the courtroom Wednesday to argue the motion to compel in front of Judge Freeman and face off against Ethan. Landon was there to provide protection, although she'd told him that she would be completely fine at the courthouse. He'd insisted and said he also wanted to see the oral argument.

Oddly, that made her nervous. He hadn't seen her in action in the courtroom yet, and what if he wasn't impressed with her lawyering skills? Her nerves were already amplified, because just this morning at the office she hadn't been able to find her prep binder. It had everything she needed, including her argument outline, key bullet points, and exhibits. Everything.

She knew she had left it on her desk last night, but it had disappeared. This was beginning to be a pattern, and she couldn't help feeling that someone was trying to sabotage her. But who? Thankfully, she still had copies of most of the key pieces she'd need for the hearing, but in a much less organized fashion. She wasn't the type of lawyer who liked to wing it, but today she'd have to do just that.

She smiled when she saw Mia walking toward her. Having a friendly face around was a boost. "I didn't realize you were going to come today."

"I just settled a case and had a little time on my hands."

Kate laughed. "Discovery motions aren't exactly thrilling to watch."

"When it's two good friends and law school classmates squaring off, and both their careers are implicated, I think it could get very interesting."

"No pressure or anything, Mia."

Mia gave her arm a squeeze. "You wouldn't have been tapped for lead counsel if you couldn't handle it."

And she'd told herself that a million times, but she still struggled with her confidence level even if she made everyone think she didn't break a sweat. So many people were depending on her.

Mia looked over her shoulder at Landon, who was standing near the entrance to the courtroom. "Wait a minute. Is that hunk your private investigator?"

"Yeah. How did you know?"

"He has military written all over him, and more important, he can't seem to keep his big brown eyes off you."

"I already told you that it isn't like that at all. We're friendly and working together, but that's it."

"Go ahead and tell yourself that." Mia leaned in closer. "But I don't want to ruffle your feathers anymore, so I'll let you get ready."

Kate settled in at the counsel's table and arranged her documents. Now wasn't the time to worry about Mia's perception of her relationship with Landon, or the fact that Mia thought Landon was a hunk—which he was.

Ethan hadn't come over to say hello, and that was for the best. Better to keep this as cool between them as possible. Their meeting had left a bad taste in her mouth, because as much as she loved being a lawyer, the interpersonal conflict was still tough for her.

And on top of everything else, she had to give her argument with her materials a cobbled-together mess. But she didn't really have a choice.

"All rise," the bailiff said.

And it was game time.

Judge Freeman took his seat and made eye contact with her and then Ethan. "Ms. Sullivan, Mr. Black, I have read your competing motions, and I'm ready to hear your arguments. Ms. Sullivan, since this is your motion, the floor is yours."

"Thank you, Your Honor. I've laid out two principal points in the motion and supporting brief. First, MPC has failed to produce any documents responsive to a number of our document requests." She looked down at her notes to make sure she got the numbers right. "Specifically, for requests ten, fourteen, thirty, and thirty-six, there hasn't been a single document produced to answer those requests. Second, MPC is engaging in tactics to produce thousands upon thousands of pages of completely irrelevant material as a means to try to sandbag us. I would argue that is borderline sanctionable."

"Let me stop you right there," Judge Freeman said.

The judge could interrupt the arguments at any time and ask questions, so Kate wasn't surprised by this.

"Is it your position, Ms. Sullivan, that MPC is willfully withholding responsive documents?"

"Yes. I will let Mr. Black speak for himself, but I believe he contends that MPC shouldn't have to produce documents in response to those specific requests. I don't think that argument holds water."

Ethan stood up. "Your Honor, maybe we should just hash this out right now."

"Why not?" Judge Freeman said. "What's your response as to why those four requests are out of bounds?"

"This case isn't about any other drug, it's only about one single drug, and that is Celix. The plaintiffs only pled allegations about Celix in their complaint, and there isn't a single allegation about any other MPC drug. I'd argue that's a strong

151

bright line for us to follow to keep an already huge document case more manageable."

"Just because the complaint doesn't specifically call out another drug by name, doesn't mean it's off limits," she said. "The federal rules of civil procedure are very broad, as everyone in the courtroom knows. We have a right to those documents."

"I've yet to hear a reason why, though, Ms. Sullivan. Why do you need documents about other drugs? I tend to agree with Mr. Black that you're being a bit overbroad here."

She couldn't exactly say, because she wasn't even sure what the documents would show. "Having visibility into comparable drugs is important. The type of testing done with other drugs before they hit the market does have an impact here—especially if MPC used a different type of testing process for other drugs than what was used for Celix. That kind of information is completely fair game, in my opinion."

"Way too overbroad, Your Honor," Ethan said.

Now on to her backup plan. "Plaintiffs would be willing to limit the other drugs to a small list of those whose development timing and lead scientists overlapped Celix. That way there is a clear limit on the number, and plaintiffs still get access to arguably extremely relevant information."

Judge Freeman raised an eyebrow. "Do you have such a list prepared?"

"I do, Your Honor. May I approach the bench?"

"You may."

She walked up and handed the list to the judge and then provided a second copy to Ethan, whose face was bright red.

"What is your response, Mr. Black?"

"Your Honor, I'd need some time to review this list."

Judge Freeman looked down at the page and then back up. "Mr. Black, there are only four drugs on this list."

"Yes, I can see that, but I'm not up to speed on every product that MPC manufactures. I have no idea whether any of these are relevant to Celix and the plaintiffs' claims."

"Very well. You have until five o'clock tomorrow to file any objections to this list of drugs, and Ms. Sullivan, you have until noon on Friday to respond. Then I'll make my ruling on those contested requests. Now, as far as MPC producing nonresponsive documents, Ms. Sullivan, do you want to elaborate further than what was in your brief?"

"Only to say that since the brief was filed, the situation has only worsened. According to my review team, we have a responsive rate of only about fifteen to twenty percent right now. I'd contend that's entirely inappropriate, and what's more, that MPC is intentionally trying to bury us in irrelevant documents."

"Mr. Black?" the judge asked.

"That is a completely unfounded assertion, Your Honor. Plaintiffs only have themselves to blame. They're the ones who came up with these overly broad and extensive document requests. When you request that much information, you're going to get just that—a lot of information. Just because Ms. Sullivan isn't finding what she wants to see in the documents, doesn't mean that MPC is doing anything wrong here. Just the opposite, in fact."

"That's not accurate, Your Honor. You can't look at that relevancy rate and make a good-faith argument."

"But that's what your reviewers think is relevant, Kate," Ethan said.

He'd slipped and called her by her first name, causing the judge to grin.

"Mr. Black, I would caution you to have another chat with your team to communicate the importance of abiding by the document requests and to operate in good faith in their review. I'm denying the motion in part as it pertains to the second point on relevancy, but this is a warning. If it continues, I'll want to get deeper in the weeds and look at further examples that I'm sure Ms. Sullivan will provide. I'll rule on the first issue after the two of you have submitted the required responses."

"Thank you, Your Honor," she and Ethan said in unison.

The judge left the courtroom, and she began to pack up her stuff. She was one step closer to victory, though, and that was important.

She looked up to see Ethan walking over to her.

"What's your angle here, Kate? Why blindside me with that list of drugs?"

"You're the one who said asking for information on all other MPC drugs was too broad. I just took that into consideration and provided a reasonable alternative."

"What do any of the drugs on that list have to do with you trying to prove your case about Celix?"

"Without the information, how can I know for sure? I think there is value in knowing how those drugs were treated versus Celix."

"It sounds like a complete fishing expedition to me."

She didn't want to admit that, but she also didn't want him to think she had something specific in mind. "Ethan, is there any point in us arguing about this?"

"I'm just trying to understand where you're coming from, because you're usually a straight shooter. Which makes me think something is going on in that head of yours, and I want to know what it is."

"You don't have the right to access my internal thoughts about strategy on the case. Remember, we're on opposing sides here, Ethan."

He ran a hand through his hair. "How could I forget?"

Once again, she wanted to be his friend, but the situation was just so awkward. "Anything else we need to talk about?"

He shook his head. "No. I'll have my objections to that list in by the deadline, and I guess we'll go from there."

He walked away, and immediately Mia popped up beside her.

"Good job. You had that fallback position ready the entire time. That was a nice move."

"Thanks. That's why you have to do so much preparation for these things." Thankfully, she'd had another copy of the drug list, even though her binder had been taken.

Landon approached the two of them, and Mia homed in on him and stretched out her hand.

"This is one of my best friends, Mia Shaw," Kate said. "She's also an attorney."

"Nice to meet you, Mia." He smiled.

And Mia smiled even wider. "I hear that you're helping Kate on this case as an investigator." Kate hadn't filled in her friends on what had happened to her, so Mia only knew about the public aspects of the case.

Fortunately, Landon was impeccably discreet. He nodded. "Yes, it's a big one, so we have a lot of things to run down."

"Well, I should get back to the office. Again, great job, Kate. I think the short drug list is a winning strategy." Mia turned to Landon. "And very nice to meet you. Hope to see you again soon." She walked away, leaving them alone.

"Your friend's right. Your arguments were solid," Landon said. "It was nice to see you in your element."

"Thanks. Hopefully, the judge will see it our way."

"Nice strategic move to get the information we need on Acreda," he said softly.

"Yeah, that was my best way to try to get at it."

"Well, I was impressed."

"Thanks. But it will all be for nothing if we can't get to those documents. So I'm not celebrating just yet."

# FOURTEEN

than arrived at the MPC building and waited in the lobby for an escort up to Royce's office.

Given the time constraints on filing his objections to the drug list, he thought it best to meet with Royce right after the hearing was over. He didn't have enough background on the other drugs to know what objections he should even be making. It also bothered him that Kate had one-upped him. She had played out the entire scenario and was ready with that list. He hated being caught off guard like that. It wouldn't happen again.

And now he had to spin this latest development to Royce while at the same time getting the factual information he needed. He'd only spoken to Royce for a minute on the phone, wanting to save the details for the in-person meeting.

A tall, beautiful blond woman walked out of the elevator and straight toward him. "Mr. Black?" She flashed a perfectly white smile.

"Yes."

"I'm Penny, Mr. Hamilton's executive assistant. I'll take you up to see him."

"Thank you." He couldn't help but think how stereotypical

it was that the CEO of a major company had an assistant who looked like a supermodel.

Penny escorted him up to Royce's CEO suite, which was nothing less than impressive. Penny had her own large oak desk in the reception area leading to multiple other offices, including Royce's private one, which was where he was taken.

He was greeted by Royce and Matt Canton. "Good to see you again."

"Likewise," Matt said.

"I'd also like you to meet my chief security officer, Bradley Cummings," Royce said.

Bradley towered over Ethan and gave him a very strong handshake. Ethan wouldn't want to get on Bradley's bad side. He looked like he could break someone in half with his bare hands.

Royce shut his office door. "So tell me what happened in the hearing about the documents."

He wondered why Royce had brought his security chief in for this discussion, but he figured Royce had his reasons. And since Bradley was an MPC employee, the attorney-client privilege would be kept intact.

"The biggest takeaway from the hearing is why I wanted to meet with you." He opened his briefcase, pulled out some copies of the list, and handed them to Royce and Matt. "In response to our argument that the other side shouldn't be able to request information about all other MPC products, their lawyer came prepared with this short list of drugs. She wants documents related to these drugs, and I have until five o'clock tomorrow to file our objections to this list."

Royce frowned and passed his copy over to Bradley, who scowled as his eyes skimmed down the page.

"And you say that your friend Kate came up with this list?" Bradley asked suspiciously.

"Kate is my friend, but right now she's my adversary. I need your help to figure out why she would be fishing around for these drugs, because I don't know anything about these products. If there's some skeleton in the closet or something else I need to know, now would be the time to tell me. Not on the eve of the trial."

"Royce," Matt said, "I think we should have a talk with Ethan. Bradley, please give us a minute, will you?"

Bradley nodded and walked out of the room.

Ethan looked at Royce and then Matt. His stomach clenched as he prepared himself for bad news.

"Ethan, we appreciate all you've done for us," Royce said.

*Uh-oh.* He wasn't about to get fired. He had to stop this. "You should know how hard I'm working on this case. It's my absolute top priority. My entire life right now."

Royce cleared his throat. "We don't want this other lawyer snooping around into all of our drugs. That goes way beyond the scope of this case, and it puts our company at additional risk we didn't sign up for when we decided to fight this thing in court."

Ethan saw an opening and took it. "Why in the world wouldn't you settle then? Take away that risk."

"Because that also sets a precedent the company can't afford," Royce responded. "We have to be strong and fight these things, or the lawsuit floodgates will be opened a mile wide, and that could have huge financial implications. We can't have every plaintiff's lawyer in the country on the hunt for a handout from MPC."

"Royce, of course you're right, but that was our analysis before this turn of events," Matt said. "If that lawyer is intent on digging into all these other drugs and using this litigation as a means to get to information they could use in future lawsuits, then we do need to consider our settlement options. Get this

159

case out of the way and move forward with our business and building our empire."

Finally, maybe they would listen to Ethan on this. "If we're going to make a settlement offer, we need to do it now. As in right now. We lose leverage if we wait until the judge rules against us on these documents."

Royce stood up. "I hadn't planned for this, so I realize I may have to adjust my expectations here. But I do have one hundred million in settlement authority from the board."

"You didn't tell me that," Matt said, his eyes wide. He seemed a little miffed.

"I didn't think it was going to come to this," Royce said. "But that is the max the board is willing to sacrifice to make the entire set of cases go away. Start your negotiations with that in mind, Ethan."

"I'll give Kate a call as soon as I leave here. But we need to think about contingencies. I'm going to fight as hard as I can to get this list of other drugs excluded, but we need a backup plan. Which drug on the list worries you the most?"

"We don't want her to have information on any of them," Royce said, "but Acreda is at a critical juncture right now. We're clearing the final regulatory hurdles, so that one matters the most to us financially at the moment. The other three drugs have already been approved."

"I agree with Royce," Matt said. "This would be awful timing to have to produce documents about Acreda when we're this close to taking it to market."

"Tell me more about Acreda." Ethan was learning that the only way to get information out of these guys was to keep pushing them.

"Acreda is one of the most promising drugs that we have," Matt responded. "If all goes as planned, it should be on the market by early next year. It was initially developed about the same time as Celix. That might be why it's on the list. We've had some additional regulatory obstacles to overcome, but we're almost in the clear."

"What does Acreda treat?"

"All types of tumors and other kinds of growths—both malignant and benign. It's a groundbreaking drug, given its wide-spectrum application," Royce said. "Which is another reason we don't want any more delays. We stand to a make a very large profit on Acreda—even more than Celix. And we have Matt to thank for that, because he's been pushing Acreda since day one."

"It's a vital drug for the company," Matt added. "It's been one of my top priorities, tasked to me by the board."

Ethan started thinking about damage control. "If we lose this fight, which is possible, we'll do a specific document search for Acreda so that anything that mentions the drug will be pulled in. Then we'll have a team review those separately to see what we have."

Royce's eyes locked in on his. "I don't want you turning over anything that could be damaging to drugs that don't even apply to this lawsuit. Do you hear me?"

Royce was asking him to do something potentially illegal. He hesitated for a moment. "I hear you. I need some time to digest all of this, and I have to get to work on these objections."

"Call me or Matt if you need anything, no matter the hour. We've gotten this far, and we can't buckle under the pressure."

Ethan nodded and stood, ready to exit the office.

Royce came around the desk and clamped his hand down hard on Ethan's shoulder. "Let me know what they say to our offer, and keep us in the loop on negotiations."

"I will." Ethan walked out and wondered how he was going to navigate these waters.

"So what's this about settlement?" Landon asked. He sat beside Kate on the large couch in her living room after driving her home from work.

"Ethan called me and put an eighty million dollar settlement offer on the table with a short fuse. That's to settle the whole class of cases in the MDL. The offer expires at midnight."

He whistled. "Eighty million? What do you do now?"

"I took it to the other members of the PSC, and everyone agreed that it's way too low. We have the power right now. This shows they're nervous about the direction the case is heading. I countered with five hundred million, knowing it would be a nonstarter, but other PSC members thought we should send them a signal that they're locked in this thing unless they bring a substantially different offer."

"That's a lot of money, though." He was surprised Kate didn't seem fazed by the offer.

"There are thousands of plaintiffs. Eighty million only goes so far."

"When is the judge going to make a decision about the documents?"

"The judge understands that we're on a very tight schedule. I don't think it's going to take long. Probably a couple days, if not sooner. He might review everything this weekend and make a ruling on Monday. The matter really isn't that complex once you boil it down. He's either going to tell them to produce the documents related to the smaller list of drugs or not."

"From a layman's perspective, your request for the other drugs that Ellie worked on seems reasonable, but I know the backstory—the judge doesn't."

"We'll see." She leaned her head back against the sofa.

"Are you sleeping enough?" She was usually full of energy, but right now she seemed exhausted. He couldn't blame her, though. It had been a crazy week.

162

She lifted her head and turned to him. "Probably not enough. I'm having a hard time shutting off my brain. And on top of everything else, I seriously think someone is trying to mess with me at work."

"Why do you say that?"

"Strange things have been happening in the office. My brief got deleted from the system, and files have gone missing. Then, before the hearing, my prep binder disappeared from my desk."

"Seriously?" He went into high-alert mode.

"Unfortunately, yes. I think it has to be someone in the firm, given all of our security measures in the building. I'd hate to think it could be Bonnie, but there's also a junior associate who got kicked off the team. Maybe he's trying to get payback."

"Sounds like the junior associate might have some motive. But Bonnie's a partner. Why would she do that to you?"

"She's disliked me from day one and still blames me for something that happened right after I started working at the firm. But I don't know what she hopes to accomplish, unless it's just to embarrass me. To show that she's still top dog. But if she was so upset, she could've said she didn't have time when I asked her to join the team. So I'm not sure how to handle the situation."

He didn't like the sound of any of this. "Maybe Bonnie's just jealous. You're doing so well, and she's not used to having the competition. But that doesn't mean she'd try to hurt a case led by one of her fellow partners. That hurts the firm too."

"You might be underestimating her ability to hold a grudge. But I can't let that issue consume me, because I have bigger problems. When I get in bed, my mind wanders back to the case and everything I'm working on and all the next steps. And then I can't sleep." She flopped back against the couch with a frustrated sigh.

"I know what you mean." He could relate to his mind wandering off at night, and it definitely wasn't to a good place. It was to a very dark desert, where his life was forever changed. He didn't have any techniques or advice for her on how to turn off those thoughts.

Her hazel eyes questioned him. "I hope you aren't losing sleep over this case too?"

"I tend to overthink all of my work." That much was true, but his sleepless nights went much deeper than that. And even though this litigation concerned him a lot, his fears were much larger.

"So this case isn't any different?" she asked.

"A bit more stressful because of the threats you're facing. Most of my cases are a lot of work but haven't had specific dangers."

"I'm sorry. The last thing I want to do is cause strain and stress in your life."

He couldn't let her believe she was the cause of all of his problems. The pain in her eyes pulled the words out of his mouth. "My sleepless nights started long before meeting you and working on this case."

"Ah." Recognition flickered in her eyes.

They'd talked about his time in the military before and the battles he faced, but she didn't know the extent of what he'd endured.

"Maybe it would help if you talked to someone about what's causing you those sleepless nights. I'm here if you want to talk, but if that someone isn't me, then that's all right. Keeping everything bottled inside isn't good for you on any level, though."

He gathered his thoughts, wondering how he could convey what was in his heart and mind. "Iraq was a very difficult place during all my tours, but my last one was the roughest." He closed his eyes. Was he really going to tell her about this? What kind of man would she think he was? Some kind of monster?

She reached out and held his hand. "You can talk to me,

Landon. I'm not here to judge or act like I can know what you went through. I'm just here as a friend who wants to listen to your story. You're helping me, so let me try to help you."

This woman was stripping him of all his defenses just with the soft tone of her words and the caring touch of her hand. "It was war, there was no doubt about that. But then it became so much more. My first tours were more about regime change. Those were tough, but my last tours we were battling against terrorism, and that was a whole different ball game. Their complete lack of respect for human life boggles the mind."

She squeezed his hand, signaling for him to continue.

"One night we were on a special mission. I can't reveal all the details, but it was high stakes. We were hunting a high-value target on the top of our list of bad guys. The order was given to move into a small house outside the city. We had solid intel that the tango we were looking for was inside that house. We were also prepared for the fact that he'd be surrounded by plenty of other terrorists, but also innocents. Women and children he would try to use as human shields."

As he spoke, the dark, awful memories of that operation came flooding back to him. A knot formed in the pit of his stomach, and his hand became clammy against her touch. "I prayed before we went in. I asked God to protect my team and me. That He would give us all wisdom and guidance in those dark places."

"And you feel betrayed by Him?"

"Yes," he said, as his voice cracked. "I was so amped up and focused on taking out the target that I reacted too quickly without taking into account all the circumstances—including the fact that there was a girl right there. I took the shot to take him out, but he used his teenage daughter as a shield, pulling her directly in front of him. I'd already pulled the trigger, and it was too late." He paused, trying to find the courage to tell her the truth of the horror that night. "I killed that girl, and to make matters worse, I was in such shock that I put my other Rangers at risk because I froze. The terrorist started shooting and seriously injured one of us before another Ranger could take him out. It was undoubtedly the worst night of my life."

"I know you've been told this before, but the terrorist is the one who put his daughter in harm's way. Her death is on him, not you."

He looked away from her. "But I should've read the situation better. I should've known he'd use that strategy, because we were specifically briefed about it. If I had waited one millisecond, instead of being overeager to take the shot, it would've been a different story. So, yes, I do feel like God turned His back on me that night."

Kate put her arms around his neck and held him tightly. Her skin was cool against his. He hadn't expected that show of affection from her, and he wasn't sure if he should respond or not. He slowly lifted his arms and returned the hug.

After a minute, she pushed back, putting a little distance between them on the couch. "Landon, this life is hard, and you were in the middle of a war, fighting terrorists who want to kill innocent people. That man purposely sacrificed his daughter in a cowardly way."

"You're right, but I wasn't at the top of my game." He took another breath. "I was off. I can't explain why, but I just was. I should've been better, done better, than that."

"Tell me something, then. How did your fellow Rangers react?"

"They knew it hit me hard. They said the same things you're saying. I just think my desire to take the shot and kill that guy was so strong that I took an unnecessary risk and got an innocent girl killed. And I have to live with that every day for the rest of my life." He closed his eyes for a second before continuing.

"So that, Kate, is why I don't sleep. It's not because of you. If anything, since I've met you, I've felt more at peace than I have since that night in Iraq."

She gave him a weak smile. "I told you that I've been praying."

Were her prayers having an impact? "If anyone's prayers would make a difference, Kate, it would be yours. You actually live out your faith. I've seen it since the moment we met."

She shook her head and looked down at her lap. "I'm far from perfect, Landon. I just do the best I can. Since I went through some times in my life in which I'm not proud of what I did and how I acted, I strive every day not to be that woman ever again. But don't make me out to be something I'm not. I have plenty of daily struggles."

"Like what?" he couldn't help but ask.

"Believe it or not, I struggle with confidence." She tucked her hair behind her ear. "Wondering if I'll ever be good enough to do what I want to do. On the flip side, though, I struggle with a strong sense of ambition and pride. There's a fine line between being proud of your accomplishments and having a big ego, and that's only fueled by the type of profession I'm in."

"I think you strike a good balance. Even if you have to work at it, it doesn't show."

"Thanks, but it's something I have to constantly monitor myself on. And I'm a very independent person, so there's no one to either check my pride or give me a boost when I need it. I don't have my parents or any extended family that I am in contact with. I've devoted my time to my career, and I've done that by choice." She paused. "But there's no one special I've ever wanted to spend time with."

"I understand that. After the debacle with Noah's girlfriend, I decided I needed to focus on getting better emotionally and dealing with my issues."

"I haven't heard you say anything about your family."

"I never knew my dad. He wasn't in the picture. My mom raised me and did her best. She passed away about five years ago."

"I'm so sorry to hear that."

Another area of common ground for the two of them. He sensed that he was just beginning to understand how many levels they could connect on. "So like you, I don't have family around. My friends and my military brothers are my family, but I've not done a good job of treating them that way."

"Your real friends will understand and accept that you've been battling some issues."

"I'm finally at the point where I can at least think about moving on. The fact that I was able to share with you what happened is a huge step for me."

She smiled. "I'm so glad I was here to listen."

There was more he wanted to say. So much more. But there was something else he had to ask first. Something that had been nagging at him. "I want to ask you a question, but I don't want you to jump to any conclusions."

"All right. I'll do my best."

"What if I wanted to explore my faith again and try to re-connect with God? What would that look like? And before you answer, this is purely hypothetical at this point."

"Have an open heart and mind. He is right there waiting, Landon. He can break the chains that you feel trapped by. Whenever you're ready, He's ready."

"What if I don't know if I'll ever be ready again?" Those words made him feel completely exposed.

"Why don't you go to church with me this weekend?"

"I don't know. I'm not sure if I can handle that."

"The fact that we're having this conversation means you're ready to explore this. If you want to connect with Him again, that's the best place to start. He knows your pain and struggles, Landon. They aren't any surprise to Him."

"I guess you're right." He looked directly in her eyes. "Thanks for listening to me and trying to understand my feelings and accept them for what they are."

"When it comes to you, Landon, I'm just speaking from the heart."

His stomach clenched. No matter what he had told himself before, he was falling hard for Kate Sullivan.

# CHAPTER
# FIFTEEN

On Monday morning, Kate heard her email ping and saw the message was from the Northern District of Georgia. Her heartbeat sped up as she clicked to open it.

Her eyes skimmed the email, and immediately she opened the PDF attachment that held the actual judge's order.

Motion to Compel . . . granted. She let out a little squeal of happiness.

She picked up her phone and dialed Landon, who answered on the second ring.

"We won!" she said, trying to not scream the news with excitement.

"That's great news."

"It is, but we can't be unrealistic about this." She had to calm down and do a sanity check about how this would all happen. "Just because Judge Freeman is ordering MPC to produce those documents doesn't mean they will—especially the ones that could hurt their case. But this gives us a legal basis for getting the information. So as an important first step, I'll definitely take it."

"How confident are you in the lawyers combing through all these documents?"

That was a good question. "In a batch of young attorneys, there are always some bad apples who don't take the job seriously. But it's impossible for me to physically look at and read thousands of pages myself. I have to rely on them, and the good thing is that now I can call special attention to this list of drugs. We'll run a special filter that will pull in all the documents that have the word *Acreda* in them. I'm not holding my breath that we'll find any smoking guns, but that won't stop me from trying."

"Keep pushing. At some point, they'll slip up. They always do. There's too much at play here to keep everything under wraps."

She hummed in agreement, then took a chance and said, "You weren't very chatty after church yesterday." She'd just been happy he'd decided to come, so she hadn't talked about the service with him afterward. It was important that she let him go at his own speed.

"Yeah, sorry about that. I needed some time to process."

"You can take all the time you need."

"It's been a couple years since I went to church. I wasn't sure what to expect. I almost bailed on you, but it was much harder getting there than it was once I got inside the building."

She was so thankful he'd been able to take such a big step. "I know it was tough for you, and I'm so glad that you did it."

"For the first time in years, I felt like maybe I could try to have a real conversation with God again. I'm not saying that everything is the way it used to be, though."

"Landon, has it occurred to you that it may never be the way it used to be? But it could be different and better. You've been through so much that has shaped you as a person and impacted your faith. If you open your heart, you might be surprised where the Lord will take you."

"I never thought any of this would be a possibility until I met you, Kate. I'd completely given up hope."

"I don't know what to say." Her heart warmed at his words.

To think that she could have any sort of impact on him, given all he had been through, told her this was much bigger than her. God was working through all of this—even using the crazy circumstances of this litigation.

"You don't have to say anything. Just know that you've made a difference." He paused. "But I don't want to distract you from getting all your work done. Good job again on the motion. Maybe we'll catch a break."

"Thanks. I'll keep you updated."

"Sounds good."

After he hung up, she sat for a moment, trying to gather her thoughts. Her feelings for Landon were growing beyond friendship, but she didn't know whether she should fight what was happening or embrace it.

Instead, she did what she always did, and went back to work. It wasn't long before she was interrupted by a knock on her office door. She looked up and saw Adam standing there, smiling.

"I got the court's notification," he said. "Congratulations. This is a big win for us."

"Come in and tell me how things are going on your end with the medical experts."

He took a seat across from her. "Really well. We have two experts to counter the argument that the tumor was related to the father's cancer. I don't think any jury will buy that argument, but I don't like the optics of it. I want to make sure our doctors are ready for that."

"I agree with you."

He grinned. "How is everything else going? What do you think of the role of lead counsel?"

"It's a lot of work, but I knew it would be. I like being able to make the strategic decisions that shape the whole litigation instead of just taking direction from someone else. I also can't thank you and Bonnie enough for stepping up to the plate."

"Of course. I'm glad I can be part of the team. I know you and Bonnie aren't close."

She couldn't help but laugh. "I guess that's blatantly obvious."

He laughed with her. "Don't take it personally, Kate. That's just how Bonnie is. She isn't close to anyone. I've known her for a long time, and she's always been that way."

"Thanks. Sometimes it's just difficult because I've wanted us to click so badly for years." She considered confiding in Adam about her suspicions of sabotage, but without any hard evidence, she didn't want to start the rumor mill.

"For what it's worth, I know you have a great relationship with William, and he's the best there is at this type of work. But if there's anything you ever need, I want you to know you can come to me. Including just blowing off steam about this case or bouncing ideas off me. You don't have to go it alone. I know I'm tasked with the experts, but I'm always happy to help on the discovery motions too."

"You've gone above and beyond, Adam, and I'll definitely take you up on that offer."

"Good. Now, I guess we both have to get back to it." He gave her another smile as he left her office.

After all her concerns about Bonnie, it felt good to know he was on her side.

---

"Nicole, we need to talk." Ethan walked into her office and quickly shut the door. He assumed she'd seen the email notification about the motion to compel, so she wouldn't be surprised to see him.

She looked up directly into his eyes. "Is this about the motion?"

"Yes." Ethan paced back and forth. "We need to filter all of our documents for those drugs listed in the motion, but I want you to pick a couple of your best people to review a subset related to the drug Acreda."

She raised an eyebrow. "Is there something I need to know here?"

He took a seat and looked at her closely. Nicole was about thirty years old, having spent five years at the firm. She was at the top of her associate class and a rule follower. She might not be able to deal with a situation that called for a blurring of the lines. "It's a complicated situation, Nicole, and I need to make sure we're completely buttoned up."

"Of course. Whatever you need. But if there is something going on, I might be of more help if I actually knew everything you know. I think there's more to the story." She leaned forward in her chair, her dark eyes concerned.

"I wouldn't come to you with this if I didn't think you were up for the job. All I can tell you right now is that I'm sure the plaintiffs have some reason to push this. I talked with the client and narrowed down the list of priorities, and we decided Acreda is the drug we need to focus on."

"And why is that?"

"It's the most high profile and at-risk drug on the list. There's a lot of money on the line here."

"What about the documents I brought to you last month about the side effects? I saw in the system that we still hadn't produced them."

"I'm holding off for strategic reasons." Under her questioning, he could feel his palms start to sweat.

Her eyes narrowed. "But we are going to produce them, right?"

"I'll make all those decisions when the time comes."

"Ethan, I know I'm just a midlevel associate and you're a partner, but I'm knee-deep in this case, and I'm the most senior person managing the document review. I'd like to think that you could level with me."

He admired her tenacity, but he couldn't go all in with her just yet. "There's a lot going on behind the scenes that I'm still working on. As soon as I can fill you in, I will."

"What about the other team members? Miles, for instance?"

"You know more than anyone else." Which was true, and he hoped that would pacify her. There was no way he would tell Miles, because Miles couldn't keep his mouth shut.

"Thanks for trusting me." She reached across the desk and placed her hand on his forearm. "I know you're the partner here, but I'm worried about you."

It bothered him that his stress was so obvious to Nicole. He needed to do a better job of keeping it in check, or at least not apparent to all who were watching—especially the client. "I'm not going to lie. This is a stressful case, and there's a lot on the line, but it's all part of the job. I just need to force myself to get some rest."

She released her grip on his arm and leaned back in her seat. "Well, my door is open if you want to talk about the case or anything."

How ironic that she was now playing the mentoring role instead of the mentee. She could have a bright future in the firm, but would she be willing to get her hands dirty?

Kate had accepted Sophie and Mia's invitation for lunch and was actually excited about getting out of the office. Given that there hadn't been other threats, last week she'd negotiated with Landon that she only needed a security escort going and coming to work and not when she ran out to do various things during the day.

Strange things were still happening inside the office though.

She couldn't find any rhyme or reason to it. Missing files, deleted documents on the shared drive, file folders put out of order. It was like someone was trying to mess with her head. And it was almost working. She was constantly looking over her shoulder at work.

She made the short drive from Midtown to downtown and walked into the make-your-own-salad place that was a favorite of theirs and spotted her friends standing in the long line.

It used to be that most of the city's action took place downtown, but most law firms, including her own, had moved to Midtown, along with a lot of other companies. There were still some great restaurants downtown, though, and it was an easy trip. She was only about five minutes late because of some random construction. At least they were holding a place for her.

"Hey," Sophie said. "Mia told me you killed it in court last week."

Kate shook her head. "Mia is being over complimentary."

"Nope. Kate is being too humble, as usual. And I heard through the grapevine that the judge ruled in your favor."

"That's a very active grapevine," she said.

Mia nodded. "You know how everyone in our community talks."

They got their food and took a seat. Kate had gotten her favorite southwestern salad with grilled chicken.

Mia leaned toward Sophie. "I also got to meet the mysterious PI Kate told us about."

"Do tell," Sophie said.

Kate laughed. "Don't even start again, you two."

Sophie lifted a hand. "Kate, be quiet. I want to hear what Mia has to say."

Mia's brown eyes sparkled with excitement. "Landon is a total head turner. Tall with dark hair and eyes. Built like an

177

Army Ranger for sure. And it seemed to me that he was quite protective of our Kate. He never took his eyes off her the whole time and was right by her side when the hearing ended."

"You two are creating scenarios that don't exist," Kate said. Or at least she wasn't sure if she wanted them to exist.

"If there's nothing between you yet, there will be soon," Mia said. "Believe me, I can tell these things. There was a lot of chemistry between you two. Major sparks."

"For right now, we're getting to know each other as friends and colleagues." She stabbed a piece of chicken with her fork and dipped it into the southwest dressing. She loved her friends, but they were relentless about her nonexistent love life. "If you had come to church on Sunday, Soph, you would've met him."

Sophie's eyes widened. "I had a friend from work singing her first solo at her church, so I wanted to go watch and support her." She paused. "Does he go somewhere else normally?"

"No. He's been on a bit of a break from church. Kind of like Mia." Kate arched an eyebrow at Mia.

"It's hard to go on a break from something you never did in the first place," Mia said. "And on that note, we can shift topics, because I don't want to get into it with you lovely ladies today. So, Kate, you're off the hook about Landon." She paused. "At least for now."

"Thanks. I wanted to get your take on something else," she said.

"What?" They answered in unison.

She described all the strange things that had been happening to her in the office. "Do you think Bonnie could do something like that? Or do you think it's the disgruntled junior associate? Or someone else entirely?"

"What about someone on the support staff?" Mia asked. "You're so kind and respectful, but with so much pressure on you, is it possible you could've rubbed someone the wrong way and now they're acting out?"

Kate racked her brain. "I don't think so. I can't think of any heated encounters I've had with anyone. And my assistant Beth is a sweetheart. She'd never do anything to hurt me in any way."

"I'd say it's Bonnie," Sophie said. "That woman has had it out for you from day one. She can't handle someone else stealing her thunder, and she sees you as a major threat to her power base at the firm."

Mia shook her head. "I disagree. Partners care about winning because it impacts their bottom lines. She would be hurting herself by trying to throw you off. That doesn't make sense to me. It's wouldn't be a rational thing for her to do."

Sophie shifted in her seat. "Hey, not everyone always acts rationally, especially when emotions run high."

The conversation lightened up a bit as Sophie told a story about a trial mishap with a forgetful witness, but they all had a lot of work waiting for them, so they ate and then said their good-byes.

Kate walked to the public garage next door to the salad place. She pulled out her parking ticket and stuck it into the self-serve kiosk along with the validation ticket from the restaurant. It spit a validated ticket back at her so she could get out of the garage.

Since it was just two flights up, she opted for the stairs. Walking after all the sitting she'd been doing lately would do her good. She probably could have done without the extra dressing, but it was her absolute favorite.

She'd made it up the first flight when she heard loud footsteps coming up quickly behind her. In a sudden burst of fear, she tried to take the steps two at a time to get away, but she only made it partway up the second flight before someone grabbed her low ponytail and jerked her backward.

She screamed as she lost her balance. She started to fall and grasped the side railing just enough to slow her down as she tumbled backward and landed across the stairs on her back.

The impact knocked the wind out of her, and she gasped for air. She looked frantically around, afraid she'd see a menacing figure looming over her, but there was no one. The person who had done this to her was long gone.

Disoriented, she tried to sit up, and a wave of nausea washed over her.

The attacker hadn't taken her purse, which made her think this wasn't a random robbery. It was MPC again. They were coming after her. She could have been seriously injured if she hadn't broken her fall with the railing. Her back and lower body had taken the brunt of the impact.

She sat on the stairs instead of trying to stand and dialed Landon. He was going to be angry because she was the one who insisted she didn't need around-the-clock security. But after the court's ruling, maybe MPC was going to step up its efforts against her.

One thing she was certain of, she shouldn't be driving and most likely needed to be checked out by a doctor.

"Hello," Landon said.

"Landon, it's Kate. There's been another incident."

Landon felt sick to his stomach. He should never have agreed to Kate's suggestion that they lighten the security detail.

When the doctor told him that Kate was going to be fine, but that she was fortunate, as it could have been extremely serious, it really hit him. He had to put her safety above all other considerations.

Upon Kate's insistence, they hadn't been totally forthcoming with the doctor about how she got hurt. She was still worried about the possible media attention that could surround her and the case if this got out.

MPC was targeting Kate. This attack had to be a reaction to the negative ruling the court had given. That much was clear to him. But if they had Ellie killed off, why were they taking a different tack with Kate? Maybe they felt actually taking Kate out was too risky. Plus, another lawyer could simply step in and take over her job. But if they shook her up enough instead, it could knock her off her game, making her perform poorly at trial, or push her into accepting a low settlement. This possibility made the most sense to Landon. They wanted to prevail in the litigation. That was MPC's chief priority.

Kate had strict orders to rest, so he drove her home and double-checked the security of her house. When he was satisfied, he found her sitting on the couch.

"The house is all good. You should probably go lie down."

"I want to talk first."

He took a seat right beside her. "You could've been severely injured."

"I know. And I'm sorry. I'm the one who pushed you to loosen up the security schedule, so I feel responsible for this."

He put his hand on her knee. "Kate, you are not responsible. You're the victim here. I should've stuck to my guns about your security protocol. If there's anyone to blame, it's me. I'm the expert, but I haven't been acting like one."

"Let's not pass the blame between us, then, but instead think about how we move forward. I have so much work to do to prepare for trial."

"But if you're not at full strength, you won't be able to do what you need to."

"I think MPC is angry about the court ruling." She sighed. "They want to show me that they're serious about pushing this trial off track, and they're willing to take pretty drastic action against me to make that happen."

He was about to go down a difficult road, but if today had shown him anything, it was that security trumped everything else. "You're not going to like this question, but I have to ask it anyway. Given everything that's happened, do you think there's any way that Ethan is involved in all of this?"

She looked at him with a furrowed brow. "I can't believe Ethan would try to hurt me. I just can't."

"And you're sure you don't want to go to the police?"

"I don't. We're too close to trial to have any publicity that isn't focused on the case. We have a good idea where the threat is coming from, so I just need your help to keep me safe."

He gave her a reassuring nod but mentally made a note to talk to Cooper. "Well, after this incident, you can't be alone like that again. It's just way too dangerous. I let my guard down once, but it won't happen again."

Kate looked away. "Arguing in the courtroom, I've got that. But being physically attacked—I don't know if I'm equipped to handle all of this." Her voice cracked, and a single tear slid down her cheek.

He gently brushed the tear away, wanting to take away her fears. And angry with himself for allowing her to feel this pain. "I won't fail you again, Kate. We're going to get your security tightened up so you can do what you do best." He rested his hand on her cheek.

She placed her hand on top of his. "MPC wants to strike fear into my heart and impact my ability to litigate the case. I've never heard of anything like this before. None of my other cases have prepared me for what I'm facing now, and I'm trying to put on a brave face, but . . ."

"But what?"

"I'm afraid."

Her words tore him up. He couldn't help himself as he pulled her close and wrapped his arms around her. Her hands fisted in his shirt. "No one is going to hurt you again, Kate. That I promise you."

As he sat there, holding her, he thought about his vow to keep her safe. Feeling this woman in his arms hit him deep inside. She was looking to him for protection. But he realized he couldn't do it alone.

He did something he hadn't done in years. He prayed.

# SIXTEEN

L andon prepared himself for a very awkward conversation with Noah. He'd been doing a lot of thinking and even praying about the situation. Since he had prayed for Kate the other night, it seemed only natural that he would pray about the situation with Noah. He wasn't expecting any immediate, quick fixes to his problems, but he wanted to take responsibility for his actions.

He'd apologized to Noah right after the incident, but looking back now, he knew it wasn't a heartfelt apology. He hadn't really been sorry at all. He was only sorry that he had been caught.

He'd asked Noah to come to Kate's house to look at the new security system before Kate got home. He didn't think Noah would have shown if he had told him he wanted to talk about personal stuff.

Noah arrived, and Landon opened the door. "Come on inside."

Noah blew right past him. "What's this about a concern you have about the system? This thing is brand-new. I installed it myself."

"Have a seat, and I'll explain."

Noah raised an eyebrow but didn't object as he was led into the kitchen.

Landon sat across the table from Noah. It was time to face what he had done. "I didn't call you here to talk about the security system. Although, while you're here, I would appreciate you running a diagnostic check just to be on the safe side."

"So what is it you really want?" Noah asked.

Landon took a deep breath. "I want to apologize."

Noah blinked. "What?"

"I know I deserve the cold shoulder plus so much more. I also know that when I told you I was sorry over a year ago, I didn't mean it, and you probably realized that."

"So why now?"

"I've had a lot of time to think about what I did. I knew it was wrong at the time, but I didn't care. When I came back from that last tour, I wanted to be as destructive as possible—to myself and even to those I cared about. I'm not making excuses for what I did—my actions were inexcusable—but I want you to know that I truly am sorry for hurting you and betraying you. You've only been a friend to me, and I can't say the same about myself to you."

Noah's dark eyes softened. "I know you went through some messed up stuff in Iraq. I worked with military guys at ATF and heard enough of their stories to understand that you came back a different man. And I should've done more when you returned. I shouldn't have shut you out regardless of what you did to me, because I knew you were struggling. Even though I tried not to, I held a grudge against you for a long time because of Gina. I've been praying that I could let it go and that we'd have this exact conversation one day."

"Funny you mention that, because I've started trying to reconnect with my faith."

"Seriously?"

"Yeah, I know it's shocking. Especially after all the things I said and the way I acted when I came back." He was ashamed of so many things.

"You were hurting, Landon. The Lord doesn't hold that against you." Noah paused. "It's Kate, isn't it? These changes in you are because of her."

He sucked in a breath as he contemplated Noah's words. "What do you mean?"

"I see the way you look at her, man. It's obvious."

Was it that obvious? Landon hadn't even come to terms with his feelings yet, but his friend was calling him out. He shook his head. "Kate is a remarkable woman, and she has helped me a lot, just by being able to talk with her about things that I haven't opened up to anyone else about. But right now, we're just good friends."

"I think you probably want more than that, though, and it's great. I just want to warn you, given the stakes involved in this case. You can't afford to have your judgment clouded because of your feelings."

"Roger that." He understood Noah's point. It was a valid one, but he wasn't sure how he was going to manage his relationship with Kate going forward—whatever that may be. He wasn't even sure how Kate felt about him.

"One other thing," Noah said. "The situation with Gina was messed up, but the fact that she was willing to cheat on me made me realize that she wasn't the woman I thought she was."

"Has there been anyone since?"

Noah shook his head. "I'm a bit wary of putting myself out there again, and our business taking off has been great. I've been able to throw myself into the work. Cooper and I are really building something."

"I'm totally impressed, but I always knew you two guys were the real deal."

"That means a lot, coming from you. We've been putting in the time and effort, that's for sure. And I think Cooper probably hasn't pushed it because of the rocky relationship between you and me, but we're going to be expanding into investigations work. There's an opportunity for you there, if you're interested."

"He did mention it, and I'm honored you guys would even consider me. Let me get through this case, and then we can figure out whether that would make any sense." It floored him that Noah was truly willing to forgive him—so much so that he'd basically offered Landon a job. "Noah, I don't deserve your friendship. You're a better man than I'll ever be."

Noah reached over the table and gave Landon's shoulder a hearty pat. "We need to put this behind us."

"I don't even know what to say, beyond thank you."

"So we're good, then. Let me take a look at the system while I'm here. Have there been any more threats since the garage incident?"

"No, but between me and Coop, we've been providing tight security for her. I'm still mad at myself for loosening things up in the first place."

"What do you think MPC's endgame is?"

"As far as endgame, it worries me to even think like that. I believe their immediate goal is to scare her to impact her trial preparation. But as Kate gets closer to the truth, if they sense that, then this could go sideways really quick."

"And who is actually behind all of this?"

"We're trying to figure that out too. We found out from Pierce that there's a guy in corporate security trying to keep the scientists in line. Whether he had anything to do with the attacks against Kate, I don't know. Also, I can't imagine someone like that acting without some direction or authorization from a person with power. Whether that goes all the way to the CEO is an open question. And to add to that, there's an extra wrinkle because Kate is friends with the opposing counsel. She doesn't think he could be connected to any of this, but I'm not so sure."

"Maybe you're just jealous?"

Landon laughed. "Maybe a little, but that's not why I'm suspicious. The whole thing stinks, if you ask me. I don't trust him at all. He's representing a company that we know has done some pretty bad stuff."

"Well, I've got the tech side covered, but whatever else you guys need, just let me know."

*Enough of the games.* Kate walked toward Bonnie's office. It was time to confront her head on and find out if Bonnie had any role in what was happening at the firm. It was clear someone was playing mind games with her. It was hurting the case, which meant the client, and Kate wanted it to stop.

Kate knocked, but since Bonnie's door was open, she walked right on in.

Bonnie looked up from her computer. "Do you want to talk?"

"Yes." Kate shut the door behind her and took a seat in one of Bonnie's fancy navy chairs. Partners were responsible for buying their own furniture, and Bonnie's office was the most stylish in the firm.

"Judging from the annoyed look on your face, something must be wrong. You really don't hide your feelings well, Kate."

"You're right. You're one of my partners, and I need to know that you're not trying to hurt me or the case."

"What are you talking about?"

Kate held back a groan. "For starters, how about my brief being deleted from the shared system? Or the binders disappearing from the war room? Or a whole set of documents that had been reviewed by the team being wiped clean of all notes?

I could keep going. And I want to know if you're involved in this."

Kate didn't think she'd ever seen Bonnie look surprised before. "I had absolutely nothing to do with any of that. I'm shocked that you would come into my office and accuse me of this. It's ridiculous."

"Is it that crazy? You've made it very clear since the day I stepped foot into this firm that you don't like me, especially after the Mitchell trial, when you didn't take my strategy advice and lost. You've never forgiven me for how that made you look. So here I am, on the biggest case of my career, and I can't help but wonder if you want to see me fall flat on my face."

Bonnie's eyes widened. "I want no such thing. You and I are nothing alike, and you're right that I didn't seek you out to become my new best friend, but I would never—and I repeat, *never*—jeopardize a case. I know I can be tough to deal with, but I am not disloyal to my partners."

The passion in Bonnie's words shook Kate. Was it possible Bonnie was completely innocent in all of this? "But if it's not you, then who could it be?"

"Putting aside for a moment that you wrongly accused me of this, it's a big problem. Could it be one of the junior associates pulling some sort of practical joke? Maybe Phil, the guy I kicked off the team? He was humiliated in front of all of his peers. That might be strong enough motivation to act out as payback against the team he can't be a part of."

"I considered Phil, but would he really risk his job over this? He has to know that the repercussions for deleting a partner's brief are a lot more than a slap on the wrist."

"Maybe, but like I told you before, Millennials are a lot different than we ever were at that age. Have you checked with security to make sure there haven't been any breaches into our systems or our offices?"

"No, but that's a good idea." Kate paused and gave Bonnie a sheepish look. "I'm sorry that I came in here flinging accusations at you."

"It's okay. You're under a lot of pressure, but it's not me. So someone else is trying to mess with you. I would call a meeting of all the associates working on the case and try to ferret out the culprit. And since you aren't exactly the scariest of people, I'll offer my services. Have you talked to Adam or William about this?"

"Not yet. I didn't want to bring them into it."

"Fine. The two of us will handle it. Set up the meeting, and I'll be there."

"Thank you, Bonnie. You have no idea how much that means to me."

Bonnie gave her a wry smirk. "Don't read too much into it. We're still not going to be bffs."

Kate smiled. "I've gotten that message loud and clear, but thank you."

She left Bonnie's office relieved but wondering if she could truly trust Bonnie. She really didn't know *who* she could trust. Someone on her own team was still working against her.

Ethan walked toward the MPC building, on his way to talk to Royce about his upcoming deposition. His cell rang, and he took the call before he entered the building because he saw that it was Kate. He wondered what she wanted.

"Hey there," he answered.

"Hi," Kate said. "Do you have a minute?"

"I'm about to head into a meeting, but I have two minutes to spare."

"Don't take this the wrong way."

"Uh-oh. Anytime you use that kind of intro, it can't be good."

"Something happened to me last week. I don't want to get into all the details, but I was attacked in the stairwell of a parking garage downtown."

He stopped short. "What? Are you okay?"

"Yes, I'm fine now, but . . ."

"But what? Kate, what aren't you telling me?"

"We've known each other for a long time, so I'm asking you this because of our friendship." She paused. "You didn't know anything about this, did you?"

"Of course not. How would I know anything about it?" He gripped his cell tightly against his ear.

"Because I have a feeling that MPC is trying to send me a signal."

"You think MPC sent someone after you?"

"It's very possible. This isn't the first incident since I started working on this case. They want to throw me off my game."

"That's insane. There's no way they would do that." As the words came out of his mouth, his stomach clenched. Would they? Could Royce be capable of something like this? Even though Royce was cutthroat, this seemed like a stretch even for him. A big stretch.

"I want to believe that, Ethan. And I hate to think that you could be involved in trying to hurt me."

"I absolutely would never do anything like that, Kate. You know I care about you." How much should he defend MPC without knowing the facts? He believed it was his duty to defend them until he knew more. "MPC is focused on the legal case, not attacking you personally. Do you have any evidence to support why you think it could be them?"

There was a pause on the other line. "No. I don't have concrete evidence. I'm glad to hear you think that they aren't targeting me, but I felt like I had to let you know what I thought might be going on. And if they are coming after me, I need you to tell them to back off."

"Thanks for letting me know. I have to run into this meeting now." He needed to get off the phone and confront Royce about this. "But take care of yourself, Kate."

He ended the call and walked into the MPC building as his mind raced, trying to piece together the implications. Royce had said he was worried about Kate nosing around, but it was a long way between that and sending someone to attack her.

It seemed like forever before Penny was able to escort him into Royce's office. When he entered, he saw Bradley Cummings was there too. That only made Ethan more suspicious. Why did Royce and Bradley need to meet so much? His imagination was running wild.

"Ethan, great to see you," Royce said.

"I need a minute with you alone," Ethan said, dispensing with the pleasantries.

Royce looked at him for a moment, sizing him up. "All right. Bradley, keep me updated on what you're working on. I'll touch base with you later."

Bradley nodded and walked out of the room, leaving Ethan with Royce.

"What is it now? You have more bad news for me? First losing this motion and now who knows what?"

Ethan tried to remain calm and remind himself that Royce was still the client—a very important client, key to his career. "Did you send someone to attack Kate?"

Royce's eyes widened. "What do you mean?"

"Kate was assaulted in a downtown parking garage. I'm asking you point-blank if you had anything to do with it."

"Absolutely not. I know you may have some reservations about my business practices, but there are clear lines that I won't cross. I haven't touched that lawyer, and I have no intention to. But I'm relying on you to beat her in the courtroom, and so far, you aren't doing too well at that."

Royce's stinging words cut at Ethan, but he did seem convincing about not having anything to do with Kate's attack. Maybe Kate was just paranoid and looking for answers. "We can come back around to that issue, but I just wanted to make sure I could look Kate in the eyes and tell her truthfully that MPC is not responsible for what happened to her."

"Of course you can. That should be the last worry on your mind."

"Good. Now, as far as losing the motion, that's one of the reasons I'm here. After the loss, the settlement demand went up to five hundred million."

Royce rolled his eyes. "That's ludicrous. Even if I wanted to agree to that, which I don't, there's no way the board would go for it. We aren't in the wrong here, Ethan. I've told you time and again. Yes, the initial version of the drug had some adverse side effects—all drugs do. But there's no evidence that Celix causes brain tumors."

Ethan considered the CEO for a moment. It wasn't unusual for clients to lie to their lawyers. But now wasn't the time to force the issue. "Understood. The other thing we need to start thinking about is your deposition."

Royce waved his hand in the air. "I don't want you stressing about that. I'm going to be a stellar witness. I've been deposed in other lawsuits before."

Ethan swallowed a sigh. Trying to control Royce as a witness was going to be nearly impossible. "Were any of them this substantial?"

Royce shook his head. "No, but I guarantee that you won't have to worry about me."

Somehow Ethan highly doubted that. "What are you going

194

to do if a problematic document is put in front of you at the deposition?"

"That's not going to happen if you do your job and make sure they aren't turned over in the first place."

"Nothing is a hundred percent when you're dealing with this volume of documents. There is such a thing as human or even computer error."

"For your sake, you better hope that doesn't happen. And even if it does, I can spin documents if I need to. You don't get to be the CEO of one of the world's top pharmaceutical companies unless you can handle things like this."

"You do realize there is something called perjury. I don't want to put you in that position. We need to be prepared."

Royce frowned. "Ethan, I'm beginning to think that you're much softer than what I need here. You're knee-deep in all of this, so you need to put your conscience aside and get the job done."

Ethan's fists clenched, and he forced them to relax. "With all due respect, Royce, I hope you didn't put your conscience aside and decide to send Kate a threatening message."

Royce's frown deepened into a glower. "You should have as much concern over the case as you do over that woman. Is there something you haven't told me about your relationship with her?"

"No. We're friends. That's it. But you didn't answer my question."

"I already answered when you first barged in here with your bad attitude. I'm not going to resort to physical violence—at least not against her—but you, on the other hand, are trying my patience right now."

There was no way Ethan could do any substantive deposition preparation with Royce today. They were both far too upset. He needed to defuse the situation and regroup. "I think it might be best for me to go and for us to find another time to work on preparing you for deposition."

Royce relaxed a bit. "You're right. Things today have gotten a bit heated. There's a lot on the line for both of us. We have to remember that we're on the same team and want the same result. That should drive us to work together and do whatever is necessary to reach those goals."

"I agree."

Except, unlike Royce, he actually had some lines that he wouldn't cross. He just had to figure out what those were.

# CHAPTER
# SEVENTEEN

K ate and Landon sat on the couch in her family room while
Jax lounged peacefully beside her. She stroked his black
fur, and she could hear him purring. Jax had taken a liking to Landon, which was unusual, as he wasn't normally that
loving with anyone except her. She was convinced Jax was a
great judge of character.

This evening routine was becoming common for them. Landon
picked her up from work most days, and when he couldn't because he was chasing down Pierce or trying to develop other
leads, Cooper was always there. They refused to let her go anywhere alone outside of her office.

The approach was a bit constricting, but being attacked in
that garage had really shaken her.

"What's on your mind?" Landon asked.

"Just thinking about everything."

He gently placed his hand on top of hers. "You're doing
amazing, Kate. Even with all of the uncertainty, you're doing
your job very well. You should be proud of yourself."

"I'm just taking it one day at a time." She paused. "I confronted Bonnie about all the strange things happening to my
files and documents."

"And? What did she say?"

"That she didn't do it, and I actually believe her." She could barely believe it herself, but she didn't think Bonnie was behind the sabotage. "And I confirmed with both the building security and our firm's security that there have been no breaches of our office."

"Which means you have a mole, even if it isn't Bonnie."

"I know. Isn't that disturbing? I have enough threats and problems coming from the outside. The last thing I need is someone working against me from the inside. I've still got my eye on that junior associate I told you about."

"We could set up a trap. Ferret them out."

"What're you thinking?"

"Tell everyone on your team about some key files or something you're working on. I could set up a camera in the war room and catch the person in the act. It's worth a shot. We don't really have anything to lose."

"Let me think about what I could use, and then we can plan it. You can put the camera in late one night after the rest of the staff is gone."

She looked down and realized they were still holding hands. Something about Landon's touch felt completely right. He steadied her, grounded her, like no other man ever had. It was like everything she'd gone through had led her to this specific place with this amazing man.

"Is there something else on your mind?" he asked.

"Yeah." Her thoughts went beyond her growing feelings for him. She felt the need to let him see her true self. The one no one else had ever really seen. But she wasn't sure how to even talk about it. "Landon, you opened up to me about your past, and based on everything you've been through, I think you might actually be able to understand."

"Understand what?"

She looked up into his eyes and felt reassured that he wouldn't judge her. He wouldn't view her differently because of her struggles. "When I talked to you before about some of the issues I've had, I left out the most difficult one." She took another deep breath, trying to find the courage to reveal her darkest secret to him.

"You can tell me, Kate. You accepted my past. Whatever it is, I'm here to listen. I want to know all about you, not just the public persona super lawyer that people know." He gave her a small smile.

She believed him. He'd only ever been honest and straightforward with her about all of the pain he went through. It was time for her to verbalize something she'd only said out loud to God in prayer.

"I've struggled with depression for years, and at times like these, with all the stress and anxiety building, I have to be extra careful, because I'm on a roller coaster of emotions."

His eyes widened. "Really? I would've never known."

"That's the thing. You can be totally functional, and the outside world can't see it, but the battle rages in your head. I'm able to put on a smile, but inside it's much uglier than that. There are days when I find it difficult even to get out of bed. I push through, and it's better now than it was years ago. I've made a ton of progress and really gotten it under control. But it's still a constant fight for me."

"Did this happen after the death of your parents?"

"I think that was the catalyst, but it got really bad in college. When I told you that my faith saved me in more ways than one, that's really true. It's still not easy, but without God's love, I honestly don't know where I'd be right now."

He squeezed her hand. "You're stronger than you give yourself credit for, Kate."

"The strength doesn't come from me. When I was only relying

on myself, that's when times were the darkest and ugliest. You're the only person I've ever told about this. It's not exactly something I'm proud of. But if you sense something is off with me, then that's why. It's one of the reasons I stay at work so much and throw myself into my cases. It's easier that way. It's a coping mechanism."

"I get it. While you're at work, you're keeping your mind busy. There's no time for you to allow your emotions to control you."

She couldn't believe the words coming out of his mouth. He understood her feelings more than she ever could have expected.

"You're not alone, Kate. I'm here, and I'll help get you through this trial. Just remember that. This isn't a solo fight."

"But that's what I'm used to."

"I know, but it doesn't have to be that way anymore." He leaned in closer to her.

She could feel his warm breath on her cheek as she stared into his dark eyes. His lips parted slightly, and she tilted her head up toward him, hopeful for what was next.

A loud buzzing from her phone startled her out of the moment. She reached for it and read the message. "It's just the review team letting me know that they haven't found anything of note yet in the current set of documents."

She set down the phone and looked at Landon, but it was clear the moment between them had passed. Sadness washed over her, and she realized just how much he meant to her.

But unfortunately, it was time to get back to business.

"When do you expect to actually see documents about Acreda?" Landon asked.

"I'm not holding my breath."

"And if you don't get anything?"

"We'll be right back in court in front of Judge Freeman."

He nodded. "What's our timeline looking like in general? What's next?"

200

"I'm going to push to get Royce Hamilton's deposition scheduled. I want more relevant documents before I depose him, because I'm only going to get one shot at it, but I can at least get the date on the calendar to put some pressure on them."

"Coop and I have been doing some digging into his past."

"Anything interesting?"

He looked down. "Sad, actually. His wife and baby died many years ago in a car accident."

She sucked in a breath. "I'm all too familiar with that kind of tragedy."

"Yeah, I wondered how you would take that news."

"Losing my parents changed my entire world, and I can't even fathom what it would be like to lose a child. I don't trust Royce, and if he's behind Ellie's murder, then he should pay. But at the same time, my heart breaks over hearing something like that. Wondering how those events shaped the man he is today."

"I've also learned the hard way that tragedy isn't an excuse, but it sometimes is an explanation. As far as we can tell, Royce lives alone in a huge mansion in Buckhead. Well, not completely alone because he has a full staff, but he never remarried after losing his wife."

She couldn't help but feel empathy for the man. They shared something that she wouldn't wish on anyone.

"Are you okay?" Landon asked.

"Yeah. Just brings back a lot of memories." She still thought about her parents a lot, but she'd come to a place where she focused more on the happy memories and not on the accident.

He frowned. "Maybe I shouldn't have told you."

"No. We need to be transparent and open with each other about what we know. I'd much prefer honesty over you trying to spare my feelings. I'm tougher than I look."

He laughed. "You've demonstrated your toughness. I would

never question that." He paused and sobered. "I just don't want to hurt you, especially if it's not necessary."

"In this instance, you did the right thing. Knowing as much as I can about Royce will help me prepare for the deposition and for the trial."

Jax hopped onto her lap, and Landon laughed again. "I don't think he wants me moving in on his territory. I better watch how close I sit to you."

"Nah. He really likes you." And as Kate spoke, Jax walked from her lap onto Landon's.

"You know, I never thought of myself as a cat person, but Jax isn't so bad." He smiled at her. "And neither is his owner."

The next day, Kate sat in her office, waiting for a meeting with Ethan. She shuffled papers on her desk, looking for the document review summary prepared by the team. She'd just had it yesterday, and now it was gone. Someone had been in her office again. Her personal space was being invaded—and most likely by someone she worked with.

*Lord, with each passing day, I face more threats. I need your strength and wisdom now to help me navigate through these troubled waters.*

Her prayer was interrupted by a knock at her door. Beth stood there with Ethan beside her. Kate had instructed Beth not to let Ethan come to her office without an escort anymore. She couldn't trust those she once thought she could.

"Thanks, Beth."

Beth smiled and left Ethan with her.

"Kate, I've been worried about you." He took a seat. He looked sincere.

"You should be, given what I've been subjected to." Her answer came out a bit gruffer than she intended.

"Listen, that's one of the reasons I wanted to meet. To assure you that MPC had absolutely nothing to do with what happened to you. There's no way I would associate with a company that was trying to harm one of my closest friends." He reached out and grabbed her hands. "You have to believe that."

"I believe that MPC would deny it."

He let go of her and sat back. "You're letting your litigation brain cloud your rational judgment. Show me one shred of evidence linking MPC to your attack. From everything I've heard, this sounds like a random assault. It happens in Atlanta all the time."

"Excuse me if I'm a bit clouded. Being physically assaulted might do that to you." She took a very deep breath, trying to calm herself, as she was getting amped up. But the fact that Ethan was completely denying MPC's involvement let her know that he was either willfully ignorant, or worse. And she didn't want to contemplate the worse alternative. "This isn't the only thing that's happened to me, Ethan." She didn't want to give him too many details, but she had to say something. "I was threatened before by someone who told me to back off of this case."

"And that's exactly what they told you?"

"Well, no. Not exactly, but it was the basic message."

"Did they mention MPC?" he asked.

"No. MPC is too smart to be that overt and leave a paper trail."

"You realize that this sounds very conspiratorial."

She shook her head. "I'm telling you the truth."

"Kate, we've been through a lot together over the years, and I would hope that we've built up enough trust and respect so that when I give you my word on something, you believe me."

"Look me in the eyes, Ethan, and tell me you are one hundred percent sure that MPC wasn't behind what happened to me."

His hesitation told her all she needed to know. Her heart broke, knowing she'd probably lost his friendship forever.

"Don't be like this, Kate. The last thing I want to do is argue. That isn't why I came. I wanted to check on you. To see how you're doing."

"So this isn't a work visit?"

"Everything is a work visit at this point, isn't it?"

"Exactly. And speaking of work, we're still anxiously waiting for you to comply with the court's order."

"Wait a minute, we have been complying. I've sent you two productions since that order came down."

"Yeah, funny you mention that, because none of the documents in those productions mention Acreda."

He raised an eyebrow. "You're really focused on that one drug? Because I was under the impression you had a short list, and that list is what we've been complying with. I bet if you pull up those documents right now, you'd find drugs from the list."

"Yes, some of the drugs, but not one specific drug, which makes me very suspicious about why you're hiding information on that one."

"If you want to jump into the abyss, then far be it from me to try to stop you. But you're wasting your time. You'll get your documents as outlined in the order, and when you do, you'll see what a waste this detour has become. But hey, it's just more legal fees for you, right?"

"How dare you? You know this isn't about the money for me. And for that matter, this case was taken under contingency fees, which you also know. Why are you acting like this?"

"I'm going to let this slide because you went through a traumatic event. You clearly think that MPC was involved, and that is causing you to misjudge the entire situation. As a friend, I can overlook that. I just wanted to make sure you were all right."

Did he really? Or did he have some ulterior motive for this

meeting? Kate held back a sigh. "While you're here, why don't we put Royce Hamilton's deposition on the calendar?"

"Fine by me. He's ready to go whenever you are."

"I'll be ready to go once I have your completed document production. Do you have an ETA on that?"

"Two weeks."

"Fine. Let's do his deposition soon thereafter." She flipped through her calendar and proposed a few dates for him to take back to his client.

Ethan stood. "Before I go, out of curiosity, why the hang-up with Acreda? Do you think you have some special theory or something?"

"I never said I was hung up. Just that I wanted the documents, and for some reason you haven't sent me any regarding that drug yet. They're relevant to what was happening with Celix. Drugs developed at the same time by members of the same team. How could I not investigate that?"

Something she couldn't read flashed through his eyes—worry, fear, anxiety? Whatever it was, it let her know that Ethan knew more than he was letting on. They both did, but he was the enemy here, with polar opposite goals. She didn't think it prudent to push him when she didn't want to be pushed.

"Anything else?" she asked.

He shook his head. "No. Just take care of yourself, Kate. Regardless of what you think, I would never want you hurt."

Those last words actually sounded sincere. Or maybe it was just that she so desperately wanted to believe him.

"What do you mean, Pierce is gone?" Landon asked Cooper. Cooper had invited Landon to the K&R office to talk.

"We've been trying to make contact with him for the past week with no luck. I've scouted out all the normal places, and I put one of my guys at his home address. No activity whatsoever. We're doing some digging to try to track him down."

"You don't think MPC took him out? Surely that would be too suspicious."

"You're right. I don't think they killed him, but that doesn't mean they didn't send him away. Maybe even paid him off? I wouldn't put that past them. A payoff is nothing."

"Pierce didn't seem like the type, though."

Cooper nodded. "Maybe under normal circumstances, but he isn't dumb. If he started to feel the heat, he could've realized that he didn't want to end up like Ellie. Maybe he thought it was the only viable option."

"What a mess." And that was an understatement. They couldn't catch a break.

"But that's not all. One other thing."

Landon's antenna went up. "What else do you have?"

"We've got the video footage from Kate's war room at the firm."

"Uh-oh. You've got something?"

"No. That's the strange thing. No one took the bait."

Landon waited patiently for Cooper to load the video and play it on the large TV screen on the wall.

"There was a lot of useless stuff, just the team working. Absolutely nothing out of the ordinary."

"Well, we made an effort. It was a good idea. We'll just have to monitor things, and Kate will have to be careful."

"Yeah. If more stuff happens, maybe Noah can come up with another solution to track down the culprit."

"That sounds good."

Cooper stood up and leaned against the corner of the table. "So I hear you two had a talk."

He let out a breath and thought back to the conversation. "Yeah. It wasn't easy at first, but I'm glad I did it."

"Noah is too. I knew that if you just took a step in that direction, he'd welcome you back."

"I got the sense he's had a bit of a rough go too." Landon paused. "I've been so consumed with my own problems that I haven't made time to care about anyone else. I'm ashamed of how I've acted." The guilt was still there even though he believed that Noah had turned the page.

"Noah has forgiven you, and he wouldn't want you to carry around that guilt. We all have enough burdens to bear."

"I guess you're right. I should probably go talk to Kate about all of this."

"Watch your back," Cooper said.

"Always."

—◅◇▻—

"I wasn't expecting a visit from you in the middle of the day," Kate said, happy to see Landon. But her mood changed quickly when she sensed that this wasn't a social call.

"There are two things we need to talk about."

"Okay. Sit down and let's talk." She closed her office door behind him as he took a seat.

"I just came from the K&R office. Cooper showed me the footage taken last night in the war room."

"Just give it to me straight." She prepared herself for the worst. Or for the possibility that Bonnie had been playing her, which would really sting.

"The videotape showed absolutely nothing."

She felt a mixture of relief and disappointment. "Then it's a dud. I was hoping to get some resolution to all of this."

"I agree, but just keep an eye on things. If anything else happens, let me know. We'll come up with another way of attacking the problem. Between all of us, we should be able to figure out something, and maybe the best-case scenario is that this was all a fluke. We're all on edge right now. Maybe it was just strange coincidences or mistakes."

"I don't think I could be that off base, but I'll definitely let you know if anything else happens."

Landon tapped a restless finger on his knee. "The second thing is not good news. Pierce has gone completely off the grid."

"What do you mean?"

He rubbed his chin. "He's gone. We can't track him down at his usual spots, coming or going from work or his home."

Fear and dread filled her heart as tears threatened to fall. "Don't tell me that MPC killed him too?"

"We don't know, and both Cooper and I believe that he's alive. It would probably raise too many flags for both scientists to be killed in such close proximity."

"What do you think happened, then?"

"He could've been bought off. MPC makes him disappear. Sets him up in a comfy beach house somewhere outside the States with a hefty dose of cash."

"Is he the type of guy who would accept that?"

"He probably didn't have much choice, if you know what I mean. The last time we met with him, he mentioned that MPC's security officer was asking around and trying to make sure none of them spoke to anyone about the case or the drugs. MPC may have decided that since Pierce worked with Ellie, he was a liability."

Her mind filled with awful scenarios. "Wow. This just keeps getting more insane by the moment. How can they do this? And who is calling all the shots? It has to be someone with power, and in my mind, all roads lead to Royce Hamilton."

Landon walked around to her side of the desk and took her hands. "I know you don't want to hear this, but I'm beginning to wonder if this is getting too dangerous for you."

She pulled her hands from his. "You can't be suggesting that I just walk away?"

"I didn't say that, but we might get to that point."

"No. I will not abandon this case or my client. Mrs. Wyman deserves justice for what MPC did to her daughter, and I will not stop fighting for her."

He gave a short nod. "Then you may have to deal with further enhanced security protocols."

"Whatever you need to do so I can see this thing through. I'm not giving up."

## CHAPTER
# EIGHTEEN

Today was the day. Kate would be face-to-face with a man she was convinced was up to no good. The deposition of Royce Hamilton was scheduled to start at nine o'clock at Ethan's office, and she arrived in plenty of time to get set up. She'd chosen to wear one of her favorite gray pantsuits with a lavender blouse.

Landon was accompanying her, but she still felt like she was headed into the lion's den. She'd prepared and prayed about this deposition, so now was the time to make it happen.

Her team still hadn't found any documents showing that Acreda had harmful side effects, but just because she didn't have documents exactly on point didn't mean she couldn't ask Royce questions. She wasn't under any delusion that he would tell the truth, but hopefully if she was persistent enough, she'd be able to catch him in a lie.

Landon seemed to understand that she wasn't in a chatty mood this morning. He gave her space while at the same time making sure she didn't have to worry about her safety. She'd told him that he would need to wait in the firm's lobby, and he seemed fine with that.

She was set up in a conference room with her stack of documents and her deposition outline. The court reporter and videographer were also there and ready to go. In cases like this, she always videotaped the depositions so that if she ever needed to play it in front of a jury, they would be able to see the demeanor of the witness. It was much more effective than merely reading the transcript.

She looked up as Ethan entered the room.

"Mr. Hamilton is running a couple minutes late," he said. "His driver is stuck in traffic coming down I-85. You know how it is for the morning commute. Sorry for the delay."

The games were already starting, but she refused to let Ethan think this would bother her. "That's fine. Thanks for letting me know." She turned her attention back to her outline, not giving Ethan another glance.

She wouldn't let this minor delay throw her off her game. She took the extra time to make some edits to her outline and organize her documents. She'd taken countless depositions in her career. Her outline just provided a roadmap, but the best lawyers listened to the answers the witness provided and adjusted their questions accordingly. Deposing a man like Royce was probably going to be like pulling teeth.

The time flew by, and before she knew it, the conference room door was opening, and Ethan walked in accompanied by Royce Hamilton. She'd seen pictures of him, but this was her first face-to-face interaction. He was a little taller than Ethan and had salt-and-pepper hair that was smoothly styled. His navy suit was immaculately tailored and paired with a striped tie.

She stood and walked over to him, providing her hand. Much to her surprise, he actually smiled and shook her hand warmly.

"Ms. Sullivan, nice to meet you."

So that was his angle. Try to be the charmer. "Thank you,"

she said. It would be a lie to say it was nice to meet him, so she didn't bother.

"Well, if everyone is ready, we can get down to business," Ethan said.

"Sure." She walked back around to her side of the table.

Royce took his spot at the head of the table. The videographer helped him connect his microphone to his suit lapel while she made final preparations.

She had a style of taking depositions, and she didn't plan on deviating from it for this witness. She wasn't a naturally aggressive lawyer, and it didn't suit her anyway. Her strength came from understanding how it all fit together and knowing when to go in for the kill. That might not happen until hours from now, and she knew she would need patience. *Lord, this is an important step today. Please give me the knowledge and patience to make this deposition successful so this man can be held accountable for what MPC has done to all of these innocent people.*

"Mr. Hamilton, my name is Kate Sullivan, and I'm lead counsel for the plaintiffs in the multidistrict litigation against Mason Pharmaceutical Corporation in the Northern District of Georgia. I assume that your counsel has prepared you for today, but I always like to start out with some ground rules."

"Of course," he said.

"As you know, this deposition is being videotaped, and we also have a court reporter in the room recording all of your answers. Because of that, the court reporter will need you to answer each question verbally so she can take down your answer. If you just nod or shake your head, she won't be able to record your answers. Do you understand?"

"Yes, I do."

"Great. If you need a break at any time, all you have to do is ask. All I ask of you is that if there is a pending question, you answer my question first before we take the break."

"That's fine," he said. His light blue eyes focused on hers.

This was going to be a battle to the last minute. That much she knew.

Methodically, she went through her outline, point by point. It wasn't until midafternoon that she was ready to home in on some of the most sensitive topics.

"Mr. Hamilton, you had a scientist who was employed by MPC named Ellie Proctor, correct?"

"Yes."

"And what happened to Ms. Proctor?"

"She was tragically murdered in our parking garage." His eyes misted up.

She couldn't believe this guy was about to shed fake tears. The thing was that if she didn't know better, he seemed truthful. "I'm sorry about the loss of Ms. Proctor, but I want to dig a little deeper. She was one of the chief scientists working on Celix, correct?"

"Yes."

She continued with a leading question. "And isn't it also true that you had concerns that Ms. Proctor might talk about her work with Celix with those outside of MPC?"

"Objection to form. Calls for speculation," Ethan said.

"You can answer," she said to Royce. Objections in depositions were purely for the record. They didn't stop the witness from being able to answer.

"I worry that all my employees might discuss their work outside of the company, Ms. Sullivan. Given the sensitive nature of our business and the vast competition in our market, that's something every pharmaceutical CEO deals with."

"Yes, but did you have any specific concern about Ms. Proctor talking about her work with Celix outside the company?"

"No, I didn't," he answered with a straight face.

He might just be the best actor she'd ever seen.

"So you don't have any reason to believe that Ms. Proctor actually spoke to anyone outside of MPC about Celix?"

"No, I don't."

"What about Acreda? Did she talk to anyone outside MPC about Acreda?"

There, the smallest flinch. He quickly made his expression neutral again. "No. And Ms. Sullivan, I'm sorry, but could we take a restroom break?"

"Of course."

She'd won this round. Royce left the room with Ethan in tow, and she exhaled. She was making progress. If only she could hear the conversation happening right now between Royce and Ethan.

"You've got this, Royce," Ethan said. "You've been stellar so far. I know you might be getting tired, but don't let Kate mess with your head. She doesn't have anything on you. She's just fishing."

"How do you know that?" Royce hissed.

Ethan was thankful his client at least had a good game face inside the deposition room, because right now his face reddened with each word out of his mouth. "Royce, you were a star in there. All you have to do is keep it going for a couple more hours. If she really had something, she'd be more direct about it. She won't pull punches. You need to start acting like the world-class CEO that you are." He figured appealing to Royce's ego was the best strategy.

"You're right. I need to get my head on straight." Royce smoothed his jacket. "Where was she trying to go with those questions about Ellie talking to someone outside the company?"

"I don't know. Maybe she suspects that Ellie spoke to someone outside of MPC about her work. I haven't seen anything in the documents that would indicate she did. You don't know anything about that, do you?"

Royce's jaw tightened. "No. That's what makes me nervous. What does she know?"

"Don't worry about it. There's absolutely nothing there. She's just throwing out wild theories to see if anything will stick. This is good practice for the trial, because it will be even worse there. You'll have an audience—the most important one being the jury."

Royce took a couple slow breaths. "I know I've been hard on you, Ethan, but you're coming through for me. I appreciate that. This woman just has a way of getting under my skin."

"You've got this. Now, let's get back in there, because I don't want her to think she has you frazzled. You go in there and do your thing, just like I know you can."

Royce nodded, and they walked back to the conference room.

"We're ready to go," Ethan said.

"Great." Kate looked at him, and he knew she was trying to determine how the break had gone.

Royce put his microphone back on, and they were ready to start again.

"Mr. Hamilton, I'd like to talk to you a bit more about another drug your company manufacturers called Acreda."

"Very well," Royce said.

Ethan's stomach was clenched in knots. He hoped the big game Royce talked would hold up under Kate's scrutiny. She didn't hit witnesses hard, but sometimes the softer approach was even more deadly, because they never saw her coming.

"What medical condition is Acreda used to treat?" she asked.

"Acreda treats many different types of growth and tumors. It has a wide-ranging efficacy."

"And is it available now?"

He shook his head. "Not yet. It should be on the market

within the next few months, if all the final regulatory approvals go as planned."

"And you're well versed in the allegations in this lawsuit against MPC, correct?"

"Yes, I am."

"That MPC's migraine medication Celix caused brain tumors that resulted in death or injury of the plaintiffs?"

"Yes."

Ethan watched as Kate skillfully led his witness in the type of questions that made for a very damaging cross-examination. She was going to be a force to be reckoned with at the trial. He figured the jury would really buy in to her approach.

"Were you personally involved in any discussion about possible dangerous side effects of Acreda?"

"No, because there are no dangerous side effects of Acreda. We have substantial testing on this."

"Are you certain about that?"

"Yes, Ms. Sullivan, I think I know the results of the testing of one of my top drugs."

"Is it possible that your scientists could have found a harmful side effect and you wouldn't know about it?"

"No," Royce responded. "I'm intimately involved with the details of all of MPC's products."

Ethan winced. He wished Royce hadn't taken that bait. Because now if Kate ever did find evidence that showed Acreda's harmful side effects, then it would lead back to Royce and implicate him. He could see the Acreda lawsuits starting to form before his eyes.

"So you would consider yourself a hands-on CEO?"

"Absolutely."

"And why is that?"

Royce's eyes lit up. "Because I take great pride in my company, and I need to know that it is functioning properly."

217

"Do you also have an employee by the name of Pierce Worthington?"

"We did, but he resigned a few weeks ago."

"Do you know why?"

"From what I understand, he said he was ready to move on to something different. As long as he doesn't go to one of our competitors, then I'm fine with it. Of course, I hated to lose a good scientist, but I'd hate even more to have a messy legal battle on our hands if he tried to jump ship to our competitors."

"Do you know where Mr. Worthington is now?"

"No, I do not."

"You have no idea where we'd be able to locate Mr. Worthington? No forwarding address or anything?"

"I'm sure human resources has his home address."

"Mr. Hamilton, you have thousands of employees, correct?"

"Yes, we do."

"Then how is it that a CEO of a large corporation like MPC has such intimate knowledge of the details of one of its scientists' departure from the company?"

Royce raised an eyebrow. "Our scientists are the cornerstone of our company. Without them, we have nothing. So, yes, I do make it my business to know what my top-level scientists are doing, especially if they are leaving the company. Pierce isn't a low-level employee. He's at the highest level of scientists we employ."

"And so was Ellie Proctor?"

"Yes, she was."

"You have stringent noncompete provisions with your employees, don't you?"

"For those employees who have access to highly confidential and proprietary information like Pierce did, most definitely. It's industry standard. You'll find it throughout Big Pharma."

Kate leaned forward. "So let me just make sure the record is clear here. It's your testimony that both of your top scientists who worked on developing Celix are no longer available to testify? One is dead and the other is at an unknown location?"

"Objection to form—argumentative, and calls for speculation," Ethan said. He needed to preserve the record. And he wanted to break up Kate's rhythm. He didn't like this entire last line of questioning.

"You still need to answer, Mr. Hamilton," she said.

"I don't agree with your characterization or insinuations. But it is true that Ellie, bless her soul, is no longer with us. And as far as Pierce goes, you'll need to look into that yourself, since he's no longer employed by MPC."

Ethan did his best to keep his cool, but this deposition had shown him one very important thing. Kate was on to something, and he had no idea what it was.

CHAPTER
# NINETEEN

Nicole's team had been feverishly screening all the documents about Acreda. Just as Ethan had instructed, she'd pulled together three of her best young attorneys to review those documents, and they'd made their way through about a third of the data in a week, as they were all working fourteen-hour days—herself included.

She was in the process of reviewing the latest batch of documents that had been flagged for her review when her fingers stopped cold on the keyboard. It was another email from Ellie Proctor to fellow scientist Pierce Worthington. She'd looked at so many documents now that she was completely immersed in all the relevant MPC employees and what they worked on. She reread the email a few more times. The body of it was highly disturbing.

> *Pierce,*
> *Please look at the lab results again for the latest Acreda tests. Its effectiveness in treating all the various types of tumors is off the chart, but I worry that may make our Celix problems much more challenging. You know the powers that be want to move forward on Celix ASAP*

*and these test results may give them the ammunition to do so. I need you to be completely sure about the results, but I want to keep these close to the vest until we have a better handle on how the testing will be used by the decision makers. We can't afford to play with people's lives.*

What did this even mean? It was clear that this document was one hundred percent responsive to the plaintiffs' document requests. They didn't have any basis to withhold it, but she needed to bring it to Ethan's attention right away.

Was this what Ethan had been hiding from her? She intended to find out.

She sent the email to the printer and hopped up from her desk. She grabbed the printout on her way to Ethan's office.

"Is he in there?" she asked his assistant.

"Yes."

Nicole knocked loudly.

"Come in," Ethan said.

She walked into his office and shut the door behind her.

"Uh-oh." He looked up at her, putting down the piece of paper he'd been reading. "What did you find?"

"You need to read this email about Acreda." She placed the document in front of him and let him have a minute to digest its contents. She watched him closely as he scanned the page. His face paled.

"I'm not sure what this means, Nicole."

It was clear to her what needed to be done. "We have to turn this over, Ethan, right? Just like we should be turning over those other documents I brought you a month ago."

"Nicole." He raised his voice. "I think it'd be best if you remember your place. You're an associate, and I am the one running this case."

She refused to back down. If she didn't show she had a backbone right now, what would he think of her? That she would be willing to roll over? No. "I don't care if you are a partner, Ethan. I'm also a member of the bar, and I know what my ethical duties are. I intend to abide by mine, and I want you to do the same."

His jaw twitched. "You're about to cross a line, Nicole. I suggest you take a moment and reconsider what you're saying."

She couldn't believe this man she admired would go down this path. "So what? You want me to destroy evidence? Hide evidence? Because if that's the direction we're going, I want to hear it from your mouth."

He ran his hand through his hair. "Can't you just do as you're told? We have a chain of command at this firm for a reason. You don't get to question that."

"That's where you and I disagree. If you want a yes-woman, then I'm not it. If you want me off the case, then that's fine, but you'll have to find someone else to get up to speed on all of the documents. Someone you can trust. Tell me where you're going to find someone like that."

"What do you want, Nicole?" His voice got even louder. "What would smooth over the situation for you?"

She didn't want to fight with him. "For you to be honest with me. That's all I'm asking. I'm offering my help again."

He walked over to where she sat and placed his hand on her shoulder. "It's not your place. Just keep up the good work you're doing. I'm still trying to find answers myself."

She looked up at him. "If I find any other troublesome documents talking about Acreda and Celix, I should bring them to you?"

"Yes, please. That's all I'm asking of you. If you do this for me, I'll do everything I can for you on your partnership track."

Nicole felt sick to her stomach. He thought she could be bribed. It disturbed her that he thought so little of her reputation and integrity.

"Nicole, remember, you have a duty to zealously defend your client."

She didn't want to hear any more from him. She stood up and walked out of his office. She had a job to do, but she also had a lot of thinking to do. Because she refused to be complicit in this unethical action.

The next day, Nicole sat alone in her office and stared at the folder of documents in front of her. Once she made this decision, there was no turning back. She'd gone through it in her head over and over again.

But there was no way around it. If she chose this path, she could be breaking ethical rules by going outside the normal discovery process. Going rogue and sending the documents anonymously, even if it was for the right reason, might not be acceptable under ethical standards. But the alternative seemed wrong and unjust.

What if she was fired? How would she pay off the remainder of her student loans? As the questions injected fear into her heart, she also thought about what she had been taught in law school, and for that matter, her entire life. *Do the right thing.*

But was the right thing sending these documents to the opposing lawyer in this way? There would be no official cover letter, no document numbering known as Bates stamping, nothing indicating that these documents came from the law firm Peters & Gomez. This would be an outside-the-box way of doing things.

Would she confess that she had done it? Because it was certain the documents would come out. That was the whole point of sending them.

Nicole liked to think she was a good person, but she didn't have a spiritual connection to any particular religion. If she did, now would be the time to pray.

She sealed the envelope. She'd only included a handful of documents, but it was enough. Once she placed the package in the mailbox, it was all over.

She jumped at a loud knock on her door. Before she could even reply, Miles walked in.

"What's going on, Sosa?"

Quickly, she shoved the envelope under a large stack of papers on her desk. "The usual, Miles. What do you need?"

"You've seemed weird lately." He took a seat in one of her two office chairs. "Are you sure everything's okay?"

She nodded. "I think we're just under a lot of stress managing all of the issues with this case."

"Yeah, but normally you're cool as a cucumber, and lately you've been jittery. And you missed a meeting yesterday. You *never* miss a meeting." Miles leaned forward in his seat. "Are you interviewing with other firms? You can tell me if you are. I won't say a word. Your secret will be safe with me."

She couldn't believe he thought she was job hunting. Although that was a preferable alternative to the truth and would most likely be the truth pretty soon. "I'm not interviewing, Miles. I just have a lot on my plate right now."

"You need to delegate more. That's one thing they're going to look for as we transition from midlevels to senior associates. You shouldn't be so down in the weeds every single day. And I know you didn't ask my opinion, but Ethan's being a bit too needy for my liking. Everyone just needs to chill."

If only it were that easy. "Miles, you realize how much pressure Ethan is under to keep this client happy and bring in more business. You should give him a break." For some strange reason, she felt like she needed to defend Ethan even though she didn't agree with how he was handling things.

Miles narrowed his eyes. "I've known you for how long? Since we were summer associates here after our second year in law school, right? And in all that time, you've never acted like this. Something is off, and I know it may seem like I'm oblivious to what goes on around here, but I'm more in tune than you may think."

There was no way she could tell Miles. He wouldn't understand, and he would definitely try to stop her. "Okay. You're clearly not going to let this go. You're right that I'm thinking about other employment." That was the truth, because once Ethan found out what she had done, she wouldn't have a job at Peters & Gomez any longer. Defying her boss on a direct order would certainly get her canned.

He slapped his hand on her desk. "I knew it! Where are you looking to go?"

"I'm keeping my options open right now."

"Would you like to work in-house at a corporation, or are you thinking of lateraling over to another firm?"

"I'm not sure."

Miles looked thoughtful. "You know, this is probably for the best. I don't think you're really cut out for the partner gig here."

Talk about a blow to the chest. "Why do you say that?"

"You're not cutthroat, and you don't care enough about making tons of money."

"Being a partner isn't just about those things."

"True, but if you don't have that edge, it's a lot harder to make partner in the first place."

She knew deep down he was right, but it still hurt to hear it. Although it made her decision about the documents that much easier.

"Don't take it as a criticism," he said. "What I'm trying to say is that you're a better person than most of the rest of us. I've always thought that you'd do better at a plaintiff's firm, actually."

"Student loans make that tough. Here we have a big salary guaranteed."

"You live so frugally, though, that I'm confident you can make it work wherever you land."

She couldn't bear to talk about her future anymore. "What about you? What are your plans?"

"I'm not even sure myself. My family expects that I'll stay here and make partner, but between you and me, I'm not sure that's what I want."

She couldn't help gaping at him. "I thought making partner was the only thing you wanted."

He shook his head. "I know my life has been pretty easy, and I've never wanted for anything, but my goals were always planned by my father. They were never my own. I wanted to go to music school, but after I mentioned that one time, I was quickly told it was out of the question."

She suddenly saw Miles in a different light. Yeah, he could be lazy and cut corners, but it was because his heart wasn't in being a lawyer. It actually made her sad. "I'm sorry, Miles. I never had any idea. I just assumed this life was what you wanted."

"Don't get me wrong, I like having nice things and the perks of the job, but there are definitely other things I'd rather be doing." His cell rang, and he looked down at it. "Sorry, I have to run. I forgot I have a conference call I'm supposed to be jumping on. But if you need to talk more about anything, just let me know."

"Thanks, Miles."

As he exited her office, she had a clearer perspective—not only of him and who he was, but of who she was and what she had to do.

# CHAPTER
# TWENTY

K ate, sorry to interrupt, but you need to look at this." Beth
stood at Kate's door, holding some papers clutched tightly
to her chest.

"What is it?" Kate was immediately concerned, because Beth
was always calm and cool.

"I was opening your mail, but this package was strange. No
return address, which made me think it might be junk mail. But
I started reading the documents that were enclosed, and I think
this is related to your case."

"Let me take a look."

Beth handed her the papers, and Kate started reading. Her
heartbeat sped up with each additional word that she read.
"Beth, do you still have the envelope it came in?"

"Yes. Let me get it."

These were emails she'd never seen before, but they were what
any lawyer who was familiar with this case would call smoking
guns. Emails between Ellie Proctor and Pierce Worthington,
talking about Celix and Acreda.

Beth brought her a nondescript legal-sized envelope. Kate's
name and address had been typed out and printed on paper that
was then taped onto the envelope. No return address.

229

"And were these emails the only thing in there?"

"Yes," Beth said. "I can tell by the look on your face that I was right. This is a big deal, isn't it?"

"Yes, Beth. A huge deal."

"All right. I'm sure you need some time to figure out what you're going to do. I'll leave you alone, but let me know if you need anything."

"Thanks. First, please take these and make some copies, then put them electronically into our system and send them to me via email." She wasn't taking any chances on these documents mysteriously disappearing. She'd store copies in as many places as she could think of.

"I already made copies, so you can keep those. I'll do the electronic filing right away."

"Thank you for recognizing the importance of this and bringing it to me."

Beth shut the door, leaving Kate alone with her thoughts. She looked down and focused on the words Ellie used in her email. *"You know the powers that be want to move forward on Celix ASAP and these test results may give them the ammunition to do so."*

She thought about what Ellie had told her when they'd met. Maybe Kate had been going about this all wrong, and it was never about Acreda's side effects.

Could it be that MPC knew Celix caused brain tumors but pushed the drug to market because they had a cure? Acreda was shown as highly effective at treating all types of tumors—and that might even include brain tumors. The pieces were starting to fall together. There were still some holes, but these emails were crucial.

She'd assumed that Acreda had harmful side effects too and hadn't considered this type of connection between the two drugs. Would MPC have done something this heinous?

Knowingly putting a drug on the market because they would at some later date have another drug that could be used to treat the side effects?

How in the world was she going to show that these emails were legitimate? She'd have to argue before the judge that MPC had wrongfully withheld evidence. Just like she'd argued the last time when she'd put forward her motion to compel.

A tiny piece of her worried that these documents could be fabricated. That this could be a setup. But who would do that? No, it made much more sense that someone on the inside at either MPC or Peters & Gomez had sent her these documents. The question was who.

Her mind immediately went to Ethan. They had a strong friendship built over years, but she had a hard time believing that he would breach his client's trust and send documents outside the normal channels. It was much more believable that he had held these documents back. Either because he wanted to or because he didn't have much choice, given MPC's direction. She'd witnessed firsthand the type of man that Royce Hamilton was. There was ice running through his veins, and she was convinced he'd already ordered a hit on one of his own employees. Maybe Ethan felt threatened.

Regardless, she had to talk to him about this and then go to the judge. But first, she wanted to call Landon. He was going to be floored at this news.

She dialed and waited for him to pick up.

"Is everything okay?" he asked instead of saying hello.

"Yes. Sorry, didn't mean to worry you."

"I'm just not used to you calling during your workday. What's up?"

She filled him in on the special delivery she'd received. "I think that even though Celix caused tumors, MPC believed Acreda would be the solution to the problem. That's why Ellie wanted me to look at other drugs and get all the testing records. She just never got the chance to explain it to me."

"You think MPC's plan was to use one drug to cure the dangerous side effect of the other? That's tantamount to making people sick to cure them for a profit."

Yes, that was exactly what it was. "And both drugs are still patent protected with no generics for years, so MPC stands to make a hefty profit—leveraging one drug against the other and profiting from them both."

"This revelation explodes the whole case. How many documents are we talking here?" he asked.

"Just five. But one of them is really the smoking gun."

"Who in the world would've sent them to you?"

"That was my first question too, and I don't have a great answer. But now I have to tell Ethan about this and hear what I'm sure will be a farfetched explanation for why these haven't been turned over in the discovery process. Then I'll have to go to the judge. Explain what happened and try to get these ruled as admissible."

"Shouldn't the other side have to face some consequence for not giving them to you?"

"Depending on Ethan's explanation, it would be proper for me to file a spoliation motion and even go for sanctions. There are even further implications for trial that would take some time to explain, but this is a game changer."

"That sounds serious."

"It is. Sanctions are a big deal, and they can be levied directly against the law firm."

"Just give me a second to think about all of this. The fact that you have these documents in your possession also increases the risks that you face. MPC may lash out if it feels like it's being backed into a corner."

"The security plan you put in place has been working."

"Yeah, but this is a major escalation on the legal side." He paused. "I hate to do this, but I do have one piece of news."

"Bad news?"

"After a lot of investigating, Cooper was able to track down Pierce leaving the country and entering Mexico. We have no idea where he went from there, but needless to say, he's long gone."

She hung her head. "I was hoping he'd turn up. I wanted to put him on the witness stand."

"Well, unfortunately, that doesn't seem like it's going to happen."

"They killed off and ran off the two people with the most intimate knowledge about Celix and Acreda—and the worst thing is that I can't prove any of that."

"One thing I've learned over the years is that there's always another way."

"Thanks. I'll keep you posted."

She ended the call and immediately called Ethan. It was time for him to face the music.

—◁◇▷—

Ethan knew something was off when Kate practically summoned him to her office. There was no lightness to her voice, none of her usual kindness. Just stern words that held the promise of something he wouldn't like.

He could imagine Kate had many gripes to confront him about. He'd just have to bite the bullet and see what she wanted.

Once he arrived at her office, however, his anxiety started to rise as Beth, who was normally polite and charming, gave him the cold shoulder. Not a single nicety as she led him to Kate's office.

He walked in, and Beth shut the door behind her.

"What's going on, Kate?" He looked at her as she stared him down. This was even worse than he had predicted.

"You should have a seat."

He did as she directed and waited for her to make the next move.

"I got something in the mail today that I want you to look at."

"Sure," he said.

As she slid the pieces of paper in front of him, he saw some of the names on the document, and his stomach sank.

"Why don't you take a minute and read," Kate suggested.

That was exactly what he did. Except one minute quickly turned into ten as he read and reread each document in front of him. Five different email strings, but they were all highly damaging. He wasn't rereading them for content, but to buy himself time. These were the emails Nicole had just found. Had she betrayed him and given these documents to Kate?

But that wasn't even his biggest problem. Right now, he needed an explanation for Kate's accusatory gaze.

"Do those look familiar to you? I assume they do, Ethan." Her cheeks turned crimson.

He couldn't admit to anything. At least not yet. Not while there was so much uncertainty surrounding this situation. "No, I've never seen these. That's why it's taking me so long to read them. I'm confused."

She sighed loudly. "Ethan, do you really think so little of me? C'mon."

This was the most visibly upset he'd ever seen Kate. What bothered him most wasn't that she was angry—it was that she was disappointed in him. "I don't think little of you, Kate. Just the opposite, and you know it." He looked her directly in the eyes, getting ready to test out his acting skills. "I have absolutely no idea where these emails came from, and I've never seen them before."

"I gave you a chance to come clean, but I hope you understand that you haven't given me any other option. I've got to take this to the judge."

"The judge? Don't you think that's a bit premature? You don't even know if these are authentic emails."

"Well, we're going to find out pretty quickly. I want you to be on notice that I will be filing a spoliation motion along with a motion for sanctions."

"You don't have to do that, Kate. We can work this out." This was going off the rails quickly. "Please give me some time to look into this. Just forty-eight hours. As a matter of professional courtesy, and as your friend, I'm asking you that."

"Okay, you have forty-eight hours. Then I'm going to the judge."

"What if I can prove the emails are fake?" He had no idea how he'd make that happen, since he knew they were in fact real, but he had to try something.

"We'll cross that bridge when we get to it, but based on everything I know and have seen, I believe they're one hundred percent legitimate."

She'd opened a door, and he wanted to test the waters. "You said based on everything you know. What exactly are you talking about?"

She cocked her head to the side. "I believe there is a link between the two drugs that MPC doesn't want us to find out about. These emails bolster that fact."

He was operating in the dark, but for the time being, he had to throw her off the trail. "You're way off base, Kate. You're talking crazy talk."

"Am I? I think I'm actually far too close to the truth, and it's making you uncomfortable."

Kate was like a dog that had clamped down on its favorite stuffed animal and refused to let go. He wondered if there was any use in continuing this charade. Maybe he just needed to go. "I'm not uncomfortable, but you've given me a lot of information that I need to run down, including the authenticity of these documents. If there's nothing else, I'm going to leave."

"Forty-eight hours, Ethan. I mean it."

He nodded and stood up, eager to get the heck out of there.

By the time he walked out of the building, he was trying to hold himself back from a full-fledged panic attack. He had to force himself to focus on his breathing—in and out.

He needed to go back to his office. He wanted to talk to Nicole ASAP. This could tank his entire case, and the threat of sanctions was looming. Kate had already set this thing up so well by arguing in her initial motion to compel that they were holding back documents. Judge Freeman was going to lose his mind over this, and rightfully so. He only hoped it wasn't the end of his career—or worse.

# CHAPTER
# TWENTY-ONE

Nicole sat in her office, trying to get work done but instead staring out the window at the Atlanta skyline. It had been two days since she mailed the envelope of documents to the opposing counsel, and it was on her mind around the clock. She'd thought once she sent the documents that she'd be able to sleep again, but man, was she wrong.

Running on caffeine and sugar wasn't good, but that was where she was. Her conversation with Miles still ran through her head. Would she be able to find another job?

That conversation had brought another revelation—Miles didn't like being a lawyer. She couldn't help herself as she laughed out loud. They were both chasing goals they didn't really want. She needed partnership for the stability and to pay off her loans. He needed it to please his family.

A piece of her wished she had opened up to him. Maybe he would have understood, but it was too late now. She would just have to see how it played out.

Ethan showed up in her office about an hour later. It was even quicker than she'd anticipated.

"We need to talk." He shut the door before taking a seat.

There was no doubt in her mind why he was there, but she was going to let him lead the conversation.

"I'm going to ask you a question, Nicole." His green eyes focused directly on her. "And I need you to be completely honest with me. Do you understand?"

She nodded. "Yes, I do." He looked even more nervous than she felt, and that was saying a lot. Her stomach churned.

"Did you send a set of MPC documents to Kate Sullivan?" His face reddened with each word out of his mouth.

She'd already decided there was no point trying to lie to him. "Yes, I did."

He let out a breath, and his shoulders slumped. "What in the world were you thinking? Do you realize what you've done?"

"I didn't make the decision lightly. I agonized over it, and I realize there will be dire personal consequences."

"This isn't just about you, Nicole. It's bigger than that."

"Ethan, it was wrong to withhold those documents. You and I both know it. I couldn't live with myself, knowing I was party to that type of behavior."

"So you thought doing something stupid was the solution?" he asked in a raised voice.

"Like I said, I knew there would be consequences, but I had to be able to get up in the morning and look at myself in the mirror." She paused, wondering how far to push this. "And I think, deep down, you wanted to do the same thing, but given your position, it was impossible. We want to win, Ethan. We want to defend our clients. But if we lose our integrity and ethics, then what do we have left?"

A vein in his neck popped out. "You really have no idea how big of a mess this is. There are going to be extreme consequences. The first being that you're fired. You need to pack up and get out of here."

"I understand."

"No, I don't think you do. Kate is going to file a motion for sanctions."

Oh no. A sanctions order was highly damaging to the entire firm's reputation as well as that of the lawyers involved in the case. It wasn't just about the money. "I didn't even think of that."

"Of course you didn't. Because you weren't thinking this through. I have to decide how to play this thing with the court, and even more important, the client."

"You can throw me under the bus."

He shook his head. "It's not nearly that simple. If I tell your story, the true story, I'm implicating myself."

"And what are you going to tell everyone here about why I'm gone?"

"That you left to pursue other opportunities." He let out a string of curses. "I could never trust you again after this. You've put me in an awful position."

The tears started to stream down her face. "I know, and for that I'm truly sorry. I don't know what else I can say."

"It probably works best for both of us if your name doesn't come out in all of this. I need to figure out what the story's going to be. Regardless, you can't breathe a word about this to anyone. Am I clear?"

"Crystal clear. I'll get out of here right away."

He stood up and took a step toward the door before turning back. "You threw everything away, Nicole. I hope in the end you'll think it was worth it."

He closed the door, and more tears started to flow. What was she going to do?

Ethan splashed water on his face in the men's restroom—a practice that was becoming all too common for him. Today was shaping up to be one of the worst of his career. He had big decisions to make, and he didn't know which path to take. None of them were good options.

There was a good chance Royce would fire him when he found out about this. No, there had to be another way. A way to argue to Judge Freeman and convince Royce that his firm wasn't behind these leaked documents and that, in fact, no one on his team had ever seen them. That they weren't even authentic.

It was a pretty unbelievable explanation, but he did have something going for him. It was also unbelievable that someone from Ethan's firm would have given those documents to the other side. No one except he and Nicole knew the truth. Well, that wasn't entirely true. Whoever reviewed the documents in the first place would know, but they were so low-level that they'd never see the courtroom or the client. He'd make sure of that. Damage control—that was what he had to do.

His larger problem was the content of the emails. He had to figure out what MPC had done with both drugs, because he suspected they'd gone well outside the law this time. He needed to understand the full story of what Ellie and Pierce were discussing in those emails.

Taking another deep breath, he exited the restroom and returned to his office. Royce was going to flip when he heard the news.

Then an idea hit him. He knew Royce was already locking things down at MPC. That he had suspicions about his employees. That was why the security guy Bradley had been so involved lately. Ethan's best and only chance was to make Royce think that someone from his own team had leaked the documents.

The judge was going to be upset regardless, but Ethan could deal with that heat. What he couldn't afford was to get fired off the case.

For this plan to have any shot at succeeding, he was going to have to go in hard at Royce. He couldn't show an ounce of fear or the possibility that this could have come from his team. He would have to be angry and act like someone at MPC was trying to bring them down.

With that strategy in mind, he grabbed his keys and headed to Royce's office. Best to show up unannounced and make a noisy entrance. If he was going to convince Royce, this had to be good.

By the time he walked into the MPC building, his confidence was building. His conscience, on the other hand, was taking a beating, but he could engage in self-loathing later. For now, desperate times called for even more desperate measures.

He strode up to Penny's desk, and she looked up from her computer. "Oh, Mr. Black, is Mr. Hamilton expecting you?"

"No, but it's an emergency. I need to speak with him right away."

"Of course. Let me go check, and I'll be right out."

He could have just stormed directly into Royce's office, but he didn't want to overplay his hand. There would be plenty of time for theatrics.

Penny came back toward him, and she had Royce by her side.

"What's all this about?" Royce asked him.

"We need to talk."

"Come on back, then," Royce said. "Matt and I were just going over the quarterly financials."

Royce ushered Ethan into his large office suite. Matt was sitting at the conference room table with stacks of papers spread out in front of him.

It looked like Ethan would have to sell both of them on the story.

"Ethan has something urgent to talk to us about," Royce said.

"We have a disaster on our hands," he started.

"I presume you're being a bit melodramatic?" Royce asked.

Ethan shook his head. "I only wish that were true. Someone

from your company sent Kate Sullivan five documents containing highly inflammatory emails. Emails about Celix and Acreda. Emails that Kate now plans to take before Judge Freeman within forty-eight hours."

"What? What kind of emails?" Royce's loud voice reverberated through the office suite.

Ethan slapped copies of the emails down on the table. "Here. I need you to look at them. They're full of innuendo, but I think I'm missing some pieces to this puzzle. If you guys have been holding back on me even when I've asked you not to, then you need to realize we're at the breaking point. Take a look at these and start telling me what you know." He watched them read, looking for any tells.

Royce walked over to his phone and hit the intercom. "Penny, get Bradley Cummings into my office ASAP."

"Yes, sir," she responded.

Royce started cursing and pacing as he reread the papers. Matt was his usual calm self, but a deep frown marred his face. So far, so good. At least as far as Ethan's plan went. His larger problem still loomed, though. He had to figure out what in the world was going on.

Royce lifted one of the papers in his hand. "I have no idea what Ellie's talking about." He looked at Matt. "Do you?"

Matt shook his head. "This is all news to me."

"You guys are the two most powerful executives in the company. I find it hard to believe you'd both be in the dark here. A jury will think the same thing and ask the same questions. All I know about Acreda is what you two have told me. I need you to fess up about how exactly Acreda is linked to this lawsuit." He paused, trying to keep his temper in check. "We are way past the point of keeping these types of secrets."

"I think what we're trying to say is that we're just as confused about these emails as you are," Matt said. "Could these have been fabricated? What if Ellie had some sort of ax to grind that we don't even know about?"

A knock on the door was followed by Bradley entering the room. "You asked to see me?"

"Fill him in, Ethan."

He gave Bradley the rundown he'd given Royce and Matt plus a few details about the documents in question.

"Bradley," Royce said, "there are two issues. The first is tracking down who in the company knows about any links between the two drugs. Second, it seems like we've got a mole, and we need to ferret him or her out ASAP. Because if they've done this, who knows what they'll do next. Do you think Pierce could've done this?"

Bradley shook his head. "No. This kind of action doesn't fit Pierce. He would never have gone to the other side's lawyer, even if he had concerns."

"Well, then it has to be another of your employees." The lie rolled easily off Ethan's tongue. "And this has put us all in a very precarious situation. I'll get in trouble because it looks like we withheld evidence. MPC will get sanctioned too, probably."

"I don't care about a monetary sanction," Royce barked.

"You might not, but I bet you'll care about an adverse inference ruling by the judge. Kate's going to go for the jugular on this. She'll argue spoliation—the wrongful withholding or destruction of evidence."

"What's an adverse inference?" Matt asked.

"The judge could structure it a couple different ways. The worst-case scenario is that the judge tells the jury they can actually presume that certain facts are true because the evidence has been wrongfully withheld or destroyed. And those facts would be very bad facts against us. Even under the best-case scenario, the judge will *allow* the jury to presume that the evidence is favorable to the plaintiffs. So even without the introduction of the evidence, it could be game over."

"You can't be serious," Royce said. "What kind of justice system is that?"

"One that doesn't look favorably on withholding evidence, and it gets worse, because in this instance, the evidence still exists. Kate could argue that these documents should be introduced, and that she should *also* get the adverse inference because other documents might have been destroyed or withheld."

Royce's face turned scarlet, and he hauled off and punched his fist into the wall. Ethan couldn't quite stop himself from flinching.

Bradley leapt forward. "Sir, are you okay?"

Royce said a few choice words as he shook out his hand.

Matt led Royce back to his chair. "Sit down and get yourself together. We need to think," he snapped.

This was the first time Ethan had ever seen Matt frazzled. He wanted Royce to get riled up, but not so much that everything exploded right before his eyes. That could also lead to Royce making a rash decision. He appreciated that Matt hadn't gone completely off the deep end yet. This was a delicate game Ethan was trying to play.

"Let's back up for a minute," Matt said. "What's the significance of the forty-eight-hour clock?"

"Kate told me she was going directly to the judge to file a motion today. I asked her for time."

"And she gave it to you, just like that?" Bradley asked.

"We've been friends for a long time. I tried to convince her that I had no idea what was going on. I also questioned the authenticity of the documents."

"So she gave you the extension out of the goodness of her heart?" Bradley asked with a raised eyebrow.

"That's just Kate."

"I'm not buying it," Bradley said. "Something doesn't add up. If she wanted to go for the jugular like you said, then why even tell you about it?"

"Because Kate plays by the book. The judge would expect her to confer with me before filing the motion. She isn't one to bend the rules, not even a tiny bit. And that kind of rule bending is exactly why we're now in this predicament."

"Enough squabbling," Royce yelled. "We need to stop the bleeding and figure a way out of this mess. I want all our scientists who were on the Celix team put on lockdown and questioned. This has to be a top priority."

"And exactly how do you think you can do that?" Ethan asked, truly curious how something like that could take place.

"Let me worry about that," Bradley said. "We have contingency plans in case of dire security breaches, and I would call this one dire."

"Is there anything we're missing?" Royce asked. "Is there any other way those documents could've gotten into Kate's hands?"

"Well, your boy here could've found them in our system through his document collection and given them to her," Bradley said with a glare.

"That is beyond ridiculous," Ethan replied. And that much was true. "That would be totally against my own self-interest. I want to win this case. There's no way I would sabotage myself. We're all on the same side here." He tried to keep his voice down, but he couldn't let these kinds of thoughts infiltrate Royce's mind.

"If you ask me, you're a bit too close to Kate Sullivan," Bradley said.

"And our closeness has only worked in our favor up to this point. Why don't you let me focus on my job as MPC's lawyer, and you on yours? Get your people in line before it's too late."

"Ethan's right, Bradley," Matt said. "We need to get our house in order. Let Ethan deal with the legal ramifications. We simply can't afford more of our dirty laundry to get out there."

But the bigger question still loomed large in Ethan's mind. "You have to figure out what's going on with these two drugs. Because if you're both telling me the truth, then someone else at this company may have made decisions that now threaten the entire corporation."

"We're on it," Matt said. "I can guarantee you that."

Ethan took a step toward the door. "If you find out anything new here, please keep me posted. My strategy will be to tell the judge that we've never seen these documents before. But I'll plan for the worst-case scenario, because it's highly unlikely he'll think we're innocent in all of this."

"Do whatever you have to do. We're at war," Royce said.

And war it was. But Ethan was no longer sure who he was fighting against.

Kate picked up the phone on the second ring because she recognized Ethan's number. The forty-eight hours she had given him was almost up, but she wasn't surprised he'd taken nearly the entire time. She also wasn't sure what he was going to come back at her with, but she figured he wouldn't outright confess to wrongfully withholding evidence. The repercussions of that admission would be too severe.

"Kate, it's Ethan."

"I've been waiting for your call." She flipped her pen around in her hand.

"You said forty-eight hours. I'm still under that."

"And what do you have for me?"

"You can file whatever you think you need to with the judge. Our position is that a rogue employee sent you these documents.

They were not collected by my firm and have never been seen in our discovery process. We were caught just as off guard as you. We're not even sure they are authentic."

*Wow.* He was digging an even deeper hole for himself. "Ethan, I'm going to give you one opportunity to take that back. As your friend, not as your opposing counsel, I'd urge you to reconsider your response."

"I'm not reconsidering, Kate, because it's the truth. I told you when you showed me the documents that I had never seen them before, and I've confirmed with my team that no one else has either. Someone on the inside at MPC who is motivated by ill will must have sent them to you."

"How would this supposed employee even have access to these emails?"

"You and I both know there are ways to get into a company's email server, especially if you're on the inside."

"Wait. Even if what you're saying is true, and I have serious doubts about that, how does that make it any better? The documents still say what they say—which means that MPC knew about the side effects and had some sort of plan to launch Celix because Acreda would be there to pick up the pieces."

"That's a leap. You're reading things into those documents that don't exist. First, we don't know that they're authentic at this juncture, and second, they're simply a back-and-forth between two scientists that contains pure speculation. There's nothing concrete or specific in them. And none of my witnesses have any personal knowledge about them. I've already asked. I will lodge multiple evidentiary objections to their admissibility."

"You've got to be kidding me." Who was this man, and what had happened to the guy she'd known all these years? Had the firm and MPC corrupted him so badly that he would go to these lengths to subvert the truth?

"I don't think there's anything else for us to discuss," Ethan said. "I'll respond to your motion once it's filed."

Kate hung up the phone and took a second to replay the conversation in her head. Would the judge really believe this concocted story? *Was* she reading too much into the emails? He was right that the documents didn't spell out an exact link between the two drugs. But there was enough there to make her believe her theory was right. Granted, the discussion was only between two scientists, but she didn't think a judge would buy Ethan's desperate attempt to explain it away.

Regardless, now that she knew what he was planning to argue, she could try to preempt those claims accordingly in her motion. She needed more coffee. It was going to be a long night, because she wanted to file this first thing in the morning.

Around eleven o'clock, she heard a knock on her office door and knew it was Landon.

"You're burning the midnight oil," he said.

"Well, technically it's not midnight yet."

He laughed and walked over to her. He placed his hands on her shoulders and squeezed. "I worry about you. You've been putting in crazy hours for weeks now."

"I told you this is just part of the lead-up to trial."

"Yeah, but I can't help being concerned," he said softly.

He gently massaged her shoulders, and she closed her eyes for a second. If she kept them closed much longer, she'd fall asleep. Even though she'd been drinking coffee for the past few hours, her energy was quickly fading.

"How's the motion coming?" He stepped back and leaned against the edge of her desk.

She forced her eyes open again. "Good, but I think I'm too emotionally invested. I want to make it perfect. I've dealt with some pretty dicey situations before in document discovery, but never anything this blatantly egregious. And I haven't even told you the best part yet."

"What's that?"

She looked up into his dark eyes and realized just how much she enjoyed sharing her world with him. She hoped that once the trial was over, they'd still be able to continue building a connection. "I spoke to Ethan this afternoon."

"Oh, this is going to be good."

"He claims he has no knowledge of the documents and that some employee from MPC with an ax to grind sent them to me, and that the emails are pure speculation. He'll try to get them excluded on evidentiary grounds."

"Would that be possible?"

"The judge could exclude them, especially since I don't have a witness to get the documents in through, with Ellie gone and Pierce MIA. It's a brilliant plan on their part. That's why this motion is so important. I need to get my hands on documents that include someone I can actually put on the witness stand."

He took her hand. "I get that. But you also don't need to stay here all night."

"You're right. I think it's good to go. I'll proof it again in the morning and then get it filed with the court."

"Then Ethan gets a chance to respond?"

"Yes. But I've framed this as an emergency motion, so Ethan will have to file a response very quickly. I've asked for a hearing to be scheduled immediately, given the nature of the issue. Hopefully, we can get in front of the judge this week."

"Let's get you out of here and home safe."

She wondered if she'd ever be safe as long as MPC had a target on her back—a target that had just gotten bigger.

# TWENTY-TWO

The week flew by, but she'd been right about the hearing date. Judge Freeman must have been so intrigued by her motion and Ethan's response that he scheduled an immediate hearing for Friday. She was glad that she'd made an emergency request instead of just letting the normal timelines dictate the schedule. Spoliation of evidence was a serious offense, and she didn't take her accusations lightly.

She needed to put on her game face and get ready to confront Ethan. Landon was all business and in security mode, but she didn't feel threatened while in the courthouse. There was no way MPC would be so bold as to attack her in broad daylight in public like that. But she let Landon do his thing as he escorted her into the courtroom. Cooper was also there to provide backup.

Ethan was already in the courtroom, seated at his counsel's table, and didn't even acknowledge her. Any hope she had for their friendship surviving this case was pretty much lost. Maybe there would be a way to repair the damage in the future, but after all the lies, she wasn't so sure. She prayed that he wasn't behind the attacks against her. She couldn't bear to think of that possibility.

She got herself settled and waited only a couple minutes before Judge Freeman entered the courtroom.

Judge Freeman locked eyes on her and started talking. "Ms. Sullivan, I have your emergency motion regarding spoliation in front of me. Given the seriousness and complexity of the issue at hand, I agreed that it was best for us to get together and have this hearing before any fuller briefing was done on the subject. Since this is your motion, please proceed."

"Thank you, Your Honor. I appreciate you acting so quickly. When I came before you last time, I argued that we believed MPC was withholding relevant documents. You provided MPC with another chance to ensure that they were fully abiding by their obligations under the federal rules of civil procedure." She paused for a moment to catch her breath. Adrenaline was kicking in, making her talk too fast.

"At the end of last week, I received an envelope of documents in the mail. They were sent to me at my office with no return address. The envelope included five emails that I attached to the motion as Exhibit A. These highly inflammatory documents were never turned over during the discovery process. I immediately contacted Mr. Black, showed him the documents, and discussed filing the present motion. He asked for forty-eight hours to investigate the issue, which I gave to him as a matter of professional courtesy. Mr. Black came back to me at the end of the forty-eight hours with excuses that I did not find reasonable, truthful, or believable. It was at that time that I filed this motion. We can get into the substance of the emails if you'd like, but I think the threshold question for Your Honor is one of spoliation."

Judge Freeman nodded. "You're right, Ms. Sullivan. I'd like to hear what Mr. Black's position is on this matter."

Was Ethan going to lie to the court? The implications of that would be staggering.

Ethan stood up. "Thank you, Your Honor. I also appreciate you taking up this important issue quickly. When I met with Ms. Sullivan in her office to discuss this topic, it was the first time I'd ever seen these emails. No one on my team at Peters & Gomez reviewed these documents. So as to the issue of Ms. Sullivan's sanctions request against Peters & Gomez, I'd respectfully argue that it should be denied, since we were unaware that those emails existed."

Judge Freeman looked at his computer and then back toward Ethan. "That's only one piece of the puzzle, Mr. Black. Let's assume that I believe your proffer to this Court. The bottom line is that these documents still ended up in Ms. Sullivan's hands. How exactly did that happen?"

"Your Honor, I believe that an employee at MPC took it upon themselves to send these documents to Ms. Sullivan. But there is a bigger issue—whether those emails are even authentic. My team has been investigating, and as far as we can tell at this preliminary stage, these emails did not get pulled into our data collection. They could have been fabricated."

"So your position is that someone at MPC was disgruntled and either fabricated these documents or found documents that your professional, top-of-the-line vendor didn't pick up? And that this employee then sent these documents to Ms. Sullivan?"

"That's exactly it, Your Honor."

Judge Freeman raised an eyebrow. "Doesn't that all seem a little farfetched, Mr. Black?"

"Your Honor . . ."

"One more thing, actually," Judge Freeman interrupted. "Has your document vendor been brought into this investigation you've undertaken to examine why these emails were not picked up?"

"We haven't had time to get them fully on board and up to speed yet. We had to conduct our own internal investigation at the firm first to make sure we had all of the facts."

Judge Freeman shook his head. "That's unacceptable. You've been accused of spoliation. You're a seasoned attorney. A partner at a highly prestigious law firm. You know that the first call you make is to the vendor who actually conducted the electronic collection of documents from your client. I fear that if I let you keep talking, you're just going to dig yourself into an even bigger hole, Mr. Black. Consider carefully before you add to this already problematic scenario."

Kate sucked in a breath. Judge Freeman wasn't buying Ethan's story.

"Your Honor, I'm presenting you the facts as I know them," Ethan said.

"And I will rule on the facts as I see them, Mr. Black," Judge Freeman said. "I think I've heard enough. We don't even need to get into the substance of the emails at this juncture."

"Your Honor, I'd ask that you give us more time to present a fuller explanation of the facts," Ethan said.

"Mr. Black, your explanation defies logic. There are too many holes in your story. You're not fresh out of law school, and you know better. My ruling is as follows. First, sanctions in the amount of fifty thousand dollars each are levied against MPC and against the law firm Peters & Gomez. Second, at the trial I will provide the jury with an adverse inference instruction, and that instruction will be included in the written order. And finally, I'm ordering MPC to immediately produce all responsive documents no later than a week from today. If more documents are wrongfully withheld, the sanctions will be tripled."

The judge said no more, and Kate looked over at Ethan, who had turned pale. She couldn't help but feel sorry for him despite the lies.

But she'd just won a huge victory. An adverse inference instruction could turn the tide of the entire case.

That evening, Landon sat beside Kate in her living room as usual. She could tell the day in court had stressed him out. She had insisted that she would be safe at the courthouse, but he wasn't so sure. As the case continued to go against MPC, his anxiety level had skyrocketed. He kept telling her that he was determined not to let her down.

"It was intense in there today," he said.

"Tell me about it. It's not every day that I go for sanctions, much less actually prevail."

"This is going to have a big impact for you at trial."

"Yeah, and it makes settlement almost impossible. MPC would never meet our demands, and we have no incentive to settle, given this turn of events. We have way too much going for us. And that means I've got to be completely at the top of my game. There's no room for error here."

"I know you can do it." He reached over and took her hand.

Warmth spread through her at his touch. "Thanks for believing in me. You told me that I wasn't fighting this thing alone, and I'm so glad you're by my side."

"Kate," he said softly. "Tell me I'm not crazy, thinking that there's something happening between you and me."

She couldn't deny it. Wouldn't deny it. "You're not crazy."

His hand tightened on hers. "I haven't had real feelings for anyone in years. Feelings built on something deeper than just superficial qualities. With each day that passes, I want to know more about you. But you have to realize that I'm a broken man. I don't know that I could ever be the man you deserve."

It hurt to hear him say that, as nothing could be further from the truth. "We're all broken. But I take it one day at a time and put one foot in front of the other, trying not to live in the past.

And I truly believe that we met each other and are working on this case together for a reason."

"You believe God brought us together?"

"I think you feel it too."

He reached out with his other hand and gently touched her cheek, sending a spark through her. "You've led me to a place where I can walk a different path. Where I can be a different man. I can't deny that. Especially when I think about the darkness that surrounded my heart and mind since that night in Iraq."

"I want to be here for you, Landon. I want to spend more time with you. I don't want this to end."

"Me either," he said, longing in his eyes.

Her pulse quickened as he let go of her hand and slid his fingers around the back of her neck, drawing her near to him.

For a moment, it was like time stood still. She put aside all thoughts of the case, all the anxiety that had gripped her, the dark nightmares that invaded her sleep. Tonight it was just about Landon.

His other hand still on her cheek, he guided her even closer to him. But still their lips didn't touch. As they stared into each other's eyes, it was like they came to a silent understanding that they were about to jump into uncharted waters. And she was ready to dive in.

Before she could say another word, his warm lips were on hers with a sense of purpose and passion she had never felt from any other man.

She kissed him back, making sure he understood her feelings for him too. During this turbulent time, he had been there for her in every way. Together they were building something that could withstand the most difficult of times.

As he deepened the kiss, she let herself get lost in him. When he eased back, she looked up into his dark eyes, not knowing what to say but feeling like words weren't even necessary at that moment.

Since he had taken the first step, she wanted him to know that she was right there with him. She took his hand in hers and squeezed, holding on tightly.

"I've been thinking about doing that for a long time," he said.

"Me too. It's nice being with you like this. Sharing our evenings together. Although I do wish it were under different circumstances."

"Yes, but one day this case will be over, and we can stop looking over our shoulders and move on. Together."

She prayed that would be true.

The next morning Ethan waited in the reception area of Royce's suite. They had to talk about the judge's order and next steps. He dreaded facing Royce again, but he had resigned himself to the fact that everything about this case was pure torture. If he had to go back and do it all over again, he would prefer to have lost the pitch and not gotten the business. He wasn't sure if any of this was going to be worth it. The firm certainly didn't like having a sanctions order on their record.

When Penny led him into Royce's office, he was disappointed to see that Royce also had Bradley and Matt with him. Ethan was beginning to think that Bradley had a much bigger role in all of this, and he didn't trust him.

"Come on in, Ethan. I filled Matt and Bradley in on what happened at the hearing."

Ethan took a deep breath. "We need to figure out a game plan, because right now the deck is stacked against us."

"There's something we want to talk to you about," Royce said. "Bradley had his tech gurus look into the situation. Tell Ethan what you found."

257

Bradley crossed his arms. "We've got no evidence of a leak on our end. We have very robust tracking of all of our employees. I can pull up a log of everything they print. No one in our internal system printed these emails. Ever. And they were never forwarded electronically. Which means that they didn't come from MPC."

"What are you implying?" Ethan asked.

"Oh, I'm not implying anything. I'm outright saying it." Bradley cocked his head to the side, challenging Ethan to defy him.

Matt held up his hand, silencing Bradley. "What Bradley is trying to say is that we might have a misunderstanding on our hands, and we want to resolve it before it escalates any further. We all have too much on the line."

"I don't understand," Ethan said, trying to play dumb.

"Now is your chance to come clean," Royce said. "Did you or someone at your firm send those documents to Kate Sullivan?"

Ethan quickly considered his options. He hadn't foreseen MPC having such a robust security tracking system on their computers. He could try to make up some other story, but that seemed unlikely to satisfy these guys.

He hated to throw Nicole under the bus, but really, did he have a choice? He'd given it his best shot.

"Your silence speaks volumes," Bradley said.

"I did not send those documents to Kate, but . . ."

"But what?" Royce asked.

"One of my associates did."

Bradley pounded his fist down on the desk. "I knew it."

"And why didn't you tell me this to begin with?" Royce asked.

"Because I knew you'd be angry, and rightfully so, if you found out your own law firm was working against you.

"But I don't understand. Why did this person send the documents to Kate?" Matt asked.

"Because they thought it was unethical to withhold them."

Royce's laughter surprised Ethan. It really wasn't something to laugh about.

"You're telling me our entire case could be blown because of one idiotic lawyer's conscience?" Royce asked.

He didn't respond because there was nothing good to say.

"Unbelievable," Bradley said.

"I fired them, so you don't have to worry about this happening again." He hoped that extreme punishment would be enough for Royce.

"For now, we need to figure out our next move," Matt interjected.

"I talked to Kate, and their settlement number went up to one billion."

Matt scowled. "That's not even a viable offer. They know we'd never get board approval for that."

"Unfortunately, they're like sharks with blood in the water right now," he said. "We're in absolutely the worst negotiating position possible."

"I want to hear alternatives other than settlement, because that number is not feasible," Royce said.

"Our best chance is to argue a new motion to limit the adverse inference ruling and try to get the documents thrown out on other grounds, but depending on how broad the adverse inference ruling is, the documents themselves may not even matter. And on that note, we need to know if there is anything else in all the data we collected that is like those documents. So far, we've come up with nothing. Anything from your end?"

"No." Bradley jumped in. "In fact, those emails were the only ones I could isolate that had both the words Acreda and Celix in them. There's nothing else. I'm sure of it."

"There has to be someone in this company who knows what's

going on with those drugs. Someone had to make the decisions. You guys need to tell me everything for me to be able to vigorously put on your defense."

"Believe me," Royce said, "we're leaving no stone unturned. But as Bradley said, the email traffic isn't showing anything, and I know that neither Matt nor I could've cooked up something like this. Putting a drug on the market with some known side effects is one thing. But those documents insinuate we did it as part of a grander plan with our Acreda launch, and that just wasn't the case."

Was Royce lying to his face? Ethan had lost all confidence in his ability to read this man. "Ellie Proctor sure believed that MPC did, and now she's dead. Kate is going to have a field day with that at trial. You guys have to realize how this looks."

"Bradley's done some digging into Ellie's background," Matt said. "He'll give you the file, Ethan. There's plenty of stuff in there to discredit her. She was very troubled and, ironically, addicted to prescription drugs. I think she was delusional about this whole thing. You'll be able to destroy her credibility in the courtroom."

"I'll do the best I can. Assuming you want me to continue as your counsel, given these latest events."

Royce stood up and loomed over Ethan, who still sat in his chair. "You're in this too deep to get out now, Ethan. I expect your full attention on this, and you better make good on this mistake. If not, you're going to have a lot bigger problems to deal with. Do you understand?"

Now Bradley *and* Royce had threatened him. There was no way out.

"Thanks for coming to dinner, Sosa." Miles smiled at her. He'd insisted on picking up the check.

"Thanks for dragging me out. It's been a rough couple of weeks."

"About that," he said. "I tried to stay away from the topic over dinner, but now that we're done, are you going to tell me what actually happened? Why you just picked up and left? Because it's obvious you don't have another job lined up."

Nicole had told Ethan that she wouldn't tell anyone. But after the solitude of the past week and the fear of what was going to happen to her career, she really needed a friend right now. And although she'd thought all these years that Miles was her chief competitor, she no longer viewed him that way.

"It's a long story."

"I'm not going anywhere."

She started at the beginning. Finding the initial email. Showing it to Ethan. The whole nine yards, all the way up through him firing her.

"Wow, Nicole. Just wow." Miles ran his hand through his hair.

"This may be the first time I've ever seen you at a loss for words."

"Because I'm in shock. I had no idea this is what was going on with you. I had all kinds of scenarios in my head, but never this. I have to ask why. Why did you risk everything?"

"I believed it was the right thing to do. I couldn't live with myself, knowing that we had an obligation to turn over that evidence and we didn't."

His blue eyes widened. "My mind is completely blown right now. What're you going to do?"

"Now you know why I was avoiding your calls and texts. I'm not sure. I need some time to come to terms with everything."

"So you believe MPC knowingly did all the things the plaintiffs are claiming?"

"I do. And without that evidence, they may have gotten off without any liability. That's not justice, Miles. That's cheating and evading the system, pure and simple. I get that what I did was also wrong, but I took the documents to Ethan and made my case. He wasn't having it, so I had to take drastic measures in order to live with myself." Just talking to someone about this made her feel better—like a load was being lifted from her shoulders.

Miles looked away for a few moments, his gaze focused somewhere in the distance. "I'm just thinking out loud here, but what if you go to the bar ethics committee proactively? Make your case before you get reported. I think they'll be totally sympathetic to the fact that your supervisor told you to withhold relevant evidence. Ethan stands to get in trouble, not you. But you want to get out in front of this, in case Ethan reports you and tells a different version of the story and tries to hold you responsible for withholding evidence."

"I'm not looking to get Ethan in trouble."

"I know you're not, but you have to look out for yourself, Sosa. You know that if his back were up against the wall, he'd blame you in a heartbeat. You need to start thinking strategically here."

She let his points sink in. Maybe Miles was right. Maybe she needed to go directly to the Georgia Bar and ask for help. "You're right. I'll go down to their office tomorrow. See what I can find out."

"That's great." He reached over and touched her arm. "I'm here for you. I know I don't come off as a highly reliable guy, but I come through for my friends when they need me."

Miles continued to surprise her. "Thank you. And thank you for dinner."

"If you get short on cash while you're sorting everything out, don't hesitate to ask."

She'd never do that, but it was sweet of him to offer. "It's getting late. We should probably get out of here."

"Let me walk you to your car."

She thanked him again for everything and then drove home to her condo. She was fortunate to have found a friend in Miles. Maybe, just maybe, she could somehow make a fresh start out of all of this.

## CHAPTER
# TWENTY-THREE

K ate was ready for trial. The question was whether Landon was. She'd never seen him so on edge. He was convinced that security needed to be tighter at the courthouse. She'd relented and let him and the guys come up with an elaborate plan, but she thought it was overkill. She'd put her foot down at Noah's suggestion of bomb-sniffing dogs. The former ATF agent was an explosives expert, but she had to be the voice of reason to rein the men in.

It was only two weeks until the first bellwether trial started. She looked over at Landon as he drove her home from the office. His hands were clenched tightly on the wheel. No doubt he was wound up.

There was no point in trying to make small talk. She was tired and he was preoccupied, but that was okay. Once this trial was over, she hoped they'd be able to have a fresh start. Be able to act like normal people instead of her always looking over her shoulder and him escorting her everywhere, thinking about threats instead of just being together.

She continued to pray for him as he reconnected with the Lord. She could see it wasn't an easy process for him, but his commitment renewed her faith as well. To know that she had a role in his emotional and spiritual healing meant a lot to her.

Bright headlights from the car behind them broke her out of her thoughts. She turned around. "Isn't that car getting really close to us?"

"Yeah," he said. "Check your seat belt and hold on. Something isn't right here."

They were in the suburbs now, only a couple minutes from her house. The winding roads didn't lend themselves to high speeds, but Landon suddenly floored it. The Wrangler accelerated and took the first curve well. She craned her neck to see the large SUV behind them.

"They're speeding up too." Her pulse thumped wildly. "This is intentional, isn't it?" She knew the answer to the question before he even said anything.

"Just hold on. I'm going to try some moves." His voice was steady but stern.

She started to pray as they took the next winding turn. It was a good thing it was nighttime, because at least there wouldn't be any children playing in the streets. She would never fly down a neighborhood road like this, but they didn't have much of a choice.

The first contact from the rear caught her off guard. Her head snapped forward from the impact. "They just rear-ended us!"

"Yeah, and they're going to do it again. Brace yourself."

This time she was prepared for the hard bump from behind, but it still jarred her body.

"Are you okay?" he asked.

She'd bitten her lip, and blood tinged her tongue. "Yeah. Just keep going." She didn't want him to slow down on her account—just the opposite. They needed to get away from that SUV.

"When I get the chance, I'm going to make a sudden turn off the street."

"Got it." Her head whipped forward again at the strongest hit yet.

"Get ready," he said.

She held her breath and tightly gripped her seat. With one swift turn of the wheel, Landon drove his Wrangler into someone's yard. The large black SUV flew by them. Landon did an immediate one-eighty turn, floored it, and started driving the other direction.

"Are they going to keep coming after us?" She looked back, trying to see the other vehicle.

He glanced over at her. "I'm not going to wait around to find out. We're getting out of here."

"Where are we going?"

"Not sure yet. I need to call Cooper, but I want to make sure the situation is secure first by putting some distance between us and them."

Her heart continued to pound as she forced herself to take a few deep breaths. Maybe Landon had been right to be so focused on her safety. Neither of them believed this was random. Someone was after her, and that someone had been sent by MPC.

They rode in silence for a few minutes, and she kept watch. There was no sign of the dangerous SUV, and she got her breathing back under control.

Landon pulled out his phone and dialed Cooper, filling him in on the details. Cooper suggested that the two of them come to his place to regroup.

They drove about fifteen minutes to Cooper's house. She practically jumped out of the Jeep when they arrived, eager to be out of the car.

Landon walked around to her side of the vehicle. "Are you sure you're all right? Do you need to see a doctor?"

She touched her neck. "I think I'll be sore, but I don't think it's anything serious." She looked up at him. "How about you?"

"I'm fine. I've experienced much worse. Let's get you inside."
He placed his hand on the small of her back and led her to
Cooper's door.

Cooper opened it and ushered them inside. "Glad you two
are all right."

"It could've been much worse," Landon said.

"Come have a seat."

They followed Cooper into his living room. Kate's head
started to ache. She didn't want to be a nuisance, but she probably needed to take something.

"Cooper, do you have any ibuprofen or aspirin?" she asked.

"Sure. Let me get it. Be right back."

"How badly does it hurt?" Landon's eyes were full of concern.

"My head's starting to pound, but mostly I want to take
something to keep it at bay."

"I think you might have whiplash. We should take you to the
hospital," Landon said.

"No. Give me some time to see how I feel and if the medicine works." The last thing she wanted to do was to go to the
hospital again.

Cooper walked back in the room with a glass of water and
a pill bottle. "Here you go."

"Thanks." She took two pain relievers from the bottle and
had a sip of water.

"What do you think the plan was?" Cooper asked Landon.

"I don't know. Maybe MPC still thinks that if they take it
up a notch, Kate will back down or make a more favorable
settlement offer."

"That's not happening," she said quickly. There was no way
she'd come this far to back down now. "I'm going to try this
case. MPC is going to pay for what they did to my client and
countless other innocent victims. Whatever steps we need to
take to get me through this trial, you have my full cooperation."

"First things first," Cooper said. "It's getting late. We should get you home safely and make sure everything is secure at your house."

"I'm not going to leave her alone tonight," Landon said.

Cooper nodded. "Agreed. We're in the homestretch. We need to institute our highest security settings at this point. The risks will only increase with each passing day."

"They were trying to send a major message tonight. They're willing to take it to the next level. We have to be prepared for that," Landon said.

*Next level* had an ominous ring to it. Exhaustion washed over Kate. Right now all she wanted to do was to get in bed, snuggle up with Jax, and try to forget this night had ever happened.

The guys must have sensed that she was ready to go home, because they gathered up their stuff.

"I'll follow you closely," Cooper said. "Call me the second you think anything might be awry. Once we get to Kate's, we'll do a security check."

—◁◇▷—

Landon was kicking himself. He'd been so preoccupied with all the things he wanted to do to protect Kate that he'd failed to see the SUV approach from behind until it was right up on them. He couldn't make that kind of mistake again.

*Lord, I know that I'm probably the last person who deserves your help, but I'm asking for it. Don't let MPC succeed in their quest to hurt Kate. Please protect her and guide my steps so that I can keep her safe.*

"House is all secure." Cooper's words broke him out of his thoughts.

He'd let Cooper take the lead in checking out Kate's house so he could stay close to her. He was worried that she was hurt more than she was letting on. She was too quiet.

269

Doubts crept into his mind, mocking him. Hadn't he already lost one innocent life because of his miscalculation? What if that happened again? He could never forgive himself if Kate was hurt—or worse—on his watch.

Noah's warning echoed through his head. Had he gotten too close to her to keep his head on straight? The stakes were too high to let his emotions get in the way of his job.

"Thanks for making sure everything is safe," Kate said quietly to Cooper.

"No problem. I called Noah and let him know what was going on too. He verified that there have been no intrusions via the security system. What he installed is state-of-the-art, so he would have known if there had been a breach."

"That's one piece of good news we definitely needed," Landon said. "I'm going to bunk here tonight and keep watch. Cooper, you should go home and get some rest. I have a feeling it's going to be nonstop until the trial is over." Although as Landon spoke, he wondered if Kate would even be safe after the trial was done. When would this be over? He had to take it one step at a time. One threat at a time. One prayer at a time. *God, I am weak. I need you.*

"Landon, did you hear me?" Cooper asked.

"No, sorry. I zoned out for a moment."

"Check in with me in the morning for a status report."

"Roger that."

"And we need to think about whether we want to bring in Atlanta PD," Cooper said.

"I don't need that type of attention right now," Kate said. "A police investigation is bound to get leaked. I can't afford to have anything jeopardize this trial going forward as scheduled."

"I understand your opinion, but we may get to a point where we don't have a choice," Landon said.

Cooper gathered his things, said his good-byes, and left the house. Landon made sure to lock up and secure the front door. Jax weaved in and out between his legs as he walked, and he had to make sure he didn't step on the cat. It was strange, almost like Jax could sense his anxiety. He hadn't felt this off-kilter since he came back from his final deployment.

"I don't know if I'm going to be able to sleep," Kate said.

"I'll be here on the couch, so you should get some rest."

"You need rest too."

"I can take a cat nap." He eyed Jax. "Yeah, like you, buddy."

"He's giving you more attention today," she said.

"Yeah." He didn't want Kate to know how messed up he was right now. He needed to remain focused on the job. Something about the physical contact of that SUV ramming into the back of them had sent him right back into the sweltering desert.

"Are you all right, Landon?" She walked over to him and placed her hand gently on his shoulder.

"Yes. I'm just a bit flustered, that's all." He couldn't explain to her that it was even more than that. "I think it might be best if we just focus on getting through this trial. I shouldn't have complicated things by kissing you. That was my mistake."

"What if I don't see it as a mistake?" She wrapped her arms around his neck.

He swallowed. "You can do so much better than me, Kate. Believe me, I'd be doing you a favor." He had so many flaws and dark spots. And all he saw in her was light. Didn't she deserve so much more?

"Don't say that. All of the pain and turmoil you have gone through has made you the amazing man that you are today. Yes, you've struggled, but you've come through it and are stronger for it. I can see it, Landon. You've changed since that first day we met. There's no longer that distant, dark look in your eyes. You're here with me, and that's where I want you to stay."

Her tender words impacted him like nothing else ever had—
and probably ever would. She tore down his walls without even
trying, but that still didn't change his concerns.

"Don't decide to bail before we've even had a real chance
to see what we could be together," she said. "I'm taking a risk
here too, but I think it's worth it."

"You're worth it, Kate. I just don't know if I am."

Before he could say another word, her soft lips were on his.
He allowed himself to enjoy the kiss. To feel something, even
if it scared him. To accept the affection that he didn't think he
deserved.

She pulled away just far enough to whisper against his mouth.
"You are worth it. Don't ever allow yourself to think otherwise."
She paused. "Shouldn't it tell you a lot about how special I think
you are that I want to spend time with you? I've told you about
my lack of relationships over the years, but for you, I'm willing
to take the risk and make the time."

He didn't understand how he could have ended up with such
a loving and caring woman, and it ate at him to think that he
could have someone so wonderful in his life when he was so
undeserving.

Keeping Kate close to him now was about so much more
than his feelings for her. As the trial approached, danger lurked
around every corner, and he wasn't going to let down his guard
again.

## CHAPTER
# TWENTY-FOUR

There was only one week left until the trial started. After the incident driving home, nothing else had happened, and Kate tried to let her trial prep consume her.

Ever since that night, though, Landon had been hyper-focused. He took what happened as a failure on his part, and she thought it was all tied to what had happened to him in Iraq. Even though the stakes weren't the same, it had reopened a deep wound.

She knew she shouldn't take it personally, but how could she not? She'd opened up to him, making herself vulnerable, and then he shut her out.

It reminded her why she was still single, so she didn't have to deal with the roller coaster of emotions. After losing her parents, it hurt to develop feelings for someone and then lose them too. Being alone had always been the safest route. The loneliness was a factor, but it had been outweighed by the fear of loss or rejection.

But her top concern now was winning this case. Her office was abuzz with activity, and she'd been working tirelessly on her opening statement. Practicing it over and over in her office. Unlike direct and cross-examinations, where you could adapt as needed or even do it on the fly, an opening statement had to be rehearsed.

Today was an important dry run. They'd assembled a team of attorneys to serve as mock jurors. The group contained a mix of experience levels, because she liked to have various viewpoints. Given how opinionated most lawyers were, she had no doubt the team would take their job seriously and provide key feedback. Kate only had one week left to get everything perfect. Mrs. Wyman deserved no less. She deserved justice.

Kate had to be the face and the advocate on the front line for her client, and this case was so much bigger than just one case. It would dictate the trajectory of the entire litigation. Thousands of other people's lives would be impacted here.

*Lord, give me the words to reach the jury.*

A knock on the door broke her out of her prayer time.

"We're ready in the conference room for you," Adam said.

She smiled at him. "You got your part down, playing Ethan Black?"

Adam laughed. "In a weird way, it's kind of fun. It's a challenge to come up with what we think their best arguments are."

She grabbed her file and undocked her laptop to take with her. "That's why I wanted you to do it. I knew you wouldn't hold back. We can't afford to take the easy road here. These mock opening statements need to be just like the real ones."

"I'll do my best."

She patted him on the shoulder. "I can't thank you enough for all you've done for me."

They walked down the hallway and entered the large litigation conference room, which was permanently set up for mock trials. A long counsel's table was positioned on each side of the room with a podium in the middle. The judge's area was up front in an elevated box, just like in a courtroom. To the side was the jury section with twelve seats. A large screen dropped down from the ceiling so they could project their opening slides.

Adrenaline coursed through Kate's veins as she realized that this was really going to happen. One week from now, she'd be standing in the real courtroom, delivering her opening statement.

But there she'd have a huge audience and a security team. Landon and his guys were locked down at K&R Security's office today, planning the trial and courtroom security strategy. It eased her nerves not to have him in the room watching and also knowing that he was coming up with a bulletproof plan to keep her safe during trial.

She opened her laptop, and one of the tech guys came over to set up her PowerPoint presentation, since she'd be going first. She took a step back so he could do his thing and saw Phil Gentry, the associate Bonnie had kicked off her team, walking toward her.

"Phil," she said, "are you going to watch?"

He crossed his arms. "After what I tell you, I don't think I'll be welcome here."

"What is it?"

He looked down and shuffled his feet before making eye contact with her. "I'm here to apologize."

"For what?"

"I'm the person who messed with your files."

A mix of disappointment and relief flooded through her. "You? Why?"

"I was so angry with Bonnie for kicking me off the team and embarrassing me in front of everyone. Then one of the other associates dared me to take those files from the war room. After I did it once and didn't see any reaction from you or Bonnie, I did more to try to get a reaction."

She tried to keep her emotions in check. In the grand scheme of things, this wouldn't take down her case, but it was still a big issue. "You realize how serious this is, right?"

He nodded. "I know it was wrong. And I figured you'd find out eventually, so I wanted to tell you what happened and why I did it."

"You hurt the client by doing this, not me or Bonnie."

"I understand that now. It was a stupid move. That's another reason I wanted to tell you. The guilt has been eating away at me."

She almost felt sorry for him. These young lawyers were under a lot of pressure, and sometimes they did stupid things. He was only twenty-five years old, fresh out of law school. "You did the right thing by telling me, but unfortunately, there has to be some repercussion for this. I'll discuss it with the managing committee, and we'll come to a determination."

"I figured as much. I really don't want to lose this job, though. I know I was an idiot, but if you believe in second chances at all, I hope you'll plead my case."

"I do very much believe in second chances, but actions also have consequences. I can't do anything about it right now. Why don't you stick around and watch? When I know more, we'll talk again."

"I appreciate you not firing me on the spot. I know you have the power to do that."

He was right. She could unilaterally make that decision, but that wasn't her style. "Go take a seat."

It took a weight off her shoulders knowing that he was responsible for the sabotage. And even more importantly, that no one on her team was trying to betray her.

She didn't like loose ends, and now she could turn her full attention to the task at hand.

"All right, everyone," Bonnie said. "Please take your seats so we can get started."

Bonnie had volunteered to play Judge Freeman, and the authoritarian role suited her well. She was even wearing a black judge's robe.

"Ms. Sullivan, are you ready to proceed with your opening statement?" Bonnie asked.

"Yes, Your Honor." Kate rose from her chair and walked over to stand directly in front of the mock jury. She no longer looked at these people as her colleagues, but as members of a jury who could render justice for her client.

"Ladies and gentleman, we met this morning for jury selection, but as a reminder, I'm Kate Sullivan, and I represent the plaintiff in this case against Mason Pharmaceutical Corporation. The plaintiff is the estate of Melinda Wyman, represented here today by Mrs. Nancy Wyman, the mother of Melinda Wyman. At the tender age of sixteen, Melinda died as a result of a brain tumor. The evidence will show that Melinda developed the brain tumor as a direct result of taking the medication Celix. The defendant, Mason Pharmaceutical Corporation, otherwise known as MPC, manufactures Celix. Melinda was a healthy and happy sixteen-year-old girl, but she did suffer from painful migraine headaches. Her family doctor prescribed Celix—a new drug put on the market by MPC that is specifically targeted for migraine headaches."

She took a breath and let her initial words sink in. She wanted to make sure the mock jury was following her. A few of them were already taking copious notes.

"This isn't just a tragic story. This story was completely avoidable, if not for the greed of MPC." She'd practiced this opening statement a million times, but saying the words—even in a mock setting—pulled at her heartstrings. But she had to keep it together. It was good that they were having this practice experience. When she did the real thing, she'd know to be prepared for the flood of emotions.

"The evidence will show that MPC knew Celix, the drug

they created, could cause brain tumors. The evidence will also show that they failed to warn about the side effects and even conspired to hide the truth. You will be presented with the facts during this trial."

She clicked to the first major slide of her presentation. "MPC destroyed or wrongfully withheld documents in this litigation." Normally she couldn't get away with this type of accusation, but after the shenanigans that Ethan had pulled, the judge would let her go pretty far.

"Judge Freeman will provide you with instructions on this matter, but know that MPC wanted to obscure the truth and did try to hide the facts. In our litigation process, we have a stage called discovery, where each side exchanges documents that pertain to the case. In this litigation, MPC purposely and with full knowledge did not provide the plaintiff with relevant documents."

Just as she hoped, her fellow attorneys were fully embracing their roles on the jury. A few of them looked horrified, while one raised an eyebrow and appeared to be skeptical of her claim.

"Ladies and gentleman, this isn't an exaggeration. You'll hear evidence during the trial about how this happened. And it means you might not see every piece of evidence that existed, because it likely could have been destroyed by MPC. But I contend that the evidence will still show that MPC knew Celix would cause brain tumors. Now why would MPC do this? Because they stood to make billions. Yes, that's billions with a *b*. But unfortunately, it goes even further."

Now was the time to reveal the kicker. "The evidence will show that MPC developed another drug called Acreda, and they were willing to put Celix on the market because Acreda is used to treat tumors. To MPC, it was a win-win. Make money on Celix and Acreda. But Acreda took longer to get to market than they expected, and it still isn't out yet."

This might be stretching the hard evidence a bit, but she was confident that once she had witnesses on the stand, she'd be able to prove this. She hadn't had the smoking gun documents when she had deposed Royce. But she felt confident that during the trial, she'd be able to break him and his fellow executives down when they were face-to-face with the jury.

She took a moment to survey the mock jury again. All twelve of them were focused on her. "I know this may sound like an outlandish story, but it just demonstrates how far one company was willing to go to increase its profits and break into a previously untapped segment of the market."

She needed to get to the legal elements, but first she wanted to play up the human element of this case.

"While MPC took nefarious actions to make more money, innocent people like Melinda Wyman lost their lives. Mrs. Wyman, already a widow, has now lost her only child because of the greed and corruption of MPC." She paused to swallow. She'd done countless opening statements in her life, but never had she been so affected by the magnitude of the situation.

"To boil it down, this is a case about MPC putting profit over the safety of the consumer. But as the plaintiff in this litigation, there are certain legal elements that have to be shown to find the defendant, MPC, liable. First, MPC had a duty to warn the general public and medical professionals of the dangerous side effects of Celix. MPC knew that Celix was unreasonably dangerous when they put it on the market. Second, MPC's failure to warn was a breach of its duty of reasonable care and safety to the decedent, Melinda Wyman. Third, MPC knew that using Celix could lead to brain tumors that could result in death. Fourth, MPC's actions directly caused Melinda's injury and death. During this trial, evidence will be presented on each of these elements. And at the end of the trial, after you have heard all of the evidence, I will ask this jury to return a verdict in favor of my client."

It was time to wrap up.

"But putting aside all of the technical legal requirements, I want to make one final point. This case isn't about a nameless victim. It's about a real person. A girl whose life was taken. It's about a mother who no longer has a daughter. Actions have consequences, and MPC must face the consequences of their actions. The choices they made as a company robbed Mrs. Wyman of her daughter. No amount of money will ever bring her back. But a verdict in favor of my client will force MPC to be held accountable so that another mother like my client won't have to face losing her child for the sake of profit. Thank you for your time and attention today."

She walked back to her counsel's table and took a seat. She'd done her job. Now it was Adam's turn as the defense lawyer to attempt to change the narrative. He would literally be playing the role of Ethan. They wanted to make this as realistic as possible.

"Ladies and gentleman, again, I'm Ethan Black, and I represent Mason Pharmaceutical Corporation, or MPC. Ms. Sullivan's opening statement no doubt has you scratching your head. She paints a pretty heinous picture of MPC and the actions they've taken. But I would urge you to take your duty as a juror seriously and not form your opinion until you've heard all the facts. Let me start with some facts that Ms. Sullivan failed to mention. MPC has produced multiple lifesaving drugs—drugs that literally have changed people's lives. Drugs that have cured illnesses and stopped pain. Ms. Sullivan would have you believe that all MPC cares about is the bottom line, but nothing could be further from the truth. Yes, as a corporation, MPC cares about being financially viable, because the more money they make, the more they can invest in research and development. They are on the cutting edge of lifesaving treatments. To develop drugs like this isn't a cheap enterprise, and MPC pours its profits back into the business."

Adam took a step closer to the jury. He wasn't holding back at all, and neither would Ethan. It was exactly what they needed. She didn't want him to throw her a softball. This was the real deal, and she was glad he was fully engaged.

Adam's expression softened as he made eye contact with the jury again. "My heart goes out to Mrs. Wyman. The death of her daughter was a tragedy. But the plaintiff has the burden of proof here. Ms. Sullivan may have the emotional element on her side, but when you peel that back, you won't find any evidence substantiating her claim—especially from the medical experts you will hear from during this trial."

As she watched him, she was reminded of what an excellent trial lawyer he was. Even though she believed she had the better facts in this case, Adam was doing an effective job of shifting the narrative. He also had a way about him that made you want to believe him. He wasn't over-the-top like many lawyers she knew, and juries found him relatable.

She could only hope and pray they would see her the same way. Because as good as Adam was, Ethan would be even better.

She listened attentively as he went through and rebutted all the legal elements in detail. He made sure to play up the fact to the jury that as the plaintiff, she would have the burden of proof. If she could not prove her case by a preponderance of evidence, the jury's duty was to rule in the defendant's favor.

"While it would be much more dramatic and exciting to accept Ms. Sullivan's version of events, the evidence will not support her claims. The decedent's brain tumor had absolutely nothing do with taking Celix. The plaintiff's lack of evidence will become apparent as we proceed, and I ask that you analyze all the facts put before you. When you do, I believe you will return a verdict in favor of the defendant, MPC. Thank you again for your time and your attention."

It didn't surprise her that they'd both opted for opening

statements on the shorter side. You could only keep the jury focused for so long.

"Thank you, Mr. Black," Bonnie said. "I think it best that we adjourn for the day and start with our first witness tomorrow morning promptly at nine o'clock."

Bonnie had also agreed to coordinate the jury comments, so she stepped down from the judge's seat and walked toward the jurors.

"All right, everyone, please take about half an hour to write down your thoughts. Be as honest and comprehensive as possible. Then we'll reconvene with a focus-group discussion."

Adam walked over to Kate. "Hey, want to run downstairs to the cafeteria and grab lunch while they're writing down their feedback?"

"Yeah. Now that you mention it, I'm starving." She hadn't eaten anything today. She'd been too worked up about the mock opening statements.

"You did really well. We'll have time to go through it all, but I thought you were highly effective." He smiled. "I can tell that you live and breathe this stuff, Kate."

"Thank you. This case means the world to me."

They walked out of the conference room and down the hall-way to the elevator bank. He pushed the call button, and her stomach started to rumble. The elevator chimed, signaling its arrival. The door opened, and she stepped in beside a man who was already on his way down.

She turned, expecting Adam to join her, but he just stood there, his face suddenly pale.

"Come on in." She reached out and held the elevator door.

"I'm sorry, Kate," Adam said.

"Sorry for what?"

"I've got it from here, Adam," the man beside her said. He

grabbed her by the arm and pulled her back into the elevator as the doors shut.

Her stomach clenched as she remembered the look on Adam's face. It all fell into place. Adam was working for MPC. He was one of them. She'd been betrayed by her friend and partner.

Something jabbed into her left side.

"If you don't want to get hurt, do exactly what I tell you," the man growled.

She held back a scream as she looked down and saw a brief flash of the gun pressed into her side, obscured by the man's navy suit jacket.

"We're going to walk out of this elevator and go down to the parking garage, and you're going to act like nothing is wrong. If you do that and keep listening to me, you won't get hurt. Do you understand?"

Fear flooded through her. Was this the same man who had come after her before? "You work for MPC."

"No talking. Just walk."

The elevator doors opened, and she stepped out as he wrapped his arm around her shoulder. Then he smiled at her. "Act normal," he said in a hushed voice.

He kept his head down, leaning into her, and he was taking her on a specific route to the parking garage elevators. That meant he knew where the building security cameras were, and he was trying to avoid getting his face caught on one.

She weighed her options. Once she left this building, it could be all over. But on the flip side, if she tried to make a break for it, he might kill her. This man was on a mission. He was hired for things like this. For all she knew, he might be Ellie's killer. *Lord, help me.*

Not wanting to risk it, she did as she was told and walked toward the elevator bank that led down to the underground parking structure. The same garage she parked in every day.

He looked at her, his brown eyes holding no hint of kindness. "If you want to live, no sudden moves."

She took his threats seriously and obeyed. They took the elevator down to the bottom level of the parking deck, which was also the most isolated. As they exited and started walking through the garage, she started to panic. Maybe she should fight. What if this was her only chance to get away?

She struggled against him as he pushed her forward.

"It's no use trying to fight me. You'll only get hurt if you do."

They walked a few more steps until he stopped in front of a large, dark SUV—eerily similar to the one that had come after them last week.

Kate's survival instincts kicked in, and she started thrashing against him with all of her might.

"I told you not to do that."

He pulled the gun, and she thought he was going to shoot her right there. But instead he brought it down hard on her head.

A blistering pain went through her body, and then there was nothing.

# TWENTY-FIVE

Kate hadn't answered any of Landon's texts or calls. He knew she was busy that morning with her mock trial, but it was unlike her to go radio silent—especially given the circumstances.

After lunch, he decided to head over to her office to track her down, just to put his mind at ease.

After another unanswered call to Kate, he called Beth, her assistant, who came down to the lobby to escort him upstairs.

"Have you seen Kate?" he asked her.

"No, I haven't. But they were in the litigation conference room all morning, working on the opening statements."

"Can you take me to that conference room?"

"Sure." She smiled.

He knew he was being overprotective, but could he blame himself? After his track record, he had to be. When he walked into the big conference room, he scanned the gathered crowd, looking for Kate. But there was no sign of her.

He strode over to Adam and Bonnie, whom he'd met briefly on occasion. "Have the two of you seen Kate?"

Adam shook his head. "No, that's what we were just talking about. She and I were going to grab lunch in the cafeteria, and she went ahead of me. When I got down there, I checked the entire cafeteria, and she wasn't there. I thought she'd come back upstairs and we missed each other."

"But I haven't seen her either," Bonnie chimed in. "We're waiting on her to start the full debrief of the mock opening statements."

A wave of nausea washed through Landon's body. "Something's wrong."

"What do you mean?" Bonnie asked.

"Something happened to Kate." He pulled out his phone and called Cooper, who said he'd be over ASAP.

"You're starting to worry me," Adam said.

"I think we should all be worried." He clenched his fists. If something had happened to her, how could he live with himself? "Kate wouldn't just bail on this meeting. You both know this case is her whole life."

"I'm confused. Why do you think something happened to her?" Bonnie asked.

"She could've been abducted." He almost couldn't believe the words as he was saying them.

"Abducted?" Adam's eyes widened. "What are you talking about?"

"There's a lot the two of you don't know about what's been happening with MPC behind the scenes. We didn't tell you for your own safety, but we believe MPC was responsible for Ellie Proctor's murder, and they've been threatening Kate. Now they've taken it to the next level. They obviously don't want her to try this case."

Adam opened his mouth, but no words came out. His skin turned pale. "I don't even know what to say."

"That's why the other guys and I have been sticking so close," Landon said.

Bonnie blew out a breath. "I had no idea. I thought you and

Kate were an item, and that's why you were around so much. Do you really think she's in danger now?"

"Unfortunately, I do."

Bonnie grabbed his arm. "Let me know how I can help."

"Thank you," he said.

She let go of him. "And I hate to sound insensitive, but we also have to figure out what to do about the trial proceeding."

"We should keep preparing as if everything is on track," Adam said.

"Then you need to be prepared to step in if the judge makes us move forward," she told Adam.

"I'll let you guys worry about all the legal implications." Landon's concern was less about the lawsuit and more about Kate's well-being. He turned to see Cooper entering the room with Beth by his side.

"We need to loop in Atlanta PD," Cooper said. "Let me start making calls."

"Is Kate all right?" Beth asked.

"Honestly, I don't know." Landon's voice cracked a little.

"I can do whatever you need me to do here," Beth said. "No matter the task, just ask."

Landon turned his attention back to Cooper. "Let's go find Ethan Black and see what he has to say."

Ethan sat in his office, tinkering with his opening statement. He vacillated on a few key points. Did he go in with the hard sell or take a softer approach? Ultimately, it was his call, and he would have to live with the consequences if he made a mistake. He could lose or win the jury in that first few minutes.

He looked up from his computer as two men he didn't know barged into his office.

"I'm sorry, Ethan," his assistant said, as she jumped in beside the men. "They insisted on coming back, saying it was an emergency."

"What's going on?" Ethan asked them. "And who are you?"

The dark-haired man stepped forward. "I'm Landon James. I'm a private investigator working with Kate Sullivan, and this is my associate Cooper Knight of K&R Security."

"Sorry, but I'm still confused about what you're doing here," Ethan replied.

"Kate is missing," Landon said.

"What do you mean, Kate's missing?" Ethan asked.

Landon pointed at Ethan, and Ethan could feel the fury just beneath the other man's skin. "That good-for-nothing company you're working for has taken her. Who knows if she's even alive?"

Ethan lifted his hand. "Whoa, now. Wait a minute." He felt his face redden as Landon's words sank in. Maybe he should have taken Kate's accusations more seriously. "Tell me everything that happened."

Landon took a step forward. "She was abducted from her firm's building this morning."

"Why do you think MPC has anything to do with this? And how do you know she was abducted?" Ethan's mind started to swim with disaster scenarios.

"She went downstairs to the cafeteria for lunch and never came back," Cooper said. "Someone took her. They're reviewing the building security tapes right now."

Ethan searched for an alternative explanation, because what Landon was saying was too awful to fathom. "This all sounds very farfetched. What if she just wanted to get away for a while? Preparing for trial can be extremely stressful."

Landon shook his head. "No way. You and I both know that Kate isn't one to run away when the going gets tough."

"I think you guys are way out of line with these accusa-

288

tions." But were they? What if they were right and Kate was in danger?

Landon walked around Ethan's desk and loomed over him. For a moment, he was truly afraid the PI was going to haul off and hit him. Landon's interest in Kate seemed to go beyond the professional. The determined look in his dark eyes. The twitch in his jaw. This man had feelings for her.

"If anything happens to Kate, I'm holding you personally responsible," Landon growled. "Do you hear me?"

Ethan raised both of his hands in a calming gesture. If there was any chance that Kate had been abducted, then he needed to do his part to help. "I understand that you're upset. And while I think you're totally off base, I'll do whatever you need me to do. I know you probably don't believe this, but Kate is one of my best friends."

"You need to confront Royce," Landon said.

Ethan's stomach clenched. "You want me to accuse my client of kidnapping? Have you lost your mind?" He was hoping for something a little less direct.

Cooper nodded. "You said you wanted to help. We'll put you in touch with law enforcement. Be waiting for the call."

Ethan looked at their faces and realized that what they were saying was true. Kate was really missing. He felt a trickle of fear for her. Could MPC be involved in this? Her prior accusations against them for attacking her rang through his head. If there was even a small chance MPC was behind it, he had to figure it out. The last thing he wanted was for something to happen to Kate.

Landon was beside himself. With each passing moment, Kate's life was more endangered—and that was if she was even still alive.

He was huddled up with Cooper, Noah, and some Atlanta police officers in a large conference room at Warren McGee. The air conditioning kept making him break out into a cold sweat.

He walked out of the room for a moment to try to clear his head. Police officers were interviewing everyone on the trial team, desperate to find any clues.

Landon couldn't believe their greatest hope for finding Kate rested with Ethan Black, a man he had quickly come to despise. But as mad as he was at Ethan, he was even angrier with himself. He had never considered that she'd be at risk inside her own office building. This had been her safe zone. After all their preparation, it had never occurred to him that MPC would be so bold as to walk into Warren McGee and take her. Only time would tell if this mistake would be another fatal one.

The firm didn't have security cameras, but the building did. The tapes weren't helpful beyond showing that Kate left the building with an unknown man. But the guy was a professional. He worked the camera angles, and with the way he wore his hat, it was difficult to make out many discernable facial features.

Landon had vowed to protect her, and once again he had failed at his duty. And this time the casualty of his failure was the woman who had won his heart. That was the other thing eating at him. The realization that something could happen to Kate and he hadn't really told her what she meant to him. He knew he'd been distant in the lead-up to trial. All the stress and pressure of the security issues had caused him to recede back into himself. It was the last thing he wanted, but it was his protection mechanism.

*Lord, please protect Kate. I know I haven't been able to live up to my end of the bargain—with you, with her, with everything. But this is in your hands.*

He walked back into the conference room and saw the other

men standing around one of the large tables. "Any updates?" he asked.

Cooper nodded. "Atlanta PD has a few officers working with Ethan right now to make sure he's ready to go talk to Royce."

"We don't really have time for a full coaching session, do we?" he asked.

"We get one shot at this," Noah said. "He needs the help."

Landon knew his friends were right, but he was worried about the timing.

"Hopefully, that contact will happen within the hour," Cooper said. "Ethan has agreed to wear a wire."

"Is that legal, with him being their attorney?"

"Yeah," Noah said. "There's a crime exception to the attorney-client privilege. Since Royce would be having these discussions with Ethan in the furtherance of a crime, he can't claim the privilege."

"And if Ethan can't get any information out of Royce?"

"We can't think like that right now," Cooper said. "Atlanta PD is also trying to track down Bradley Cummings. It doesn't appear he is at the MPC office."

"Do we have pictures of him to compare to the man in the security camera tape?" Landon asked.

"We're getting that now, but I think it's a strong possibility Bradley is the culprit." Noah gave Landon's shoulder an encouraging slap. "Man, I know you're upset and worried, but we're working every possible angle here. We're going to find her."

Landon could only pray that Noah was right. He couldn't even consider the possibility that he had seen Kate alive for the last time.

CHAPTER

# TWENTY-SIX

Ethan was a mess. His heartbeat was racing, sweat rolled down his back, and his hands were clammy as he entered the MPC building. He'd agreed to this because his gut was screaming at him that something was wrong.

He'd pushed down thoughts and questions about his client before, but the more he spoke with authorities, the more he thought there was actually a possibility that Royce was dirty.

So maybe, just maybe, he could turn this thing around.

Penny escorted him in to see Royce. There was no sign of Bradley this time, and Ethan was glad for that, but he did see Matt sitting at the large table across from Royce. This would make his task all the more awkward and challenging.

"Wasn't expecting to see you today. Thought you'd be deep in trial prep," Royce said. "Matt and I were just talking over development plans for the next year."

Ethan didn't care at all about MPC's plans. "We've got a huge problem. Kate Sullivan has gone missing."

Royce raised an eyebrow. "What?"

He took a breath. "Royce, if you had anything to do with this, I need you to come clean right now while we can still fix it."

Royce cocked his head to the side. "Ethan, this is the second time you've accused me of doing something to that woman, and I've never taken any action against her."

Ethan clenched his fists. "I'm having a hard time believing you."

"You're turning red. You need to calm down."

Royce was right. The police had told Ethan to remain calm, get to the facts. He wasn't supposed to fly off the handle. That wouldn't help anyone. He needed to use Matt to his strategic advantage to get Royce to confess. Matt was always level-headed.

He shifted his attention to the COO. "Matt, please help me. Talk some sense into him. If he's gotten himself into something, let me help him out of it."

"Ethan's right," Matt said. "We're all in this together, Royce. I know the extreme pressure you've been under in this litigation. If you took things too far, we can figure out a plan. But we need you to tell us right now."

Royce shook his head. "I've taken many actions to protect this company, and some of them might be legally questionable. But I have not crossed the line with Kate Sullivan. I'm telling you both that." He shifted his eyes to Matt. "C'mon, Matt, tell him he's out of his mind."

"The police are all over this," Ethan said. "Royce, you're living in a delusional world right now if you think you can get away with actually hurting people."

Matt pulled out his cell phone. "I'm texting Bradley to inform him that we have a security situation on our hands, and we need to do damage control ASAP."

Matt had just provided Ethan with the perfect opening. "Royce, the police believe you're behind Kate's disappearance and that Bradley is doing your dirty work." He followed the script the police had given him.

Matt looked up from his phone. "Do they have any proof?"

"Yeah," Ethan said. While they didn't exactly have proof connecting Royce to this, he felt the need to bluff. "Please, Royce, just tell me where Kate is." He hoped he could appeal to whatever humanity Royce still possessed.

Royce threw up his hands. "I don't know what to tell you. I have no idea where Kate Sullivan is!"

"That's enough," Matt said loudly.

Ethan looked at Matt and sucked in a breath as his eyes locked on the muzzle of the gun in Matt's hand. The gun was pointed right at him.

"It wasn't meant to go this way," Matt said.

Ethan swallowed hard. "Matt, please, don't do this. Let's talk."

"Matt, what—what have you done?" Royce's voice cracked, and a wave of realization washed over his face. "This was all you, wasn't it?"

Matt turned his attention to Royce. "You didn't have it in you to take the company to the next level. You're too soft to make the decisions that have to be made to ensure success. We have so much more we can accomplish, but you were standing in the way."

"Even if it means risking people's lives?" Ethan asked. If he could keep Matt talking, maybe they had a chance to get out of there alive. But if he was going to die, he needed to understand why Matt had done this.

"Someone had to be willing to push forward with Celix." Matt looked at Royce. "And you wouldn't have done it if you had known the real test results. I had to tell you that we'd re-solved all the issues because MPC stood to turn a hefty profit from Celix and Acreda. Record-breaking numbers. I was willing to risk the collateral damage. A risk you would've never been man enough to take."

"You shouldn't have kept me in the dark," Royce said.

Matt's face reddened. "Everything would've worked out just

fine if Ellie Proctor hadn't started snooping around. I thought Bradley had handled her, but I didn't account for all contingencies. Including one of our own lawyers selling us out and sending documents to the enemy."

The accusation hit Ethan hard. This man was not only dangerous, he was out for revenge.

"You want my job," Royce said flatly.

Matt took a step forward. "I deserve your job."

Ethan watched as Matt shifted the gun toward Royce and fired. The bullet struck Royce in the head, and he dropped to the floor with a loud thud, a pool of bright red blood forming around him.

Ethan instinctively stepped back and to the side, but it was too late. Another gunshot rang out, and the bullet tore through his flesh, sending searing pain throughout his body. Lights flashed in front of his eyes.

Then the world went dark.

Cooper's SUV came to a screeching stop in front of Warren McGee. Landon picked up his bag and opened the backseat door.

"Get in," Cooper said. "We're ready to go."

Details were still murky, but they'd just gotten word that Royce was dead and Ethan had been shot. More officers were already en route to MPC, and Landon and Cooper planned to be right behind them. Noah was riding up front.

Before Landon could close the door, Adam Fox came running toward the vehicle. His face was bright red and wet with tears. "I need to talk to you."

"Jump in." He didn't really want to deal with Adam's emotional breakdown, but he didn't have time right now to do anything else. He slid over to let Adam into the vehicle.

Cooper hit the gas, and they were off.

"I'm responsible for this," Adam blurted.

Landon looked at him. "What do you mean?"

"I'll tell everything to the police, but I need to explain it to you first. I never thought that Kate would be harmed."

"What have you done?" Anger simmered as he looked at the traitor beside him.

"I didn't have a choice. I'm being blackmailed by MPC."

"Blackmailed?" Cooper chimed in.

"Yes. Bradley Cummings is the security officer at MPC, but he is also their hired gun. I have a gambling problem and got on the wrong side of some dangerous people when I couldn't pay my debts. Bradley found out about it and paid off the money I owed. Then he held it over my head. I was to serve as MPC's inside man. All I was told was that Kate would be kept out of the picture so that I could try the case. They said they wouldn't hurt her. I was a fool to believe them. Especially after what Bradley did to Ellie. But they claimed it would be different with Kate. That all they needed was for me to take her place as lead counsel."

Landon clenched his right fist. It took every ounce of discipline he had not to strangle Adam. "You need to tell the cops the entire story. You understand me?" He gripped the turncoat's arm as hard as he could.

"I'm sorry," Adam whispered, squirming.

"That's not enough. But in the meantime, keep talking. Tell us everything you know."

Kate said a prayer as she silently waited for the man to come back and hurt her. She was locked inside a hot, dark basement with no way out. She'd tried everything, but there was no exit except the locked door at the top of the stairs. Literally, her life was in God's hands right now, and she had come to terms with the fact that she might die today.

She started reciting Psalm twenty-three quietly. The Lord was with her. She knew that much. But she also was prepared for the fact that she might not make it out of this room alive.

She'd had plenty of time alone in the darkness to mull over MPC's plans—and Adam's stinging betrayal. He'd probably been playing her the entire time. And with her locked away, Adam could naturally step in and take her place at trial. No one would know that he was working with MPC. He'd be able to make it easier on them. Especially on the link between Celix and Acreda.

What a disaster. She simply couldn't let that trial move forward with Adam as lead counsel if he was on MPC's payroll. Tears welled up in her eyes as she thought about Mrs. Wyman and Melinda. There had to be a way to stop MPC before it was too late.

The door opened, and she scooted back as far as she could into the corner. It was the same man who had taken her. He jogged down the steps and walked toward her.

She stood up to face him. "Please," she said. "Just let me go."

"We've gotta move now." He grabbed her by the arm.

She saw the gun tucked into his waistband.

"Please," she begged. "Don't do this. Don't hurt me." But as she said the words, she realized he might do just that. "You don't have to do this. You can just walk away."

"Do you really think I'm paid to just walk away? My job isn't over yet."

She started to pray, because that was all she had left. "You killed Ellie Proctor, didn't you?"

"I'm just a good soldier following orders. I don't make the calls."

"So Royce gave you the order?"

He leaned down and chuckled into her ear. His breath sent a chill down her spine. "You really have no clue, do you? You must not be as bright as everyone says you are."

She didn't understand his response, but she had to keep trying. "There's always another way. You can make that decision."

"Start walking. Upstairs—now. The decision has already been made. I've been given my orders, and it's time to get out of here."

She closed her eyes, fearing the worst. If she didn't make a move now, she may not have another chance.

Taking a deep breath, she started to climb the long staircase. She wanted him to believe that she was afraid and wouldn't fight back. But she was a fighter and refused to let him take her. *Lord, I need your help.*

She waited until they were about halfway up the steps. Then she quickly turned around and shoved him. Hard.

He lost his balance and fell backward.

Not wasting a second, she started to run up the rest of the steps. She'd almost made it to the door when he grabbed tightly onto her left ankle and pulled her down.

She hit the stairs hard, banging the side of her head. But she kicked and screamed, refusing to let him drag her off. She was able to break his grip and make another run for it, her heart pounding, her breathing heavy. But he was right there again. Grabbing her right calf, he yanked her down.

Her fingers dug into the wooden steps, desperate not to let go. He flipped her over on her back and stood over her. He pulled out his gun.

This was it. He was going to kill her. She closed her eyes.

A loud gunshot rang out. She expected to feel pain, but she didn't. Opening her eyes, she saw the man lying on the steps below her. She hadn't been hit. He had.

Police officers rushed past her, down the stairs and into the basement. Shouts and sounds echoed loudly all around her. She lay frozen in shock. The next thing she knew, Landon was there. His strong arms pulled her up and wrapped around her.

"Kate, are you all right?" He looked down at her.

"Yes, I think so."

He helped her stand. She looked down and saw her captor groaning in pain. "Is he going to make it?"

Landon turned her head gently back to face him. "Don't worry about him right now." He led her up the steps and took her outside. "Are you hurt?"

"Nothing too bad. Just a bit sore."

He pulled her into a tight hug, and she let the tears flow freely.

"It's okay, Kate. You're safe now."

"What happened? I'm so confused."

"We're still working through all the details, but it looks like Matt Canton is the puppet master behind all of this."

"MPC's Chief Operating Officer?"

"Yeah."

He had seemed so mild mannered in his deposition. She'd been so focused on Royce that it never occurred to her that Matt could be calling the shots.

"Why do you think it was Matt?" she asked.

"Ethan confronted Royce, thinking he was responsible for taking you. But really it was Matt, and then Matt shot Royce, killing him, before turning the gun on Ethan."

She gasped. "Is Ethan all right?"

"Thankfully, Matt missed the mark. An inch over, though, and the bullet would've struck a main artery. Ethan's in the hospital having surgery, but he should pull through."

"So Royce is dead?"

"Yes. Gunshot wound to the head. But Matt didn't realize Ethan was wired and that law enforcement was outside waiting for him. He didn't get very far."

It was all coming together in her mind. "So that's why he said that," she murmured.

"What are you talking about?"

"The man who abducted me. I was trying to keep him talking, and I asked if Royce gave him the order to kill Ellie. He said that I didn't have a clue. That's what he meant. That it was never Royce. He was innocent this whole time."

"As far as the attacks against you and the murder of Ellie go, it certainly appears Royce wasn't involved. That's not to say his hands were clean, because we don't know yet the extent of his involvement with the decisions made about Celix. But it looks like Matt was the mastermind behind the rest of it."

She realized she was shaking. "Where's Matt?"

"In police custody. He provided your location in an effort to cut a deal. But I doubt there will be one. We'll know more once the police fully interrogate him and the guy who took you, who I believe is the MPC security chief, Bradley Cummings."

Her mind swam. "I don't even know what to say."

"You don't have to say anything." He paused. "But I can't let another moment go by without saying something to you."

Her fingers tightened against the fabric of his shirt. "What? Please tell me there's not more bad news."

He shook his head. "Kate, when I thought that I could lose you, I went crazy beating myself up over how I've treated you these past few weeks. I realized that I cared so much about you that I pushed you away because I was afraid. But I don't want to live in fear, and I don't want to hide my feelings from you. There's been so much darkness and pain in my life over the past few years, but you've shown me there's another way. And somewhere throughout all of this, I've fallen totally in love with you."

She stared into his dark eyes and let his words sink in. "You love me?"

"Yes, I do. I didn't know if I would ever find someone to love, someone who would accept me with all my baggage and issues. You never discounted my past, you listened to my words, you actually heard me, Kate. You showed me that God hadn't given up on me. You and I make a great team. I want to continue what we've started. I hope you do too."

Tears slid down her cheeks, but this time they weren't tears of fear, but joy. "Landon, I love you too. And I do want to build on what we've started. There's so much more ahead for us."

"Roger that." He gave her another quick hug. "Let me get you out of here."

She smiled. "Can we go by the hospital before you take me home? I'd like to check on Ethan."

"You're a good woman, Kate Sullivan. I knew from the moment we met that you were one of the good guys."

Kate walked out of the conference room and shook hands with Ethan and the two board members from MPC who were present at the settlement negotiations. It was official. MPC had settled the entire multidistrict litigation for a staggering 1.5 billion dollars. The MPC settlement would be one of the top five Big Pharma settlements of the year.

It was unclear whether MPC would be able to weather the storm, especially with the criminal penalties they would most certainly be facing. But they were going to try to make a fresh start, including a completely new leadership team that had been instated immediately after Matt had been taken into custody.

"Kate, can I have a word?" Ethan asked her.

"Sure." She followed him down the hallway. He still wasn't up to full speed after being shot, but he'd come back to work on the settlement.

He turned and looked at her. "Kate, I know I've said I'm sorry

302

multiple times, but I'm going to say it again. I should've taken your accusations about MPC more seriously. I was blinded by my need to win the case, and I have to live with that fact every single day."

It had been almost a month since Matt's arrest. Kate still couldn't believe everything that had happened. Matt thought taking Ellie out would solve his problems, but little did he know, a handful of emails would open the door to the Acreda issue. Ethan had told her that one of his associates, a woman named Nicole Sosa, was the brave person who sent Kate the documents despite knowing she would lose her job.

"Ethan, I don't want you to live like that. Yes, I got hurt, but I also know that once you found out about what MPC was up to, you did everything you could to help me. Including endangering your own life."

"Then maybe I can start trying to earn your trust back," he said. "Your friendship does mean the world to me, even though I haven't done a very good job of acting like it."

She couldn't help but feel warmth toward Ethan. He'd been through a lot. She took his hand and squeezed. "We're going to be okay. Focus on making a full recovery. That's the most important thing right now."

"Thank you." He paused. "Looks like you have company. I'll head out now."

Kate smiled when she saw Landon waiting for her at the other end of the hallway.

"Thanks, Ethan. We'll talk again soon. Please take care of yourself." She left Ethan and walked to meet Landon. "Hey," she said.

"Is the settlement done?" he asked.

"Yes, it is. We'll put out a statement for the press within the hour. I still can't believe it."

Landon nodded. "It just shows what the thirst for power

can do to a man. Matt was already working board members to put the idea in their heads that he was the future and Royce was the past."

"You know what, it probably would've worked if it hadn't been for Ellie and Nicole. Have you heard anything about Pierce Worthington?" she asked.

Landon nodded. "Pierce is safely back in the country and fully cooperating. He's providing very useful information about how his family's lives were threatened, which just adds to the charges against Matt and Bradley. Pierce had no choice but to flee for his family's safety."

"It's truly mind-boggling." She didn't think she'd ever be the same again. "And Adam's betrayal still stings."

"Yeah, but Kate, remember, he was being blackmailed."

"He would've thrown the entire case to do their bidding. I'm so thankful it didn't come to that and the victims will now have justice. The settlement money won't bring Melinda and the others back, but it sends a strong signal that companies like MPC can't get away with treating people as if their lives have no value. Money isn't everything."

"But it's finally over. We can start moving past it all." Landon took her hand in his. "Let's get out of here. I want to take you out to dinner."

Her heart filled with love. "It's a date."

# EPILOGUE

The past eight months had gone by in a blur. The details of Matt's plan had finally been completely exposed, and he was facing the rest of his life in prison pending trial. Kate had no doubt he would be convicted—the evidence against him was substantial, especially given Bradley's corroborating testimony.

MPC was still operating as a company, and the new CEO vowed to make things right by trying to instill public confidence with a new PR campaign. She wasn't certain that would ever be possible, but with all the players who wreaked havoc gone, they might have a fighting chance. MPC would be under the microscope for years to come, though.

She walked into the private room they'd reserved at the restaurant for Sophie's birthday party, and saw Ethan walking toward her.

"Kate." He hugged her. "Thanks for inviting me to Sophie's party."

"Of course." Their friendship had survived the MPC case. He'd put forth the effort and time to rebuild her trust.

"I've decided to extend my sabbatical from the firm."

"Really?"

He'd taken a much-needed sabbatical once the MPC settlements had been completed.

"Yeah. I've had some time to evaluate everything about my life and my priorities, and I'm still not content with where I am. I'm thinking of giving teaching a try. I don't think I can ever look at Big Law the same way again, and I don't want to do a disservice to my clients."

"I'm so proud of you for taking a stand like this."

"I always thought you were naïve and idealistic, Kate, but now I see that I want to be more like you. I was the one who was naïve to think I could make any decision I wanted without facing the consequences. I'm not saying I'll never go back to the firm, but just not right now."

"You'll know if the time is right."

Landon walked up to them. Fortunately, Landon and Ethan had patched things up and were even friendly with each other.

"I wondered where you had run off to." Landon wrapped his arm tightly around her. "Good to see you, Ethan," he added.

"You too. Hope you have a fun time tonight. Let me go say hello to some friends. I'll catch up with you guys later."

Kate smiled as she looked up at Landon. The two of them had fallen into a normal routine, and she had never been happier. She was under no illusion that their road together would always be easy, but she knew she could count on him to be by her side no matter what.

She watched as Ethan walked up to Nicole. After the settlement, Kate had asked Ethan to introduce her to the brave woman who helped turn the tide of the case. She and Nicole had immediately clicked, so much so that Kate had offered Nicole a job on the plaintiff's side, and Nicole had gladly taken it. Kate had also spoken on Nicole and Ethan's behalf to the bar ethics committee. Given the extenuating circumstances, the committee had let them off with only warnings.

Sophie joined them, and Kate gave her friend a big hug. "How's the birthday girl?"

"I'm great. So glad the two of you could make it." Sophie grinned and then gave Landon a wink. Kate wondered what that was all about.

"We wouldn't want to be anywhere else," she said.

"I better enjoy tonight, because I'm going to be working around the clock if we decide to file charges in this case I'm working on."

Kate didn't push, because she knew that as a prosecutor, Sophie could only say so much. But she hoped her friend would be ready for this big challenge. Being a prosecutor was extremely stressful.

"We're about to do the cake," Mia yelled from across the room. "Come on, Soph."

Sophie walked up to the center table. A large chocolate cake with pink frosting was brought into the room, and everyone started singing "Happy Birthday." Sophie's bright blue eyes sparkled as she blew out the candles.

"Everyone, thank you so much for coming tonight to celebrate my birthday. It's amazing to spend time with such awesome and caring friends. Everyone should have some cake and enjoy the rest of the evening. But first, there's something Landon needs to say, so I'll turn it over to him."

Kate realized everyone had stopped looking at Sophie and instead was looking in her direction. What was going on? The room quieted down.

Landon took her hands. "Kate, I've thought long and hard about this. I know you're a private person, and so am I. But I also realize how much our friends mean to us. They're really our family, since neither of us has close family anymore, so I believed that they should be here for this. And Sophie thought this would be the perfect time, since everyone is here."

He dropped down to one knee.

Her heartbeat sped up. *Is this really happening?*

"So in front of all of our friends, I want to ask you the most important question of my life." He took a deep breath. "Kate Sullivan, will you marry me?"

He pulled a sparkling diamond solitaire out of his pocket and presented it to her.

Peace settled over her as she let his words sink in. *Thank you, God, for sending this man into my life.* "Yes, Landon. Definitely, yes."

He slid the ring onto her finger to shouts and applause. She pulled him up off his knee.

He leaned down and pressed his lips to hers. "I love you, Kate. You have my heart."

"I love you too, Landon." As she looked into his eyes, she knew she'd found the only one for her.

# ACKNOWLEDGMENTS

Sarah—I couldn't ask for a better agent. I can't believe it's been four years since we found each other. Time has flown by! I've grown so much as a person and a writer during our time together. I appreciate your willingness to fully embrace my journey, even if it has turned out a little different than we first envisioned together. As I've told you before, I believe with all my heart that I am on the right path now, and you have supported me each step of the way. You've been with me through the lows and the highs. Thank you for always having my back.

Dave—Thanks for taking a chance on me and welcoming me into the Bethany House family. I remember attending the Bethany House spotlight at my first ACFW in 2013. At that point, writing for Bethany House was only a distant dream. And now, just a few short years later, that dream is a reality. I am so appreciative of you and everyone at Bethany House.

Jessica—You are a complete pleasure to work with. I appreciate how much time and effort you've put into making this story the best it could be. Thank you for fully embracing my story and providing amazing input.

To Rachel's Justice League—You ladies bring me so much joy and make the writing journey even more special. Having each and every one of you in my life is truly a blessing. I look forward to each day that I get to spend time in our group, talking with all of y'all. Your enthusiasm, fellowship, and friendship means the world to me. I hope I can continue to write stories that will inspire you and others.

Susan—Seems like just yesterday that we met in seventh grade and realized we shared the same birthday. It's been a crazy ride ever since! I hope that we get to spend many more birthdays together. Thanks for always being there for me. Through life's ups and downs, you are always a constant.

Alison—Who would've thought that us meeting on Twitter would have turned into such a wonderful friendship! Thanks for making me laugh, listening to me vent, and empathizing with the struggles and joys we share as authors.

Dana and Lee—You are a constant source of encouragement, and even more importantly, fun. I'm looking forward to reenacting more scenes with you for years to come at conferences.

Aaron—I love you. Thank you for being fully supportive of my writing and even reading all my books. You have always encouraged me to follow my writing dreams. You get my crazy writer mind and still love me for it.

Mama—Words can't express how much I love you. You've always been my biggest supporter and have believed in me no matter what. You instilled in me the idea that if I set my mind to something and worked hard enough, I could achieve my dreams. Thank you for all you have done for me.

Daddy—You were the man who first prayed with me, showered with me love, and showed me the way. I know you're in heaven right now, but I couldn't be writing the stories that I write today if it hadn't been for the strong foundation of faith that you laid for me.

And finally, to the Lord, for all You have done for me. No matter how many times I fall, You're always there to pick me up. Thank You for using writing to open my eyes to even more of You and Your unfailing love.

Rachel Dylan writes Christian fiction, including legal romantic suspense. She has practiced law for over a decade, including being a litigator at one of the nation's top law firms. She enjoys weaving together legal and suspenseful stories with a romantic twist. A southerner at heart, she now lives in Michigan with her husband and five furkids—two dogs and three cats. Rachel loves to connect with readers. You can find her at www.rachel dylan.com.

# Sign Up for Rachel's Newsletter!

Keep up to date with Rachel's news on book releases and events by signing up for her email list at racheldylan.com.

---

# More Romantic Suspense

When a terrorist investigation leads FBI agent Declan Grey to a closed immigrant community, he turns to crisis counselor Tanner Shaw for help. Under imminent threat, they'll have to race against the clock to stop a plot that could cost thousands of lives.

*Blind Spot* by Dani Pettrey
CHESAPEAKE VALOR #3
danipettrey.com

# You May Also Like . . .

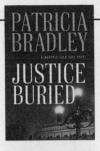

Sparks fly when security specialist Kelsey Allen and cold case detective Brad Hollister work together to find a murderer—until their attention must turn to keeping themselves alive.

*Justice Buried* by Patricia Bradley
ptbradley.com

While Detective Evie Blackwell and her new partner, David, investigate two missing-persons cases in Chicago—a student and a private investigator—their conviction that "justice for all" is truly possible will be tested to the limit.

*Threads of Suspicion* by Dee Henderson
An Evie Blackwell Cold Case
deehenderson.com

Four years ago, Kate O'Brien and her twin were attacked by a serial killer—and only Kate survived. When new evidence is found suggesting the wrong man was convicted, Kate is terrified. With a target on her back, can U.S. Marshal Tony DeLuca keep her safe until the new trial begins?

*Dark Deception* by Nancy Mehl
Defenders of Justice #2
nancymehl.com

Defense Attorney Ian Wells is struggling to build a law practice. When a new client offers a huge sum to take on a simple trust fund case, he can't afford to say no. But when the investigation leads to a decades-old mystery linking the trust to dangerous criminals, he realizes this case could cost him his career.

*Fatal Trust* by Todd M. Johnson
authortoddmjohnson.com

BethanyHouse